Tempted by a Rogue
by a

lauren smith

DEDICATION

To my wonderful Street Team, you guys are some of the best fans and friends there are! Your support and dedication to my stories makes living this wonderful dream possible.

TABLE OF CONTENTS

CHAPTER ONE   1

CHAPTER TWO   12

CHAPTER THREE   29

CHAPTER FOUR   46

CHAPTER FIVE   67

CHAPTER SIX   84

CHAPTER SEVEN   92

CHAPTER EIGHT   106

WICKED DESIGNS EXCERPT   124

OTHER TITLES   138

ABOUT THE AUTHOR   139

Chapter One

Midhurst, West Sussex 1817

White and pink roses formed spots of striking color against the dense green hedges as Gemma Haverford walked through the gardens of her home. She let her fingertips touch the petals of the roses as she headed toward the center of the garden. Twilight was her favorite time of day. Birds began to quiet their singing, the sunlight softened, giving everything a soft glow. Gemma took a seat on a cool marble bench at the center of the maze of hedges and rosebushes. Her hands trembled as she smoothed out her skirts. She was anxious enough that her knees knocked together too, but she couldn't banish her nerves.

It wasn't every day that she wore her best gown,

an almost sheer sky blue silk, for a secret garden rendezvous. Everything needed to be perfect. She'd gone to great effort to have her lady's maid tame the wild waves of her hair and help to slightly dampen her gown to cling better to her form, which bore only the veiled protection of a single filmy shift.

She had to look her best tonight. At twenty-five she was past the age where most women found it easy to marry. One of her distant cousins had callously remarked earlier that year that she was so far back on the shelf that she was collecting dust. Gemma, feeling a little too irritated at the remark, and having one too many cups of arrack punch, had sneezed at him as though he was the one covered in dust. Not her finest moment, she had nearly dissolved in a fit of unladylike giggles at his horrified expression when he'd struggled to find the handkerchief in his waistcoat to wipe his face.

There was a very good reason she hadn't married, but she couldn't tell anyone, not even her parents why she'd turned down more than one suitor over the years. For eleven years she had kept herself out of the hunt for husbands, believing, *knowing* that she would marry one man, James Randolph, her childhood sweetheart.

He and his best friend, Jasper Holland, had enlisted in His Majesty's Navy as young midshipman. James had been fourteen and Jasper, half a year older, had been fifteen. For eleven long years the two men had been gone, making their fortunes on the high seas, but now they set to return home, to marry and settle down. She'd not seen them in all that time, but she knew in her heart of hearts, that James was coming for her. His letters to her had been steady and filled with reassurances of his affection and his intent to marry her as soon as he came home. And now it was time.

What would he be like after so many years? Had he changed like she had? Grown taller, more muscular, more handsome than the wild young man who'd dashed off to sea? Would he be stern as a husband after commanding men and war ships? Or would he be gentle with her after so many hard years at sea, and want nothing more than a quiet country life full of friends and family within an easy walk of one's home? It was what she'd always wanted. She'd never cared for London and the fast pace of the city. She adored the country, the birds, the green lands, the sheep, even the garden parties that her neighbors threw often were an amusement she enjoyed. Would James want the same thing?

Gemma nibbled her bottom lip, glancing about the gardens. Wisteria hung over trellises to the entrance of this particular part of the garden, the thick blooms almost like wildflowers strung on green vines over the white painted wood. How lovely it was here tonight. How perfect too. She couldn't resist smiling.

Just that morning she had received James's latest letter, telling her he would seek her out in the gardens tonight, for a private audience, away from the eyes of parents and chaperones.

Tonight. The one word held such promise. Enclosed in James's letter was a soft strip of black gauzy cloth embroidered with silver stars. The letter instructed her to wait until twilight, and then blindfold herself for his arrival because he wished to surprise her.

A wave of heat flooded her cheeks at the thought of being so vulnerable and alone with him in such a manner, but another part of her heated in strange, unfamiliar places. She knew meeting him here like this wasn't proper and if anyone found out, she'd be compromised. But this was James, her James. The man she trusted more than anyone else in the world, except for her father. The temptation to meet him here, even in secret, was irresistible.

What would he do when he came upon her? Remove the blindfold? He might touch her face, her hair, her neck…Gemma trailed her own fingertips over her neck, wondering how different it would feel to have a man's hands there, ones worn with callouses from years of working the ropes while tacking the sails of a great ship.

A shiver rippled through her and she hastily dropped her hands back to her lap, feeling a little foolish. It was so easy to get carried away when thinking of James. When she first read the portion of the letter that told her to meet him like this, being compromised was her first fear, but James was a good and noble man. He was not the sort to ruin a lady, especially not when he intended to marry in good standing.

Even though she had not seen him since he set off eleven years ago, she had faith that he would not damage her virtue with this garden rendezvous. He would be a gentleman, wouldn't he? Gemma was all too aware that she knew little of the hearts of men, or how deeply they could fall prey to their desires.

Perhaps I ought to go back inside and wait for him to call upon me tomorrow morning? That would be the proper thing, after all.

Proper yes, but she wanted to see James alone and didn't want to wait another moment, even one night. If she were to be caught in a position that sorely injured her reputation, well, her father would demand a marriage immediately, James would comply, and all would be well.

Yes, all would be well enough. We need to be married, and mayhap it matters little how the deed comes about?

Perhaps that was what James intended, a certainty of compromising her so he could ensure they would be married. It was indeed a little unorthodox, but that might be his intent. To conquer her like he'd conquered his enemies upon the seas, swiftly and surely. If that were the case, then he was certainly a rogue. Another little smile twisted her lips.

Am I to marry a rogue? Wouldn't that be... She giggled unable to stop herself from thinking of how wonderfully wicked that would be. It would be scandalous, but if it was James, he would be *her* rogue.

So with that reassuring thought, she pulled the blindfold out, carefully put it over her eyes, and tied it into a small bow at the back of her head. She fiddled with her hair, tugging the loose untamable ringlets a little so they coiled down against her neck. Mary, her maid had done her best to fix it, but they both knew it would always look a bit wild. James would have to forgive her for appearing a little unruly. At least her gown had turned out well.

With the blindfold secure, she found she could see the vague outline of shapes through the thin gauzy cloth but her eyes were, for the most part, shielded from any clearer perceptions. Gemma smoothed her gown again, shifting restlessly as her stomach flipped over and over inside her. What if James had met with some delay, for he was not *officially* due to arrive in Midhurst until tomorrow where he and Jasper would be toasted and celebrated at Lady Edith Greenley's country estate garden party.

Gravel suddenly crunched close by as someone trod along the garden path leading straight toward her. She held her breath, sitting very still. It had to be James. Her heart fluttered so wildly that her ribs hurt from the hammering beat.

Jasper Holland cursed for the thousand time as he fumbled his way through the maze of the Haverford Gardens. It was a bloody mess, this whole situation. It was James who should be here, not him, yet he was the one who was trapped in the situation of compromising a thoroughly decent young lady because his best friend was acting like a cur. Straightening his blue naval coat around his waist, he took another right turn, facing a dead end.

"Who designed this damnable thing? I'll likely lose my way and be eaten by a Minotaur," he muttered, stumbled back and took a left down another path. Someone should have drawn him a map to this—

He heard a feminine giggle some distance away and halted. The sound was light, a little husky, and it had the strangest effect on him just then. He could almost picture a woman beneath him in bed, just as he was about to enter her and ride her to their mutual pleasure making that sound. It was the best sort of sound in the world and one he hadn't heard in a long time. On the sea, there were often chances to visit the docks when in port, and pay for a night at a brothel. James had done that often enough, but Jasper never liked it.

There was something sad about the painted faces and the quiet resigned looks of the prostitutes that betrayed the way they felt about the manner in which they earned their living. More than once Jasper would pay to simply talk to them and then leave for the night, unsatisfied. After that, he'd taken to staying on the ship, leaving James to cavort on his own.

It still amazed him that after all these years he and James were friends. Many men were separated at sea and went years without seeing anyone. Losing touch often resulted in friendships waning. However, that hadn't happened with him and James. They'd been assigned to the same frigate, the *HMS Neptune* as midshipmen after attending a naval college. They'd both been promoted to first lieutenants and by the time they were ready to leave service, they were both still on the same ship.

Due to the influx of men joining the service, the waiting list to be promoted to captain was extensive and neither he nor James had enough peerage connections to curry favor for a quicker rise in officer status. Ergo they'd both agreed the time was good enough to leave service and return home. James had always been a bit of a rakehell, even as a young man before they'd left for the sea, but time had hardened both him and Jasper in different ways. He'd been more hesitant than Jasper to return to Midhurst and even the day before was talking about moving to London once he'd selected a pretty wife, one he could easily tire of and take mistresses later if he so chose. London was much better for mistresses than a little town like Midhurst.

"Love is for fools. Lust is what keeps a man going."

It was something James always said, something he'd taken to believing after so many years at sea. The women in ports had turned James into a jaded man and he'd abandoned dreams of marrying Gemma Haverford, the sweet little country gentleman's daughter he'd left behind.

"Jas, do a man a favor, write Gemma and break it off," he sneered under his breath in imitation of James's plea all those years ago.

It had started out so simple. A favor for a friend.

"And I'm the fool who took over writing those bloody love letters," Jasper growled in self-directed frustration.

He'd written one letter to Gemma, doing his best to imitate James's poor handwriting, but the words to end things…well they just hadn't come out on the page. Instead he found himself sharing details of his day, thoughts and impressions he had of the islands they'd visited, the strange lands and natives they'd encountered, the battles they'd faced. His fears, his hopes, his own dreams. And he'd signed that first letter with a single letter J. Not as James, but Jasper, the man he was. He hadn't wanted to deceive her any more than he had to. Her response to his first letter had been almost immediate. A letter back to him found him so quickly through the post that he had to assume she'd written it the second she'd received his letter.

The Gemma he'd met through her letters had fascinated him, amused him, and changed the way he thought of Midhurst. The little girl with ginger hair had changed so much. She'd become a woman worth knowing. Her stories and descriptions of the town, the village, the countryside, everything that was so easy to forget at sea, had kept him grounded and reminded him of home. It was no longer a place he'd escaped from to live a life of adventure, but become a wonderful place of refuge for him, a sanctuary to someday return to when his service was over.

But the game was now at an end.

James had found out on their last week aboard ship that Jasper hadn't broken off the secret engagement and that he'd continued to write to Gemma for the last ten years. James had been furious to learn that Gemma was now fully under the impression James was going to propose to her and that she'd saved herself for him and him alone. Jasper had read every letter where she'd detailed the passing London Seasons and how she'd felt a little pressured to marry, but had insisted she loved him and would wait. For James. Not him. The thought summoned a black cloud over Jasper's thoughts, but it wasn't going to change what he had to do tonight. He had to end it with Gemma while pretending to be James. Compromise her so that tomorrow morning when she met with James, he could discover she'd kissed another man and break it off with her forever.

Yes, it would ruin her, but Jasper had every intent of making things right, of marrying her himself. He would just have to convince her of that once the dust settled from James crying off. Jasper could wait, *would* wait for as long as he had to for Gemma to be his wife, his lover, his world. His only fear was that she would despise him for his deception all these years, but it was a risk he would have to take. He'd led her to believe he would marry her in his letters and he'd meant every word. If only he hadn't hidden behind the facade of being James.

I should have confessed my identity from the start, before I wove this tangled web, but 'tis too late now.

A bitter taste coated his tongue. Scowling, he peered through the nearest bush. He could just make out a feminine figure seated on a bench. It was a sight he'd never forget. The woman was lovely. She had a full figure, hips just the right size for a man's hands, and the perfect indent of a narrow waist. From where he stood, he couldn't see her front, but the twilight highlighted the riotous ginger colored waves of her hair that were escaping the nest of pins atop her head.

She looked like a delicious little minx ready for a tumble into the nearest bed.

Lord, he wanted to be the man to take her to bed, to explore Gemma in a way he'd only fantasized about for years. Of course that had been purely dreams, he hadn't thought she'd look so tempting in real life. He remembered the little ginger-haired girl that had followed him and James about when they were children. He'd never had much interest in girls, but James had rather enjoyed the way she'd gazed at him with those sweet calf eyes. Adoration, no matter where the source came from had always been something James enjoyed and it had been only too easy for him to woo little Gemma with his smiles and teasing. Jasper had been far too busy to deal with girls at that age, he'd been more interested in exploring the hills and forests of Midhurst and getting in the sort of trouble boys were prone to do.

The woman on the bench sighed touched the blindfold over her eyes. It was made from a strip of cloth he'd found just for her in a little shop in a seaside port only a week ago. It was to be his tool of deception, a way to keep her from seeing him clearly, so she'd look back upon tonight and have to admit it was not James who'd visited her. It was a cruel plan. James's plan, not his, but Jasper was equally a bastard for going along with it.

"Hellfire and damnation," he muttered, squared his shoulders and walked around the nearest hedge. The time to compromise an innocent lady had arrived and he couldn't put it off another moment.

Forgive me, sweet Gemma.

Chapter Two

"James? Is that you?" She called out, her heart beating wildly with the excitement of the moment.

Her face warmed with the heat of a blush when she heard a soft intake of breath a few feet behind her. This moment was a decade in the making. She had dreamed of this deep into the night, and she could scarcely breathe with the abundance of joy inside her. Every letter, every anxious day waiting for a messenger to bring her news of him, had finally led to this night. Her life could begin again, this time with James by her side.

"Good god, is that you, Gemma? What a glorious creature you've grown up to be!" a low masculine voice uttered breathlessly.

It was curious, she had expected to recognize his voice, to hear it be just the same as the boy's voice she had carved into her memory, but it was not. The voice that spoke was that of a man, changed to a rich baritone, which rumbled sensually from behind her. She started to turn around on the bench but suddenly a body sat down behind her, arms circling her waist and lips brushing against her ear.

"Don't turn around," he whispered. "I want to see you like this, drink in my fill of you."

The shock of that intimate caress of his lips against her ear sent her jerking forward in panic. Sparks of sharp heat shot down between her thighs. Gemma tried to wrest herself free of his grasp because the way he held her made her feel so…queer.

"James, wait, I want to see you." Her hands flew to her face to remove the blindfold and get a glimpse of him. James, however, had other ideas. He snagged her arms, securing them at her sides as he jerked her back down against his lap on the marble bench. That forced closeness shot her heart into her throat and made her lightheaded with an unsettling mixture of emotions and physical awareness. He was a little rough, but rather than frighten her, it heightened her awareness of his strength. He touched the bare skin of her arms with his calloused palms.

Why didn't I wear gloves? A lady always wears gloves. But she hadn't tonight because she'd wanted to feel him, to touch him without a layer of silk between her fingers and his skin. Now she felt a skin to skin sensation, perfect, arousing.   Arousing… yes that's what she felt. Arousal. Mary had explained it to her in whispered tones when preparing her for tonight, she'd explained a kiss could do strange things to a woman's body if the man were skilled. It seemed Mary had been right.

James's arms tightened about her body to keep her from escaping, now were tight in an entirely different way. His breath turned heavy and he snuggled up to her.

"James, what are you doing?" She gasped, trying to pull free again.

"Shh…be still my lovely Gemma, embrace this twilight dream with me…" The words were honey smooth and delivered in such a perfect poetic cadence that Gemma was too entranced by the romance of it, to bother fighting off the amorous embrace of her love.

This was the man from the letters, the one who wooed with his words. Now he wooed her with his hands. She found it easy to relax beneath that soothing voice despite the clearly compromising position of her body fully against his. If no one came upon them, her reputation would be safe enough.

"It is good to hear your voice again, eleven years is such a long time. I was worried you might not find me…desirable," Gemma said, barely above a whisper. Not a young lady anymore, she was older, a little wiser, and she'd never been one of the prettiest girls in Midhurst, let alone London.

The fear that he'd replace her with someone new, a more beautiful woman was a fear she didn't want to admit, but it was there, clawing at her heart, making it hard to breathe. Would she be enough for a man like James? Or would he find her lacking? She'd never measured her worth in looks before, and certainly had never valued herself by a man's affections. That hadn't changed. But if James didn't want her, it would hurt. Deeply. The eleven years she'd spent in their secret courtship through letters would have been a waste, and the decent, eligible men she had turned down now were all married with wives and babes of their own.

Lightheaded with the sweet swell of heat in her body and the slow growing ache between her legs, she bit back a moan when James slid one hand down from her waist along her thigh. Struggling to catch her breath, she tried to paw his hand away in an effort to ease the effect it had on her senses. James slid his hand off her thigh, to cover her own protesting hand and guided it down to her own leg. With this simple switch of hands, she felt a little more in control. He led her hand downward onto the smooth tenderness of her inner thigh, stroking the silk against her skin. He made her caress herself, in the way she had only ever done when alone in her bath.

Her head spun and little tingles skittered beneath her skin just knowing that he wished to touch her there, to explore the hidden skin of her legs. She leaned back against his chest, and he stretched his fine long legs out on either side of her own. He surrounded her, enfolding her completely in his embrace. She resisted the urge to touch him back, even though she wanted to feel him and ensure he was real. Gemma put her other hand tentatively on his right thigh. The heavy muscles, strong beneath her grasp, sent slow ripples of heat through her and her heart jumped in her chest. The muscles beneath her hand tensed, and he shifted a little behind her.

"Not find you desirable? Gemma, you are breathtaking!" He pressed his lips on her throat in a kiss.

Then he laughed softly, and he moved his other hand up to caress her breasts. Her flesh tightened beneath his touch and Gemma drew in a deep breath. James pulled her back harder against him, and she felt something hard, his arousal against her backside. That, too, Mary had warned her about, how a man's groin area would stiffen when he was ready to take a woman to bed. The idea had been laughable at the time, but now Gemma's lungs burned and her hands shook at the thought. Would he want to take her to bed? Would he try tonight? Did she want him to?

Gemma was not a wanton woman, but she was tempted by this...rogue. The way he handled her, the way he knew just how to make her body flood with heat and desire.

Jasper's hand on her thigh started to coil her gown, raising it past her calves, up over her knee until bare skin was revealed. If he touched her any more this way, she would surely faint, fall right off the bench and ruin her best gown...but if he stopped, she was sure she would die from unfulfilled yearnings.

"James...I don't think we should..." she tried to speak but he caught her chin with his hand and angled her head to the side so that he could kiss her on the lips.

It was Gemma's first real kiss. She remembered James kissing her once, long ago, when they'd been children. He'd caught her by the back door to the kitchens of Haverford and pressed his lips to hers. A brief flash of a smile later and he'd run off, leaving her to stand alone and confused by his actions. She hadn't much liked that kiss, but what respectable girl of ten years old would? Now though, everything had changed and James's kisses had too it seemed.

This was a true kiss, with melting fire and the sweet taste of passion's first bloom. His warm mouth on hers was a fascinating sensation. Soft lips that coaxed and teased, sending shivers through her in places she didn't know could tremble. When his tongue parted her lips and teased her own tongue, something deep in her belly twisted and clenched and a flash of heat shot through her like a fire in a pan. Quick, startling, making her gasp. She gripped his leg tighter, feeling the taut muscles of his thigh beneath her when she strained to kiss him harder. It would be so easy to lose herself in his arms, to the feeling of his mouth on hers. His lips twisted upward and he smiled between kisses.

"You taste divine, Gemma," he whispered huskily, as his hand drifted higher up her leg, straying close to dangerous areas.

She knew she should have tried to close her legs to prevent him from going further up. When his hand abandoned hers, it moved steadily onward beneath her gown, lifted her petticoats as though they weren't even there.

"Oh!" Gemma gasped when he stroked the tight coils of the dark triangle hidden between her legs. Tingles of pleasure shot up her spine, yet she squirmed a little at that touch, afraid of the mounting tension in her lower body. James caught her mouth with his, absorbing the little gasp, still smiling as he did so.

"I have waited years to touch you, Gemma…" he confessed in a soft sigh and nuzzled her cheek.

Gemma wanted to face him, wanted to see what she knew had to be a handsome face. But he caught her hand as it strayed toward the blindfold, kissing the inside of her wrist, before moving her palm to his neck. She was able to twine her fingers in his silky hair and hold his head close to hers while he let his lips stray from hers down to her neck and then her shoulder. His hand between her legs moved a few inches deeper, caressing the entrance of her moist center and the violently pleasurable sensations that rippled through her made Gemma tremble. James paused in his deep caress to kiss her.

"Are you all right?" His touch gentled as he waited for her to answer.

Gemma tried to nod, but she still trembled. She knew if she tried to stand she'd sooner fall than walk. He pulled his hand away, seeming to realize just how affected she was.

"Gemma…" he cooed softly, his hand pulling her gown back down over her legs.

"James…I'm sorry. I'm not used to…" Gemma tried to explain herself, so ashamed that she wanted to sink into a hole in the ground and hide from him. She'd waited years for him, for this moment and now she was inexperienced and unsure of herself. Would he want a woman more experienced? Shame made her face heat and tingle. She closed her eyes, trying to breathe. Who would have thought her innocence would have become a burden?

"There's plenty of time for you to get used to this and to me," his soft voice purred without the slightest hint of annoyance. He was compassionate to wait, to not press her until she had grown used to these new passions he'd lit within her body. How could she have ever thought to doubt his intentions?

When he got up and let go of her, the warm heat of his body vanished. The deprivation of his close proximity had a startling effect on her, she had to still her own arms from reaching out to bring him back into her embrace. Gemma turned around instinctively but the blindfold kept her ignorant of her love's appearance.

"Will you be at Lady Greenley's party tomorrow?" She tried to sound casual, as though he hadn't just changed her entire world in a matter of a few caresses and kisses.

"Yes, but promise me you will not speak a word of what has transpired tonight. Our meeting must be kept secret."

"A secret?" A flicker of insecurity flashed through her but she dispelled it. This was James! He would do right by her, there was no question of that.

"Yes, until I can ask you to marry me properly." James placed a tender kiss on her forehead and his footsteps retreated in the distance.

She pulled the blindfold off in time to see the tall fine figured back of a man with dark hair vanish around the garden's edge. Gemma clutched the beautiful blindfold to her chest, her entire body quivering with joy. James was going to marry her! To think that she would be blessed with years of tender words, and soft hot kisses…she was the luckiest woman in the world to know love at James Randolph's hands. The years of faithful affection they'd shared through words created by pens on paper had only made their future passion a mighty fire waiting for the chance to burn.

Jasper arrived at Randolph Hall and left his horse with the groom. He was immediately granted entrance and shown into the evening room where James Randolph stood beside the marble fireplace, one hand braced on the mantle, swirling a glass of brandy. He didn't seem to be at all surprised at Jasper's arrival because he nodded toward a waiting glass of brandy on the mantle. It did nothing to ease the black mood that rolled through Jasper like summer storm clouds. Listening to Gemma gasp another man's name. James's name, made his blood burn. It should have been only Gemma and him in that garden without the specter of his friend between them.

"Jas, you devil, what took so long?" James asked, offering a second glass of brandy to him.

"I was delayed…" Jasper took the brandy from his friend and drank greedily.

"And your meeting with Gemma? How did it go?

I'll wager that blindfold did the trick in disguising that it was you and not me who made love to her just now." James chuckled and sipped his brandy again.

It took everything for Jasper not to bloody his friend's nose. This whole scheme was dreadful and he despised the way it made his insides wither with guilt.

"James…are you sure you want to do this to her? I mean—"

His friend held up a hand to silence him. "Now, now, Jasper. Remember, we are in this tangle because *you* didn't do what I asked you to." James shook his head in reproach.

Unfortunately he was right, Jasper had done something incredibly foolish and now it was a thorn in his side to handle and a nasty blockade against James's marital plans. Not to mention Jasper's intentions to have Gemma for himself. Both he and James were trapped, one wanting to escape her and the other wanting to claim her with every fiber of his being. But there was no easy way of going about this. A man couldn't cry off an understanding even as fairly secretive as the one Gemma had, without a damned good reason. Ergo, she had to be compromised by another man, which would give James his honorable out, and hopefully Jasper would be able to swoop in and snatch her up.

I have to. She loves me, she just doesn't know it's me.

That was probably the worst part of this plan, convincing Gemma the man she loved wasn't James, so that she'd let him go on his merry way without her. James had decided to get married after all, despite being the jaded lover he'd become to many a woman in many a port. He'd settled on some chit with a vile temper and an odious manner, but she turned a pretty ankle. That was all James cared about now, a lady's looks and her desire to have a bit of fun. Gemma was not the sort of girl James would have sought out for a bit of fun.

Gambling hells and boxing matches, and other lower forms of entertainment weren't something that would ever interest Gemma. She and James were so ill-suited it was a blessing the marriage between them would never happen, but it still wasn't fair that Gemma was being treated so poorly. Of course that was still Jasper's fault, he admitted that. It had been his letter writing that had left Gemma with hope of matrimony because he had every intention of marrying her, if she'd have him after what he'd done tonight.

"I wrote your letters to her like you asked me to, but I couldn't follow through with breaking her heart." Jasper flung himself into the nearest chair and glared up at James.

He knew they could have been mistaken for brothers, with their tall forms, dark hair and brown eyes. Each of them bore the fine proud features of the sons of English country gentry with sculpted chins, straight noses and strong jaw lines. The years spent toiling at sea had forged muscled gods of them and their newly won fortunes lent them both an air of recklessness that often resulted in trouble. More so for James than Jasper, of course.

"It's not my fault, Jas, that you couldn't let her

TEMPTED BY A ROGUE

down easy."

James was the more dramatic and outgoing of the two men, but he was not the leader between them. His flair for drama drew women to him, and he rather enjoyed the benefits of the opportunities this gave him. Jasper knew James had cared for Gemma Haverford when he was a boy, and he wrote to her sporadically that first year they were away at sea.

But by the time he'd reached seventeen, he'd fully immersed himself in womanizing like any decent rake, and no longer wanted to be burdened with the marital expectations of a dear, innocent little country girl like Gemma. James had therefore enlisted Jasper to pen a few letters to her pretending to be James and eventually break off the relationship.

However, Jasper had found he enjoyed his correspondence with Gemma, she had a ready mind and a quick wit and whatever worldly knowledge she lacked could easily be remedied. He never would have imagined she would become something he dreamt about every night, that her letters would get him through storms and fierce battles... Gemma, forever a sweet young girl in his eyes; an innocent country child who would never grow up...*had grown up*. And now the depth of his deception had him fairly torn in two where his loyalties were concerned. He would do whatever James wanted without question, but Gemma? How strong was that sweet child's hold on him, now that she was a sweet woman? Too strong. So much so that he wanted to marry her.

"So, did you see to it then?" James asked, smiling crookedly at his friend.

"You mean, did I lure her into the garden and compromise her?" Jasper's words came out more acidic than they should have, but he couldn't help it, he was not a fan of this whole wicked plot James had worked up, which, given their rather reckless youth and daring acts in the service of God, King and country, was saying something.

"Well, did you?" James walked away from the fireplace and joined Jasper in the chair next to him.

"Take comfort in this, James. She is completely and thoroughly compromised. The poor creature is so madly in love with you that it will crush her tomorrow when you call her out for being with another man."

Jasper's loyalties were uncomfortably tight at the moment between his best friend of more than twenty years and the girl to whom he'd been writing love letters to for a decade. He wouldn't have agreed to James's scheme if Gemma would have been truly hurt. The worst of it would be a broken heart, and she'd recover soon enough, and then he would win her for himself. And James would be free to propose to Arabella Stevens, his current "heart's delight," and intended betrothed.

Jasper thought Arabella was nothing more than a fast little chit that James had met at Brighton. Unfortunately the girl had an uncle who lived only a few miles away from Midhurst. Jasper had no right to begrudge James his choice in women, he'd often sampled the pleasures of ladies of less than perfect reputation, but to marry one, when the likes of Gemma Haverford could be taken instead? It was nonsensical, completely, totally nonsensical. Of course now that he'd seen Gemma, well more than seen...he'd tasted her quite deeply...the thought of James standing at the altar with her made something in his gut churn uncomfortably. It was oddly reminiscent of when he'd been a lad out on the ship that first month, suffering from sea sickness.

"Excellent." James didn't seem even remotely concerned about Gemma and what Jasper might have done to her in the garden. In fact, it had been his idea for Jasper to do "more" than just meet with her.

"How was she? Our blushing country girl?" James smiled wickedly over the top of his brandy glass, brown eyes warm with mischief.

Jasper's brow furrowed as he debated on how to answer.

"She was very sweet, but she's completely green, poor thing. I barely touched her before she was shaking like a leaf. I didn't dare go all the way with her," Jasper said, a little wave of guilt rippled through him. He'd done a tad more than touch, but could anyone blame him? A ripe fruit hanging from a vine, he couldn't resist...

"A green girl? How is that possible at her age? No, wait, let me guess, she's too plump, and not at all attractive? Is she an ugly freckled little thing? She must be, with all that ginger hair I remember she had as a child." James chortled.

Jasper grimaced at his friend. He didn't like hearing Gemma talked about, especially in such a cruel manner. He didn't love her, that would be nonsense, but he did *care* about her, deeply, the way one does a favorite spaniel and he didn't like it when another man kicked his dog. He wanted to protect Gemma from the world, the way he would anything he cared about, even if it meant keeping James's callous remarks away from her little ears.

"You would be surprised, James. She's quite a beauty."

"Oh? Then why didn't you finish the deed, Jasper? We agreed…" James watched him curiously now.

Jasper clenched his fists automatically, his body aching to suddenly throw a vicious right hook into James's smug face. He forced his self-composure, uncoiling his tightened fists and relaxing again.

"She was so…I've never made a woman shake before James. I didn't like it, knowing that she was only letting me do those things to her because she thought I was *you*. She's kept herself for you, and I couldn't just rip that innocence from her in less than an hour." Jasper rubbed his eyes, wearily, as he tried to erase that creeping guilt again. Her voice, crying out James's name, echoed in his head and that nausea returned again. He wanted Gemma to love him, to know it was him and not James she'd kissed.

I must bide my time. Wait until all of this is done, then I shall go after her.

"How amusing…that she would affect you so. Perhaps you ought to have a go at her Jas, keep yourself entertained until I can secure Arabella," James mused and rubbed his chin.

"No, I've already damaged her enough. Almost making love to her while pretending to be you was bad enough. I won't do more than that."

"Aww, come on Jas, do a friend a favor. We both know what Gemma is like. She won't let our engagement drop without putting up a fight. I need you to entice her away and offer her something… sweeter." James looked at him pleadingly and Jasper huffed loudly.

"Sweeter? Good God, James, you want me to act the libertine to distract her away from you?" What a wretched notion, but he owed James.

"Jas, please. You know I can't marry Gemma. She's not what I want out of life. Not *anymore*." James met him with an even stare, and Jasper knew what his friend said was true. He didn't want love, didn't want that vulnerability it could give a man. They'd both seen men driven mad by love and James had made it clear years ago he wanted nothing to do with loving a sweet country girl like Gemma. Better to wed and bed a viper like Arabella and have no expectations of heartbreak. At least that was James's thinking, as far as Jasper knew and he knew his friend well.

Their friendship ran deep. James had risked his life more than once to save Jasper and he'd done the same in return. Over the boom of canons and through the fog of war, they'd stayed together, been wounded together. Their blood had run in twin rivers, mixing upon the floor of a cabin after a cannon ball had torn through the hull of their ship. That wasn't something easily dismissed when it came to a question of loyalty. But he did not want James to know how much he cared about Gemma. He didn't want his closest friend to make things difficult for him when he pursued Gemma.

"Fine, I'll keep her occupied so you can have your damned Arabella," Jasper said, watching his friend's pleading face turn to ecstatic excitement.

"Wonderful! I must write Arabella and tell her to be at the garden party tomorrow." James finished his brandy, and Jasper got to his feet.

"I'd best be going, before it gets too late," Jasper said and both men clasped hands. He left Randolph Hall, with the strange sensation he'd just made a pact with the devil to steal poor Gemma's innocence. He didn't like how that made his stomach churn. But promises were promises. With any luck, however, he would be able to make it up to Gemma by marrying her.

Chapter Three

It was nearly impossible to keep a secret. Especially one involving a relationship with a man. Gemma found that out in the most difficult way possible the morning following her meeting with James in the garden the night before. Only Mary, her lady's maid, had known she'd met with him in the maze-like sprawl of her father's country estate gardens. Still, it hadn't escaped her notice this morning that her mother hummed while they broke their fast and watched her with a devious twinkle in her eye.

"James arrived in town last evening, did you know that Gemma, dear?" her mother asked while she spread some orange marmalade over a slice of toast.

Good heavens, is nothing secret here? Gemma bit her lip before replying.

LAUREN SMITH

"He did? How wonderful! I take it he'll be sure to attend Lady Greenley's party today then."

The white painted door to their small breakfast room opened and Gemma's father, John Haverford strode in, a newspaper under one arm and a stack of letters in the other.

"Morning, my heart." He bustled over to her mother and kissed her cheek before he winked at Gemma. "Get a good night's sleep, Gemma?"

"Yes, papa, and you?"

"Oh yes. I almost went for a walk in the gardens, but thought better of it. The weather was nice though, wasn't it?"

She swallowed hard, choking on the bit of egg she'd just slipped in her mouth. Her father had almost come across her and James in the gardens?

"Gemma, you're flushed, too much time in the sun this morning?" Her mother's concern was sweet, but Gemma knew she'd faint flat out if she guessed the real source of Gemma's high color.

"No, I just walked through the fields to the village and back, and not too fast." It was a lie, but not a bad one. She'd actually run through the fields for a bit before coming back home. She loved to run, there was something wicked and wild about dropping one's silly bonnet and just sprinting through the grass with only the wind as her companion. Last night had left her in such a wonderful mood that she hadn't been able to resist running most of the way back from Midhurst to her home this morning.

"I think it will be interesting to attend Lady Greenley's party today. I suspect there will be much to talk about Mr. Randolph and Mr. Holland's glorious return from the high seas." Her father laughed and settled down at the table across from her mother. He retrieved a pair of silver rimmed spectacles and perched them on the tip of his nose so he could read the paper he'd spread out beside his plate.

"Indeed," her mother agreed. "This town does know how to gossip, doesn't it?" Her mother chuckled.

The small market town of Midhurst barely held seven hundred people, and so naturally everyone knew *everything* about everyone else. From seventy-five year old Lady Edith Greenley, the highest level of Midhurst's society, right down to the poorest farmer's family, there were few, if any, secrets. Gemma knew this better than anyone, so she resolved to keep her mouth shut like James asked her to. She was excited to see him today at the Garden Party.

Every year Lady Greenley held a garden party, inviting all the local gentry and some of the better off merchant families to attend. Gossip was shared, tea drank, crumpets and scones devoured and engagements announced. There was an unmistakable stirring of pride in her breast that she would finally be able to count herself among the lucky women who had earned engagements. Of course, the secret of her soon-to-be-engaged state had left her rather more excited than was perhaps wise. She nearly bounced on her heels like an eager spaniel while she finished breakfast. After that, she dashed back upstairs where Mary helped her dress.

"Good luck, miss." Mary winked. "And don't be getting into too much trouble you hear? I'm afraid your hair won't stand for much mussing with this style."

"Thank you, Mary." Gemma giggled. James would have to behave whilst they were at the party, no sneaking off, however much she might want to do just that if he tried. It wouldn't do to come back to the party looking thoroughly compromised, even if the engagement was announced today.

"Will Mr. Randolph be speaking to your father?" Mary asked and handed Gemma a bonnet with lovely blue ribbons dangling down in silk tendrils.

"I..." She honestly didn't know. He'd have to, wouldn't he? But it would need to be done before the announcement so unless James met with her father at the party early, she might not have her engagement announced there. The thought was a depressing one.

Mary touched her arm gently. "There now, Miss, no need to worry. I'm sure your young man will have it all planned and proper."

"I hope so," Gemma whispered and then left her room to meet her mother at the entrance of the house to wait for their carriage to take them to Lady Greenley's. So much depended on how this party would go and she hated how excited she was to see James again. Eleven years was a long time to wait for a man to come home, a man she loved fiercely, with every part of her body and soul.

Her mother placed a calming hand on her arm to indicate she stop fidgeting. "Calm down dear, today will be a good day, I just know it."

Shooting a glance at her mother, she tried to smile. Her mother was the sort of woman who saw silver threading to every dark shadowed cloud, and could take any pie that was too tart, and find a way to sweeten its taste. Gemma had a tad more of her father's sardonic nature in her. In other words, she tended to fret, not too much of course, but enough every now and then that her mother would have to remind her not to be so restless with her worries.

"Mama, do you think James will…" She glanced down at herself, trying to see how she might look from his point of view.

Her mother's eyes twinkled. "He will." She didn't have to say anything more. Mothers had an uncanny way of doing that sometimes, seeing right through to their child's innermost thoughts.

"I hope so," she replied more to herself than to her mother and once more studied her appearance. She wore her best sprigged muslin gown and had her hair tamed into a respectable Hellenic fashion. But she had to heed Mary's warning and not let James muss her hair too much.

The carriage pulled up in front of the entrance and her father appeared just in time to assist her and Mama inside. As she settled into her seat, she clutched her reticle. Inside it she kept the blindfold cloth. It was a token of the passion she and James had shared. She felt a little foolish, but she'd never been so happy, so *in love* before. Without the presence of James there, Gemma pushed her mind to other thoughts, more specifically to thoughts of the letters James had written her.

For the first few years of his absence, his replies had been scattered and brief in subject matter, which she had attributed to his chaotic life at sea. But for the last several years his pace and length had changed. His penmanship had improved, as did his ability to express himself. She had begun to look forward to his monthly letters, hearing amusing anecdotes about his fellow sailors and harrowing adventures of foreign lands. His prose had often been poetic and deeply romantic toward the most recent few years of her letters. It had been such a dramatic change from the ill-expressed thoughts of a boy starting his life's journey to a man who'd lived a full exciting life and had learned much about himself and his fellow man. Life at sea had matured James greatly and she was never more ready to give herself to him in every way.

She hoped he would see marriage as the next great adventure. That love and someday children, could fill a void he'd not yet satisfied in his life. It was something she longed for, but only with him, not with any other man. No one else understood her the way he did, listened to her when she spoke of things, and when he agreed or disagreed, the discussion was always intelligent, frank and completely unguarded by fears of what the other would think. Of course, this had only been through letters, but she knew deep inside her bones that the man in the letters would be just as wonderful in reality. They had become partners in their thoughts, and now she wished more than anything to become partners fully in life.

The carriage took a narrow path through the wooded glen and past the village to the other side of

Midhurst. Cutting through another small forest, the vehicle rumbled around a bend and a sweeping expanse of beauty stunned Gemma. No matter how many times she saw Lady Greenley's lands she was always amazed at the sheer effect it had on her.

The tan sandstone house sat atop a hill, the many windows reflecting the noon sunbeams, making the glass wink and sparkle like distant diamonds. A large lake lay below the house, the waters dancing with the light breeze, and golden rushes at the water's edge waved back and forth in slow ripples. A large lawn led to a garden maze much like her garden back home and colorful tents and tables already dotted the landscape of the lawn in the distance, appearing so small that they seemed more like colorful toadstools that fairies would sit upon during a midnight revelry.

When she and her parents arrived at Lady Greenley's grand estate entrance, her gaze swept expectantly over the milling crowds gathering on the vast lawn. There was no sign of James, or even a tall dark-haired man who could be him. Perhaps he was deep in the garden, waiting for her to seek him out, or maybe he was running late, his horse having thrown a shoe.

A crowd of people exited the garden and gathered near the tables by the garden entrance. Two tall men stood with their backs facing her, talking with her fellow Midhurst neighbors. She knew the look of them right away, no other men of her acquaintance in this little town had such a striking appearance. James and Jasper were here. *Finally*. The boys of Midhurst had come home as men.

Against all her control, she smiled, fully, unable to contain it.

James. She sighed and grinned again like a silly girl still in the schoolroom.

"Gemma, your mother and I are off to the tea tables, we shall meet up with you later." Her father winked at her before he gently secured his wife's arm, tucking it into his while leading her to the nearest tent where a beleaguered young footman set out tea for the guests clustered around him.

Her father, no longer a young buck, still bore the vestiges of his youthful good looks, like her mother. As a pair, Gemma's parents looked lovely together. They inclined their heads toward each other and whispered softly. Her parents had been married for thirty-one years and were still loving and affectionate toward each other as ever. They had the sort of love and marriage born of years of friendship, passion, and now, deep love. She'd been blessed to have grown up in such a house, fostered with such love.

"Gemma dear!" a familiar feminine voice called out.

Lily Becknell, one of her dearest friends, strode toward her. Lily was the town's true beauty with fair blonde hair and blue eyes, with a soft womanly form that drew only admiration from every male eye when she passed. With Lily came a shorter woman with black hair and shiny little black eyes. It made Gemma think of a rat she'd seen in the gardens once, all beady black eyes and gnashing teeth. She shivered in revulsion at the memory. This stranger flashed Gemma a calculating sort of smile that caused an undercurrent of unease to move through her. It was not the type of look one young lady ought to give to another, not if they were meant to be on friendly terms.

"Lily! How are you?" She clasped hands with her friend and smiled politely at the other woman.

"Gemma, this is Miss Arabella Stevens. You recall a Mr. Stevens who lives a few miles north of Randolph Hall? This is his niece," Lily informed her.

"Oh yes, of course! Miss Stevens, it is so nice to meet you," Gemma greeted with genuine warmth. Mayhap the woman was nice once a person got better acquainted with her. Then again, perhaps not. Gemma bit her lip to hide her frown.

The other woman smiled, but it wasn't exactly a friendly expression when it was displayed on her face. There was something almost vicious in the feral glint of the woman's dark eyes and her smile revealed teeth that smiled seemed gritted together as though in great displeasure. There was no way that Gemma would be able to keep from picturing that rat in the garden when she saw this woman.

"It is a pleasure to meet you, Miss Haverford," Arabella replied, her rosebud lips pinched into a little simper.

Rattish eyes and teeth aside, Gemma had to admit Arabella was attractive and dainty looking, nothing like Gemma with her fuller figure and taller body. Her father used to call her Little Diana because of her beauty and her strong looking form, like the Goddess of the Hunt. But men did not want such women, they wanted petite delicate flowers that depended upon them for protection. Men were silly though to toy with such flowers, for they often had the sharpest thorns. And Arabella looked very thorny indeed, at least to Gemma.

I should be ashamed to be so petty in my thoughts. She knew that, but she couldn't stop herself from thinking them. Sometimes a person simply didn't strike her as genuine and that always bothered Gemma.

Lily broke through Gemma's prickly thoughts. "Have you seen Mr. Randolph and Mr. Holland? They are just over there, talking to Lady Greenley." There was a hint of mischief in Lily's tone. She and only she, outside of Gemma, knew of the understanding between her and James.

"I have not…" She craned her head about toward the two tall men again, vastly distracted by their handsome forms. The way their navy overcoats and buckskin trousers molded to such strong, athletic forms. A little shiver rippled through her at the memory of touching James's muscles, particularly those of his thighs and the way it felt to clench them while she rode through a seemingly endless wave of pleasure at his knowledgeable hands.

"James came by my carriage, with my uncle of course," Arabella supplied to the conversation and Gemma's head snapped back to her. Why would this woman think she could take such a familiarity with James, when only Gemma had that right?

"Yes, it was kind of you to provide such transport for him," Lily added diplomatically. Gemma decided to believe what she wished, that Arabella had *no claim* to James. Perhaps Arabella's uncle lived near James's family home, and offered a ride out of kindness.

Yes, that was it. She couldn't help but smile. All would be well, she was going to see James. She turned back to her friend, seeking any bit of information about James, but she would have to ask about Jasper too, in order to prevent any speculation by Arabella that she and James had an understanding.

"Well Lily, how did you find them? Are they much improved from those darling boys of our youth who used to tug our braids and put frogs in our pinafore pockets?" Gemma ignored Arabella now, eager to hear what Lily had to say about the two prodigal men of Midhurst.

Lily smiled secretively and leaned in close and conspiratorially to Gemma. "Never have you seen such a finer pair of men. If I had not married my Henry last year, why I'd be setting my lures to catch one of them." Lily winked at her and Gemma suppressed a laugh. Lily had always gotten into arguments with the boys when they'd been younger, whilst Gemma had tried eagerly to catch up when the young men had run off on their much longer legs. The mere idea of Lily marrying either one of the two bucks was laughable. She'd spend too much time arguing with them if one of them ever became her husband.

"Oh really, Lily, you are too much!" Gemma smiled and bit her lip, looking over Lily's shoulder toward the pair of men again.

Turn around James, I want to see you, she silently begged. *Let me put a face to the dreams I've had for years. Let me see the lips that brought forth such passion last night.*

Lady Greenley's screech jerked Gemma out of her thoughts.

"You, Haverford! Come here at once!" Lady Edith Greenley's bonneted head bobbed up and down when she waved at Gemma and demanded she come to her like a general in His Majesty's army. The ancient yet formidable Lady Greenley stood near the two men, who both turned at Lady Greenley's shout, in order to see Gemma.

Her heart stopped and she sucked air into her burning lungs after what seemed like ages of being frozen in time. Funny, she'd never had this happen before in her life, but seeing the faces of James Randolph and Jasper Holland after eleven years... Her world spun on its axis, as though she were a celestial planet shifting in its orbit, thrown into a spin by seeing these men. Side by side, they stood, almost an equal height, proud and strong in looks and demeanor. And both of them stared directly at her, equally curious to see her as she was to see them.

The resemblance of the two men to each other was startling. Only her childhood memories dared to find differences between the manly faces turned toward her. James had a fuller mouth, quicker to smile, but Jasper, quiet, calm, Jasper had eyes like liquid caramel that smoldered so powerfully when he stared at her that her mind simply blanked of all thought.

A rapid play of inscrutable emotions danced across his eyes, touched lightly upon his mouth as though he nearly smiled, but caught himself. Why on earth would Jasper smile at her? When he'd been a boy he'd always avoided her and had shouted rudely at her more than once that she was a nuisance and ought to go home and practice her needlepoint and sketching rather than gallivant off into the wooded glens after him and James.

Not that I ever listened to him. She almost smiled back at Jasper. She had the strangest urge to needle him, challenge him for daring to smile at her.

"Now Haverford! I could keel over and die waiting for you to grace me with your presence," Lady Greenley snapped, prodding the ground with the tip of her closed parasol. Gemma excused herself from Lily and Arabella and walked quickly toward Lady Greenley. She tried not to stare at the men when she reached them.

"What can I do for you, Lady Greenley?" Gemma asked.

"Can I depend upon you to rescue me from these unruly young bucks? Take them about the garden, and see that they don't scandalize my party, won't you?" Lady Greenley demanded of Gemma, a wicked glint in the older lady's gray eyes. With her crafty mannerisms and being rather boisterous for her age, no one dared to cross her.

"Of course, Lady Greenley," Gemma answered politely.

Both men grinned at her. The direct attention from both James and Jasper heated her skin with an embarrassing blush. There was nothing decent in either of their gazes. She could understand a look like that from James, after what they had shared, but Jasper? He should not be eyeing her form with such a bold look of appreciation like he did at that exact moment.

Lady Greenley watched this odd triangle of looks with an arched brow of interest, and Gemma thought she saw the old woman hide the beginnings of a smile beneath her ridiculously foppish bonnet. Where James's gaze seemed to outline every curve of her body with speculation, Jasper's gaze had the deep sensual sweep of such force that she almost felt his *hands* stroking her rather than his eyes…it was a knowing gaze, like he knew just how the flesh of her breasts would tighten, her legs tremble and her breath quicken beneath his touch…

"Why, is that really you, Miss Haverford?" James exclaimed with a broad smile and a deep bow. It did little to dispel the ensnaring enchantment of Jasper's heated gaze which distracted her from James.

Gemma forced a soft laugh, letting James take her hand and kiss it, but the tingling rush of contact she expected did not come. His voice did not seem quite the same as the night before, perhaps because it was disguised by his whispering tone…

"Mr. Randolph, Mr. Holland, I'm so glad to see you both returned to Midhurst in good health." Her gaze was strangely drawn back to Jasper, who watched her in deep concentration and she didn't know what to make of his scrutiny. She nibbled her bottom lip, studying Jasper intensely. His shoulders were wide…a little wider than James's now that she compared them so diligently.

James dropped her hand and glanced between her and Jasper, one brow raised.

"Er...we're quite glad to be home, Miss Haverford," James added, trying to draw her attention again. "I see Midhurst has treated you well over the years, Gemma." His voice deepened, but still Gemma didn't tear her gaze away from Jasper.

Was it possible to have a battle between a man and woman based on eye contact alone? She did feel as though she were battling this man, what she couldn't understand was why. His lips twitched, her eyes narrowed and her heart gave a strange little flip in her chest when his gaze lowered, inch by inch to focus on her lips.

We're strangers, after all these years. I should not be fascinated by him.

When he spoke to her, however, her body responded with a terrifying thrill of recognition.

"You are looking well, *Gemma*." The way he caressed her name...she went suddenly pale. That voice! Jasper's voice was the voice in the garden, the voice that belonged to the body which had...

No, no! He could not be the man I... Gemma wavered on her feet when a cloud seemed to cover her mind and she couldn't quite control her legs enough to stay standing.

"Now you've done it you rogues! Gone and frightened the girl. Shame!" Lady Greenley struck Jasper in the chest with the pointed end of her parasol.

Jasper grunted with the impact of the parasol's blow to his navy waistcoat and doubled over as

43

though in pain. James ducked when Lady Greenley's parasol whirled through the air where his head had been moments before.

"Have at you, you devils!" Lady Greenley cried, waving the parasol aloft like a saber as she started forward to continue the attack.

Both men got control of themselves and flashed smiles in Gemma's direction and looks of amused fright at the crazy, old battle-axe before turning tail and running toward the garden like any sensible rogues would do when threatened by the likes of such a woman aiming a parasol at their jugulars. Once Lady Greenley had clearly vanquished them, at least enough that they had sought safe haven in her garden, Lady Greenley turned to face the recovering Gemma.

"Now, Haverford, what's all this fainting nonsense? Tell me what's gotten your shift in a twist?" the elderly lady demanded in an all-knowing whisper. Had Gemma not grown up around Lady Greenley, the bold vulgarity of her reference to undergarments would have been shocking and not amusing. But this was Lady Greenley after all and no one would be surprised at her wild behavior after knowing her a short time.

Lady Greenley was far too smart for her age and saw far too much. Gemma shook her head, not wanting to breathe a word of what she'd discovered, especially if those words spread, as they often did in Midhurst. She still couldn't believe it. Jasper, not James, had met her in the garden, had deceived her, had compromised her... Why? How? A thousand questions beat inside her mind so harshly that it made her eyes ache and she shut them, rubbing them with gloved fingertips for a few moments while she struggled to regain her composure.

If James knew the truth, knew that she'd been compromised by another man, his best friend no less…knew that it was Jasper who had kissed her, touched her… It didn't matter that she thought it was James the whole time, he would not forgive her.

Fury boiled inside her. She distinctly remembered saying 'James' in the garden, several times, and her 'love' had not corrected her. He had wanted her to believe he was James! Lady Greenley was right. Jasper, at least, was a rogue. Not a good one either, not the sort of rogue a woman would sigh and swoon over then whisper about in giggles to her friends. But not Jasper. He was the sort of rogue who would end up on a dueling field, likely shot for having stolen his best friend's future wife's virtue. A wave of nausea followed her churning fury.

"Excuse me Lady Greenley, I have a man to strangle," she growled softly and started off toward the garden where she'd seen both men flee. She was going to find Jasper and ring his bloody neck. After that, she was going to cry for a very, very long time.

"Remember dear, use both hands, cuts off their air quicker!" Lady Greenley's advice warbled across the lawn when she cut through the garden's entrance. At any other time in her life, Gemma would have been fascinated to stay and hear just how Lady Greenley had gained such useful knowledge of the strangulation of rogues, but not today.

Chapter Four

The Greenley gardens were expansive, a huge array of mazes and gazebos marking various points of the gardens. It was easy to get lost especially if one was angry as Gemma was. She took several wrong turns and only just stumbled upon James who chatted quietly with Jasper near a white laced gazebo. Their heads were close to each other while they whispered, their shoulders squared and arms crossed, in that pose men take when no woman is around to scowl at such blatant displays of masculinity. They both looked far too handsome and rakish as they shared soft snickers and smiles. Gemma despised being left out of that loop of friendship they shared, at any other moment she would have given her left leg to know what they were saying. Right now, she wanted to throttle both of them.

"Miss Haverford?" James asked, his lips curving slightly when he saw her. Gemma tried to smile but it withered quickly. How was she going to do this? She had to tell James. She would not continue to be secretly engaged to a man when lies lay between them. He needed to know what sort of man his best friend was.

"May I speak to you, Mr. Randolph? In private?" she asked, trying to stay cool and calm. It didn't work. Her hands trembled, and her lungs couldn't seem to take enough air.

"Er...yes, of course." James came over to her, leaving Jasper alone to lean back against the gazebo, watching them with hooded eyes. She wished Jasper would go away, far away where she would never have to see him ever again. But that did not happen. The man stayed right where he was, watching her with a smirk on his face.

"Did you...come by my house to pay a visit to me last night?" She worded the question carefully. There was still a possibility, however infinitesimal, that it had been James and not Jasper, they were so alike after all. She just had to be sure.

"Come by your house? No, I'm afraid I did not...why?" Suspicion darkened his eyes and shadowed his face.

"Oh, no reason," she said quickly, trying to sound nonchalant.

James grabbed her hand. "Did you expect me to come and see you?"

"Well, in your last letter you said you would, you

even sent this..." She retrieved the black and silver star embroidered cloth and held it out to him. He took it from her, sliding the cloth over his fingers, a scowl etched into his full lips. Lips she hadn't kissed last night.

Oh, Lord, this cannot be happening. I couldn't have kissed Jasper.

"I did not send this...who gave you this?" he demanded sharply, his face flushing and his fists clenching "Another man has been sending you letters and gifts? I'll *kill* him."

"I..." How stupid could she be? She'd let him see it and now the whole incident had turned into her fault. His almost violent response made her take a hasty step back.

"Did you meet with someone last night?" he asked, his lip curling in a soft snarl.

Her heart dropped clear down to her toes with dread.

"No, I—"

James thrust the cloth back at her. "I see the lie in your eyes, Miss Haverford. I cannot attach myself to someone who has clearly been with another man and lied about it. It makes me wonder what else you have lied about." James leaned in close, his eyes narrowed to slits.

"But I haven't lied! I came here to ask you the truth, the letter was signed with your name! How was I to know it wasn't from you?" She wanted to hit him, hit the arrogant man right between the eyes, for assuming she would betray him and their love, a love she had built her dreams and future around. Her heart splintered, each fracture pinching her chest with pain.

"Lies or not, you have granted your attentions to another man, I have little interest in marrying a deceitful creature like you…however." His cold eyes heated up again when he reached to tug a curl of her hair before letting his fingers drop to her throat. "I would be more than willing to offer companionship whenever you tire of this other man."

His words hit her like Lady Greenley's parasol, right in the stomach, her breath knocked completely out of her lungs. She slapped his hand away and took a step back. He wanted to sleep with her, but not marry her? Who was this man? This was not the man she'd written love letters to for eleven years…James Randolph was a coldhearted ruthless stranger.

"I am an honorable woman, and you dishonor me with your accusations and your… *offers*," she added for lack of a better word. She hated herself for the way her voice shook when she took another step back from him. She was going to toss her accounts if she had to spend another minute around this man.

"Suit yourself, Miss Haverford," he replied almost sulkily and stalked off, leaving her alone.

"James, wait!" she called, but he was already gone. Should she run after him? What could she say to erase that accusing glare in his eyes, or remove her own damning desires for the man she'd kissed in her garden? Nothing…and what's more…she didn't *really* want to. There was nothing left to say to him, not after he'd revealed his true nature. Rather than listen to her explain what had happened, he'd made a scandalous and frankly disgusting offer to take her as a mistress. The man she'd loved for so long was a cruel, insensitive brute of a man.

Gemma's eyes filled with tears, she hadn't known, she hadn't meant to disgrace herself or him. How could he just walk away from her, after all these years...it wasn't fair. That awful cloudiness seemed to fill her head again and she couldn't quite get enough breath...

"Gemma?" A concerned male voice, one she recognized all too well, jerked her out of the fainting spell and filled her with cold fury.

She slowly turned around to see Jasper still leaning against the gazebo but he looked ready to come straight to her if she fell. His handsome face was dark with an emotion she couldn't read; it was something between anger, lust, and concern if she could interpret the fire in his eyes and the pursed line of his lips. He straightened up and started walking toward her.

"Bad luck, Gemma," he breathed in soft apology and started to leave.

Oh no, he was not going to just walk away after shattering her so wonderfully planned dreams. No man should ever be allowed to walk away after such a crime.

"You! It was you!" she hissed, grabbing his arm, forcing him to spin around and face her. The muscles of his arm, covered by his jacket, still felt warm beneath her gloved hand. His touch shocked her and she let go immediately.

"I don't know what you're talking about," Jasper said, but his caramel brown eyes were sharp.

Gemma, normally restrained and reserved in her manner, could not contain herself any longer. What was it about this rake in particular that turned her mild-tempered self into a raving heathen full of anger and desire?

"Don't lie to me, Jasper Holland!" She shook him by the shoulders rather violently, not caring that she breached propriety by breathing his first name. Her show of violence did not affect him at all, rather he seemed impassive, a sea of ice compared to the hellish inferno that raged within her. Yet there was no coldness in his eyes, they were hot like melted honey and they revealed his precarious grip on his self-control.

"Calm down, Gemma, there's a good girl. Don't make a scene," Jasper warned.

When he moved to grab her, Gemma stepped back, away from him. At that moment if he had succeeded in touching her she would have slapped him.

"Gemma, come now, you must get control."

"Control? Where was your control last night in the garden? How could you!"

She couldn't stand the sight of him, so she tore away, and started running blindly. The sound of him coming after her, the crashing of the bushes, made her run that much faster. Gemma collided with a prickly bush and briars dug into her stockings at the ankles. A half-strangled cry of pain escaped her lips but there was no time to stop and pull them out because in that brief hesitation she heard his booted feet thundering after her.

Hoisting her gown up past her knees she jumped over the offending bush that had snagged at her gown and kept running.

Jasper's muffled curse came moments later when he ran into that same bush. Her heart beat frantically, and her ragged breathing gave this moment a thrill, one reminiscent of the garden when he'd caught her about her waist and pulled her to him. Gemma had no desire to be caught, least of all by that devil Jasper. She needed to be pursued, to feel wanted, desired, after the heartache she'd just suffered at James's condemning hands. She needed this. And yet, needing it made her feel terrible. She should be weeping and wilting, not running away from the man she'd kissed the night before, the man she wasn't going to marry.

After a mad dash, leaping over flower beds and ducking around hedges, Gemma skidded to a stop in a small clearing. A garden shed sat at the farthest end of the garden away from the party. She ducked inside the dusty tool filled shed, trying to find something with which to secure the door behind her so she might be left alone. The little shed appeared to have been abandoned. Dust coated every surface and the windows were thick with years of grime. A trapped bee buzzed against the window, trying to escape back into the garden. A little pang of sympathy moved through her and she wished she could open the window to free the insect, but from the looks of the window, it was the kind that did not open.

"We're both trapped aren't we," she muttered to the bee as it continued to collide with the glass.

Outside the window Jasper strode into view, panting slightly, his large chest rising and falling. That impossibly dark hair, the hair she remembered touching last night, was wild and windblown with his chase. She ducked behind the wooded shed walls while he scanned the various other garden entries and exits from his location. When his head slowly turned in the direction of the shed, she held her breath, praying he could not see her hiding in the shadows inside. His eyes narrowed and he started toward the shed with purpose.

"Blast!" she hissed and frantically glanced about the little room.

A rusted, wood handled garden hoe rested against the wall in one corner. She snatched it, raising it defensively when Jasper burst in after her. She swung the hoe at his chest, he lunged back, and the shed door slammed shut beneath the force of his body smashing into it as he evaded the hoe's path.

"Gemma! What in God's name are you doing? Put that bloody thing down, before you hurt yourself," he admonished, facing her and lifting his palms, attempting to show her he wouldn't come after her. She lunged for him again, but he leapt aside, barely out of reach.

"Who would care if I did hurt myself? Certainly

not James, you made sure of that!" She was losing that fire of hate against him and in its place was despair. Thick, cloying, choking despair for everything she'd lost.

His warm eyes pleaded with her to calm down, but all she wanted was to erase what had happened last night. To take away every kiss, every caress Jasper had given her. Why couldn't she forget the unspeakable pleasures he'd given her with his hands and his mouth? Those were memories she shouldn't have, shouldn't long for… Everything she dared to remember, it was a betrayal of her heart, a betrayal of the man who'd written to her for eleven years. James should have been the man meeting her in the garden last night.

Jasper ducked from another swing of her garden hoe and then expertly wrenched it from her shaking hands. He set it down, well out of her reach by the door of the shed. Then he turned to watch her, drawing his brows together. Gemma inhaled in a slow shuddering breath, feeling the slow press of tears in her eyes.

Everything is falling apart. I can't even escape the man who ruined my life.

"Don't cry, Gemma darling. I can't bear to see a woman cry," Jasper said, his voice strangely rough, as though something was caught in his throat. He took a step toward her, his black boots made a soft scraping sound over the gray stone floor of the small shed.

She fell back against the wall farthest from him, using her hands to support her behind her back when she bent over a little, sucking in aching breaths. She tried to find the right words to respond.

"How can I not weep for what I've lost? All my dreams, my hopes...you've *ruined* me. Could you not tell James the truth, convince him to take me back?" she pleaded softly. His dark hair gleamed in the dim light of the shed and he shook his head slowly.

James take Gemma back? That was the last thing Jasper wanted. It was also the last thing James wanted. He had his sights on Arabella now and would be announcing their engagement soon.

"No, he would not hear of any excuse, no matter whose lips did the begging. He's not the man for you anyway, there are *better* men out there. Men who would love you to distraction, who would want to spend every night in a garden with you. Forget James. You'll thank me for it later." He prayed she'd understand one day that his deception would help her. It had hurt him to betray her like he had, she was so damned lovely, so perfect in so many ways, and knowing he'd taken away her dreams hurt him as much as she was hurting. As soon as she opened her heart again, he would be there to claim her.

"Please Jasper..." she begged softly, her sweet voice a plaintive bird's frightened trill. The shattering pain in her eyes killed him. She was a strong woman, and he'd broken her.

Hellfire and damnation, I ought to be hanged for what I've done.

"It would do no good..." he repeated, wishing for her sake she would not cry.

She did. The well of tears came first, glistening in her eyes like vibrant, shining jewels, then the trembling shoulders, and at last the choked sound in her little throat.

It broke him into a thousand pieces, scattering like dust in the breeze. All that cool restraint he'd been gripping tooth and nail to keep was gone.

Gemma tried to step around him, to flee the isolated confines of the small garden shed. It was too intimate a space for them both to share, not while her despair and his desire wreaked havoc on them both. Their bodies brushed against each other, fraying his control with the soft promise of what it would feel like to hold her, to ease her pain.

He blocked her path to the door, but she tried to slip to the left, one trembling gloved hand reaching for the iron door handle, but he flung his hands out barring her way to freedom. The moment he wound his arms around her waist she railed against him, fists curled tight, beating his chest. The blows didn't hurt though, and he let her strike out, deserving every stinging punch she gave him.

"Gemma, I'm sorry, truly I am." *Take out your anger on me, little one, I'll still hold onto you for the gift you are.* The gift he wished he could lay claim to now. Knowing he couldn't, created a sharp ache inside his chest. She would need time to come to terms with James, and he still had the problem of his confession with the letters. He didn't want to tell her, but he knew he had to. He was damned either way.

"How could you? How could you do this to me? I hate you! Do you hear me? I hate you Jasper!" she hissed, her fingers digging into his chest, clawing uselessly at his well-protected body. Her voice had risen in pitch when she'd shouted her last statement. Jasper sighed, thankful she'd fled to a place where no one would find them…or hear them.

He pulled her tighter to him, holding her firmly, but gently while she cried herself into a soft exhausted state. Having her in his arms felt so right. He knew he shouldn't be thinking that, and not just because he was the one who'd made her cry. This woman was too good for a man like him. He'd done a lot of things in his life he wasn't proud of. He'd killed men in the heat of battle, he'd seen friends blown to pieces when cannon balls exploded across the decks of his ship.

Every minute he'd been fighting for his life, trying to save himself and his crew from being killed, captured or drowned; it had been this woman here in his arms that had kept him alive. Jasper had fought to stay alive because of her. Her letters had given him courage and strength. Before every battle at sea, he'd wrapped her latest letters in a flat package and secured them against his heart beneath his shirt and uniform. Like a romantic fool, he'd wanted to have that little bit of her close to him, should he perish.

And she'll never know, can never know how much I needed her these last few years. How she saved my life by simply writing back to me. And I'm the bloody bastard who ruined her because I couldn't say no to James.

James had forced him to choose between him and Gemma. Could he deny the man who'd saved his life countless times whatever he asked and in turn hurt the woman he'd come to cherish more than his own life. A devil's predicament with no easy answer except that he was damned no matter who he chose. And he had the sinking feeling he should have protected Gemma over James, not that it would have helped. James would have broken her heart no matter what because he wouldn't let himself fall for any woman, not when it would create a weakness in him that could be exploited.

His throat tightened and he closed his eyes, hating that so many lies rested between them, lies she didn't even know he'd told.

"There now, shhh," he hushed her gently, whispering against her ear. Every little choked sound escaping her lips was slicing him deeper and deeper inside. "Please, darling, I need you to dry your eyes."

If she didn't stop crying soon, he'd do something they'd both regret and enjoy. He'd have to kiss her and make her smile.

Jasper stroked her hair, while her tears soaked through his dark waistcoat. She shouldn't be touching him, shouldn't let him hold her, but his very presence, his very body against hers was thrilling and calming all at once. She wanted to burrow into him even deeper, press every inch of her against him and let his body heat warm her up.

With a little shiver, she rubbed her cheek against his waistcoat, sniffling. That enticing, masculine scent that made her think of the woods, with a hint of sandalwood and a touch of leather. A scent that wrapped itself around her and made her feel safe. How strange that she should feel such things for him? Safe with the man who had just destroyed everything she'd dreamt of having. But it was true, she felt protected by his hold on her, the way he cradled her to his body.

It had been so long since anyone had held her like that. The last time she remembered being so protected, she'd been a child. She'd skinned her knee when she'd sprinted across a stony path too fast and fallen. Her father had found her crying. He'd picked her up, cradling her on the front step of the house until the pain had eased and she was able to let him clean the little scrape. It was so strange that Jasper could make her feel safe. But she didn't feel like a little girl, not while he held her. The way he touched her made her feel like a woman, one that mattered to him. Her heart gave a little jolt when she realized she was thinking about Jasper and not James.

Is my heart so fickle that I should fall for Jasper only minutes after losing James? She clenched her hands into fists and she tried to convince herself she wasn't fickle, that everything that had happened hadn't changed her character in the last half hour.

She opened her eyes again, taking in the dusty interior of the small shed, the thick brown dirt tracking over the gray stone beneath her slippers and Jasper's boots. Their feet were tucked together in a little pattern of boot, slipper, boot, slipper. They remained so tightly pressed against one another that they shared the same breath, almost the same heartbeat. Her skirts tangled between his trousers and he threaded his fingers through the loose curls of her hair. Somehow this felt more intimate in a way than what they'd done the previous night in the garden. Was it because she'd bared her soul, and he could see her heart bleeding? Gemma couldn't help but wonder, what sort of man had Jasper become? How had the years changed him?

As a boy, he'd always been distant where James had been attentive, but then Jasper was a year older and the more dominant one of the pair. James had gotten all the attention because of his natural charm and Jasper had gotten all the responsibility. Gemma had loved James for his smiles and boyish antics which had amused and excited her. She hadn't given much thought to Jasper at all, not when James tugged her curls and wrote her love letters which he snuck through her window in the evening by climbing the trellis outside her window. But somehow all of that ceased to matter when Jasper held her now.

Jasper had shown her what it was like to be with a man, not a boy, and the differences were staggering. She wanted more of what they'd shared in the garden, the breathless kisses, the wild headlong rush toward pleasure when he'd slid his hand between her thighs and touched her in that secret place.

Gemma raised her head, to look up at him, to

better see the face of the man who had brought her body to the trembling brink of ecstasy the night before. James was lost to her now and all she could think of was feeling Jasper's hand on her thigh, sliding across her bare skin. She needed to feel that again. Jasper tightened his hands about her waist the slightest bit and he gazed down at her with his stunningly bright eyes.

"I...I never noticed before..." she whispered to herself, not realizing he heard her until he spoke.

"Noticed what?" His warm breath flushed across her skin like a southern breeze, exotic and exciting.

"You look so much like him, or rather, he looks like you...but he's the apprentice's etching...and you...you are the artist's masterpiece..." Her gaze traced his handsome face. He was beyond beautiful, words could not capture that breathless flutter of her pulse, or the heat that spread from head to toe when he dared to even just glance her way... He was so much more handsome than James. How had she not seen that before? Even as boys, he'd been the more attractive one, always an inch taller, a little larger.

"*You* are the most beautiful thing I have ever seen, like the goddess Diana...the fair huntress..." he breathed, and she felt a strange stirring in her chest, that he knew to call her a name which only her father had ever done before.

She rose up on tiptoe to kiss him. That brush of her lips on his sent spirals of giddy delight through her. The secret thrill deep at her very core, churned to life when he wound one hand in her hair at the nape of her neck to hold her closer for his kiss. Little tingles seemed to shoot out from the point where their mouths met and a little gasp escaped her.

She frantically clung to him, kissing him wildly and her world began to blur. Jasper rotated her around so she had her back up against the shed door and he pinned her there with his body, kissing her deeply, ravaging her mouth. She parted her lips for his questing tongue and responded eagerly to his silent, sensual instruction. Their lips moved together, playful, nipping, sucking, caressing.

Jasper settled one of his hands on her outer thigh, snaking her gown up. The fabric of her dress and her petticoats became bunched up around her hips. He lifted her bottom away from the door and crushed her gown up high on her waist before he pushed her back against the door. He kept her gown tucked up and out of the way so he could trace his fingertips around the edge of her stocking on her lower thigh and play with the ribbons that fastened them in place. That little touch tickled and she couldn't help but let a little breathless giggle escape.

"Do you like it when I do this?" he whispered against her mouth while his fingertips stroked little teasing circles on the bare skin of her outer thigh.

"Hmm, yes," she managed to get out between little blissful sighs. The soft touches were wonderful. Every part of her body seemed to be building in a low hum like a hive of bees awakening in the early morning hours.

"Did you like what I did to you last night?" He slid his hand between her legs, questing between her undergarments until he found the slit in the fabric and he cupped her mound.

She could only nod and throw her head back when he applied a small amount of pressure, rubbing his palm against her as he did so. *More*, she needed more of what he'd done last night.

"Please, Jasper, please do not make me beg." She gasped at the same instant he stroked one fingertip around the edge of her channel. She whimpered but couldn't prevent the wetness that rushed to greet his touch. He hissed softly before he took her mouth with his again.

His lips turned almost feral. That rough, ungentlemanly kiss made every tiny hair upon her body stand at attention and her womb clench in eagerness for him. She didn't want to think about what it meant that his edge of roughness excited and thrilled her.

He stroked her once, twice, three times, before his finger sank deep within her. Using his hand, he brought her to the edge, finding some spot inside her that with each little brush of his finger, made her legs jerk and a spark of flaming heat shoot up her spine.

"Let me inside you, Gemma, please." His gruff plea sent riotous frissons of pleasure through her. He begged to have his pleasure too. It ought to be fair, this sharing of intense physical joy. Last night only she had reached a fulfillment. She wouldn't do that to him again, leave him to satisfy her needs alone.

"Yes." It was the only word he seemed to need to hear before he began to undo his buckskin colored trousers. He lifted her leg up around his hip.

"Grip me, just there." He patted her calf.

"Understand?" he said in a breathless voice.

She nodded, tightening her leg around his hip, loving the way it kept them close together. Then he fussed with her skirts with one hand and his lower body with the other. Before she could get too distracted, he kissed her, wild and hard.

Gemma shook all over, her body reacting to the rush of sensations. She couldn't prepare herself for his entry and bit back a cry of pain as he thrust into her. The sensation of fullness overpowered her. The painful stretching mixed with a lingering sense of pleasure. She wriggled her hips, trying to escape the feeling of being pinned, helpless and vulnerable while enduring that throbbing pain between her legs where he'd sheathed himself. His mouth broke away from hers. Her eyes flew open to find him gazing at her. He moved inside her, then stilled suddenly.

"How much does it hurt?"

"It doesn't," she lied, too ashamed to admit it did, but the pain eased a little.

"Gemma, darling, I've seen enough hurt in the eyes of others in my life that I can recognize it." He threaded one hand in her hair, and nuzzled her cheek. "Try to relax. The pain should ease." He pressed his lips to hers, then spoke again. "Breathe with me."

In. Out. She drew in breath after breath, matching his. He kissed her neck and everything below her waist seemed to turn to liquid fire.

"I'm much better." She sighed in delight when the pleasure began to build along with the strange pressure in her womb.

"Thank God." He chuckled. "Hold on to me,

darling." That was her only warning before he started to move inside her, faster, harder. He bent his knees, lowering himself a few inches then jerked his hips up, so he could bury his length deeper into her. He tore through her body and soul, as a surge of ecstasy built, overtaking her pain.

There was something masterful and mesmerizing in the way he stared at her while he took her. Those caramel eyes captured her, held her entranced like his voice had in the garden the night before and she couldn't look away. Their bodies moved in unison now, and she learned to open herself up to him and cling tighter at the same time. The wood beneath her back burned into her skin, but she didn't care. With each thrust, Jasper moved faster and fiercer as though possessed by some animal spirit that could not be stopped.

They ceased to be two separate souls, but became something infinitely more complex and yet singular. She curled her arms around his neck, and fisted one hand in his hair, tugging tight on the strands, desperate to keep hold of him. It would be so easy to fly away, she felt light enough that a breeze could carry her off.

"Don't let go of me, Jasper," she gasped. The world around her spun like a child's toy top.

"Never…" he vowed "*Never.*"

For the briefest instant she wished his uttered promise were true, that he would never let her go, that she could belong to him for the rest of her life.

Gemma gave in fully and completely, her body aching so terribly she thought she was dying. She would have screamed out but Jasper's lips found hers again and she saw stars. Brilliant lights and fiery tingles ruptured through her entire body. Jasper shuddered against her and slowed. Gemma felt a spreading of deep heat, his heat and she knew something forceful, unchangeable had happened between them. It could never be undone, this fire that burned, this fire that would spark, flash and turn them both to ash, and it was all for the wrong man.

Chapter Five

They stayed connected to each other for a long moment, their faces close. Jasper leaned in, stealing the softest kiss from her lips, which trembled along with the rest of her. She couldn't help it. Every muscle, every bone, everything seemed to be liquid and unstable. If he let her go now, she'd melt into a puddle at his feet.

"I thought I was going to die…" she whispered. He half-smiled and kissed her again, this time deeper.

Each kiss seemed to be her undoing. She never wanted them to stop. The way he tasted her mouth, played with her tongue, gently, like he was enjoying the experience after they'd made love and simply wanted to keep himself connected to her. Something deep inside her felt warm and soft every time his lips brushed hers. Like coming home after a long walk back from the village and spying the front garden gate of her home, with lilacs thick in bloom and birds clinging to the fence posts, singing. There was no other way to describe Jasper's kiss except that it felt like coming home…

"It does that first time, the French call it the 'little death,'" he explained quietly and very slowly pulled out of her body.

Her channel stung from his withdrawal and she shut her eyes and Gemma winced. Everything that had felt so wonderful seconds ago now seemed sore and sensitive.

"It is supposed to hurt like this?" she asked, watching him fix his breeches.

"Only the first few times. Here, lift your gown, darling." He pulled out his handkerchief and got down on one knee.

She lifted her gown, wondering what he meant to do.

A small line of blood trailed down her left inner thigh. Jasper wiped her skin with surprising tenderness and dabbed at her throbbing core. Embarrassment heated her cheeks and she looked away, ashamed. Was bleeding normal? Had she done something wrong?

He rose and she dropped her skirts hastily, but he didn't move away. Catching her chin, he tilted her head up so she was forced to meet his gaze.

"I'm sorry I hurt you. The first time usually leaves a woman with some bleeding. Take care of yourself for a few days, no riding. Be gentle with your body." He spoke so frankly of the situation that she jerked back, hitting the door behind her with a little *oomph!* Jasper sighed and crowded her against the door.

"I know most men don't speak of such things. I'm sorry that I'm not more gentle with you, darling. It's just that I've grown accustomed to the lives of men bleeding out in front of me on the deck of a ship. I'm not very good at being respectable. I say things I shouldn't. Clearly" —he gestured between their bodies— "I've done things I shouldn't."

That comment made the lingering taste of his kiss upon her lips turn bitter.

"I understand." She raised her chin, trying with every shaking breath not to let him see that his words were stabbing her heart to pieces. "I am a mistake."

With a low growl, he tossed the bloody handkerchief on the floor and scowled at her.

"That's not at all what I meant, and you know that." He paused, his heated gaze turned soft, and he lowered his voice, smoothing out the gruffness. "I meant that I've wronged you, Gemma, not the other way around. We both know that you being with me here, agreeing to let me have you, has ruined what little chance you had of marriage with *anyone*."

Not just James. The weight of those unsaid words burned her straight through like a blazing fire on dry tinder. What was she supposed to do now? Live the rest of her life alone with her parents? She'd never defined herself by marriage, still didn't. Living as a spinster might have been something she could have tolerated before she'd been with Jasper. Now she wanted things, dark, wonderful, powerful things, and a spinster wouldn't get a chance to experience that pleasure ever again.

"But you and I…" She dared not ask him to do the proper thing and propose to her. She couldn't marry Jasper, even if he wanted her to. She couldn't be with a man she'd been forced to marry due to their circumstances. He would despise her for such an entrapment and she couldn't bear to have him hate her too.

"Gemma, you and James have just called off your understanding, now isn't the time to be thinking about…anyone else. You need time to heal your heart." His sigh seemed heart-heavy and she couldn't help but wonder what made him believe that. The handsome features of his eyes and mouth seemed to darken with a grim resignation.

Swallowing the lump in her throat, she nodded. "I suppose that's it then, we go our separate ways. I should fix my appearance before I return to the party."

Gemma found her strength returning to her and with trembling hands she checked her gown. Thankfully it was unmarred by dirt or blood. She'd been lucky. He returned to his knees, once more lifting her gown, but this time he only touched her ankles, prying away the brittle briars which lodged into her stockings during her flight from him. His gentle touch made her both hate and adore him at the same time. How could this man make her feel such wild extremes?

When he got to his feet again, he stared at her for a long moment. The sunlight coming through the windows of the garden shed seemed to fill the room with heat and she knew a blush crept up her neck to her cheeks. A century seemed to span between them, colored with a thousand thoughts that passed between their eyes along with the hints of words upon their lips that went unspoken. Everything was full of promise, yet tinged with a sense of desperation and melancholy she couldn't understand.

Without a word, he wrapped his arms around her waist and tugged her up against the length of his body. He buried his face in the groove between her neck and shoulder with lips pressed tenderly against her skin while he held her. The shock of his sudden embrace had her tensing for several long heartbeats before she finally relaxed. Gemma touched him back, tentatively at first.

After a few seconds, the pressure of his hands on her back made her feel feminine and protected. She'd never thought a man's embrace would make her feel like this or that she'd enjoy it so much. It wasn't that she felt weak or fragile, she simply felt safe in his arms. The way he held her, with such desperate pressure, made her feel like he was trying to erase all the ways he'd hurt her that day. As if his arms alone could protect her from whatever would come next. Silly, she knew to think that, because the moment they left the shed, her world would shatter all over again.

But here, now, it was easy to forget that the world around them existed. The idea that life continued outside these small dusty walls of the shed was impossible. The only thing that really mattered to her was what she'd just experienced with Jasper. The pleasure of that spirited union when she surrendered her innocence to him. And then his desire to hold her, the clash of tempers...All of it had been worth it, to feel such an enchanting moment of bliss within his arms and the sweet taste of his mouth against hers. But even the strongest spells could be broken...

"Just tell me the truth Jasper, it was you in the garden last night wasn't it." She needed to be sure it was him. She had to hear him say it. When'd he'd touched her, kissed her here in the garden shed, it had been just like the man who'd come to her in the garden, rough hands, soft lips, drugging kisses...

Jasper pulled back from her. "What difference does it make if it was me?" He looked at her, his face inscrutable.

"It matters, because I need to know if I have been with another man besides you, I need to know!" She met his gaze, bravely fighting off the urge to cry. She had a right to know the truth.

Jasper released his hold on her, putting distance between them.

"Bloody hell, Gemma. Fine, it was me. Does that make it any better?" He crossed his arms over his chest and scowled.

Gemma bit her bottom lip and blinked rapidly, hoping no more tears would escape her eyes. The moment they'd shared was over and she had to accept it and move on.

"Thank you for your candor. Now excuse me, I have to return to the party." She tried to push past him to exit the garden shed.

"Gemma...stay." Jasper put out a hand, but she

knocked it away.

"No…" she gasped, her throat constricted and her lungs burned. "I have to get out of this dreadful place…I can't breathe!" Gemma shoved him away and almost ripped the door from its rusty hinges in her flight to freedom.

Part of her wanted to never see him again. To her shame she looked back after a few steps, but he leaned against the frame of the open doorway, not moving. He did not try to stop her. The other part of her wanted him to chase after her, catch her and tell her that his promise to never let her go was one he would keep. But he didn't. He let her go, broken heart and all.

Jasper remained in the little garden shed for a long while after she'd gone, staring out the window. He had just cornered her and taken her like some beast, without a thought to her pain until it was too late. Seeing her tears, quarreling with her, when all he wanted to do was hold her and kiss away every glistening drop on her cheeks was enough to destroy the last of his sanity. How could he have so little control when it came to her?

I've survived scurvy, starvation, fire ships, pirates who slit the throats of men while they sleep in their hammocks, and yet I cannot seem to withstand Gemma's tears.

He'd robbed her of the one thing she'd protected and held for the man meant to love her. It should have been given on her wedding night to her husband, the man he wanted to be more than anything, but he'd acted too early, too rashly. The worst part was he didn't feel guilty enough for a man who'd done what he'd just had, in fact, he had loved every single kiss and heated thrust of that short but powerful moment with Gemma. The innocent wantonness of her response had been his undoing. The way she responded to his touch, his kiss, every little shiver and sigh had made him hot all over and aching to be inside her body in whatever way he could.

What was he supposed to do now? Did he just walk away from her until she was ready to love again after James? He wanted nothing more than to tell her everything, but for the first time true fear cut him deep. He could lose her if she chose to hate him after everything he'd done. What if he wasn't enough for her? Assuming she could get past the lies he'd told her, and the letters he'd written claiming to be his closest friend, would she want him?

A lack of confidence had never been one of his weaknesses but now he was afraid he wouldn't be enough for her. All he had was his parent's home, a little country mansion, half a dozen servants and a respectable income. The dreams of returning glorious with a vast fortune hadn't been possible, and he couldn't stay at sea another decade. That life had taken much from him and now all he craved was a measure of peace. Would that be good enough for a woman like Gemma who deserved a wonderful life?

He'd been raised to be the sort of man who did the right thing by people, but the years spent serving in the navy had changed him. He had learned that people could be sacrificed, that men could be betrayed and that you had to look out for your own interests. Gemma was most certainly one of his interests. He only wished he could tell her everything at that moment, confess his lies and win back her trust so he could be that much closer to winning her heart.

I'm damned for craving something far beyond my reach...

"Gemma, there you are!" Lily cried out when Gemma emerged from the gardens. "Oh dear, what's happened to you?" Lily took her friend's hand and pulled her aside, no one seemed to notice them at any rate. Most of Lady Greenley's guests huddled around the tent where tea was being served.

Licking her lips, Gemma stared at the tea. A cool cup of tea would ease the burn in the back of her throat. "I'm fine, I just fell ill in the garden and had to rest. I shall be better as soon as I've had some tea." Gemma tried to convince herself, but she hurt in all sorts of places below the waist and she felt exhausted.

"Come then, let's get you some." Lily led her to the tent where they were served two cups by a footman.

The tea was cold and pleasant, soothing her throat which was still tight and raw from her crying. While she sipped her tea, she turned her attention to the guests. Most of them seemed to have herded themselves into a small crowd near the entrance to the garden. The ladies grouped together, their colorful gowns striking against the rich green of the lawns. The light breeze played with their skirts, billowing them out like the sails of a dozen small ships.

A short distance away, some of the older gentleman bunched together, murmuring to each other, occasionally chuckling. Their cheeks were rosy and despite their best attempts to hide it, more than a few men seemed to be drinking glasses of sherry whilst their wives were otherwise occupied. She would have smiled, except she noticed that the women were focused on something that sliced her heart into tiny pieces. James and that awful woman Arabella seemed to be in the middle of a group of women who were chittering and clucking like little birds.

"Lily, what is happening over there?" she asked, her head spinning with a heavy sense of sudden doom.

Lily glared at James before turning back to her. "Mr. Randolph has just announced his engagement to Arabella Stevens."

"What?" Gemma's voice out dreadfully shrill, but thankfully no one had the least bit of interest in her. All eyes were on the new happy couple. *Couple.* The word cut deep. How had he moved so quickly to Arabella when just a half an hour ago she and James were supposed to be engaged? The tea she'd been sipping seemed suddenly bitter and she flinched, setting her cup down on her saucer hard enough that it rattled.

"It seems." Lily cleared her throat. "That Mr. Randolph and Miss Stevens have met before, and that they have been courting this last month."

Courting? James had been courting another woman while writing love letters to her?

"How? How could he do this to me?" she said in a hoarse whisper. Her heart shattered into even smaller pieces beneath the weight of James's betrayal. All those letters, each word she had cherished had been nothing but lies. To move on from her so quickly? It made no sense, what sort of man had she fallen in love with? Everything she'd worked for, planned for, every hope and every dream had been spurned by James, and tricked by Jasper. She wasn't sure which man she hated more at that moment.

"Apparently he met her several months ago in Brighton and has been in love with her ever since," Lily informed Gemma in an acidic whisper. "What a wretched man. If Henry only knew, he'd…oooh!" Lily kicked at a tuft of grass with her slippered foot. "Do you want me to have Henry draw his cork? I'm sure he'd be happy to."

Gemma shook her head. "No, you mustn't. I just… Oh, Lily…it was supposed to be me," she whispered to her friend.

Lily alone knew of the depth of Gemma's and James's secret love letter affair. The secret stack of letters had never been bared to another's eyes save for Lily's, because there were often passages that were so amusing, or impressive, and often romantic that Gemma felt compelled to share them with her closest friend. Lily would often comment on them, tell Gemma her thoughts on what she believed certain things meant, and it was part of Lily's impressions that had led her to believe James would marry her. Had they both been so utterly wrong on that account?

"Look not to him, not any longer Gemma. Perhaps you ought to adjust your gaze to finer, better company?" Lily cupped Gemma's chin and turned it to point to the person who had just emerged from the garden. Jasper Holland. How he could look so devilishly handsome in his blue coat and buckskin trousers? It was dreadfully unfair. Gemma blinked back tears and pulled free of Lily's hand.

"No, no. I detest Mr. Holland. He's a ruthless rogue!" she declared vehemently, even if the sight of him did make her mouth suddenly go dry and make her body shudder with a confusing twist of feminine interest and near abject misery. How could a man make her want to cry and to kiss him at the same time? What was a woman supposed to do when a man tugged her in two completely different directions?

It was as though he heard her words because his gaze met hers. A flash of intensity and dark brooding passed between them. He clenched his hands into fists and took one step in her direction, then froze when he seemed to realize she would attempt to turn him to stone like Medusa if he dared to come closer.

Lily's gaze darted between him and Gemma, her lips pursed into a confused moue. "That is a pity. I thought he seemed rather taken with you, Gemma. He's done nothing but stare at you since you've arrived," Lily said, eyeing Jasper with an arched brow.

Gemma tore her eyes away from him, wanting to remove that creeping feeling of need, of hunger for newly discovered pleasures. She couldn't want him, couldn't want to make love to him again, not when she was so determined to hate him for all eternity.

Henry Becknell, Lilly's tall, blond-haired husband trotted over to them. "Lily, my love, come quick, the archery contest has been set up."

He was the sort of man a woman could love immediately. All smiles and boyish charm without any of the danger that someone like James or Jasper would pose to a girl's virtue. Henry was older than James and Jasper by two years and had been away at school before Lily had grown up into the town beauty. When he'd returned home, it had been inevitable that they'd fallen in love. Gemma was filled with envy sometimes when she watched them, but she was happy for her friend too. Lily deserved to be loved by a good man, and Henry was the finest there was.

"Miss Haverford," he greeted Gemma warmly.

She smiled a little; Henry was so good-natured that it was hard to keep one's spirits depressed when he was near. "Mr. Becknell," she replied.

"I know you love a bit of archery too. Come and join us, give my Lily some competition, eh?" His teasing challenge made it irresistible to refuse.

"Oh, very well." She laughed. Archery was one of her pleasures at parties like these and it would do her some good to get her mind on other things. There was nothing as satisfying as handling a weapon when one was in a foul mood. When she pictured shooting James in the rump with an arrow, she stifled a giggle. It was too tempting a notion.

Henry escorted them both to the part of the lawns where ten targets had been arranged and bows laid out for those interested in competing. James and his new bride-to-be refrained from the contest, choosing instead to linger near the tea tables and gossip with others not participating. Gemma didn't want to have to face that embarrassment of having to speak to them and congratulate them. It was actually a relief that they stayed far enough away that she could focus on the archery. She and Lily both slipped on leather vambraces and shooting gloves to protect their arms and hands.

Jasper had recovered somewhat from her earlier glower at him to keep his distance and now strode toward them, a purposeful gleam in his eyes. Glancing away, she did her best to pretend she didn't notice him. It didn't stop her body from sensing him. Each of the fine hairs on her neck prickled and she felt his focus on her.

"It's a pity you despise Mr. Holland, he seems keen to be your partner for the first round," Lily remarked in a low whisper behind her hand.

Gemma determinedly looked away from the clearly interested gaze that Jasper kept shooting her way. How the devil was she to avoid him if he came over to join her in the game?

"Would your husband care to partner me?" she asked Lily.

With a sigh, Lily waved Henry over to them. "Gemma, dear, we shall have to have a talk about you avoiding eligible men," she whispered softly so her husband wouldn't overhear.

"Henry, my heart, would you partner Gemma? She's in need of rescuing." Lily's smile to her husband earned a chuckle from Henry.

"Of course." Henry winked. "Assisting ladies in distress is my specialty."

"Thank you." Lily glanced about, apparently seeing no one watching them and planted a kiss on her husband's lips. The barest touch, yet it made Henry turn an amusing shade of red. Gemma longed to have that sort of relationship with a man, where a hint of a kiss would be a reminder of the passion that burned between them when no one was around to witness it. It was romantic, and sweet, and deeply full of love, and it made her chest ache to witness it.

After making sure Gemma and Henry would be fine, Lily left them and went to claim a different partner.

Gemma took up a bow and joined Henry at one of the ten targets, ready to match herself against him to see who would advance in the contest. She was a skilled archer and was better than Henry, who loved the sport but lacked Gemma's natural skill. One more reason that her father called her a fair huntress. She and the bow were well suited.

She took her shot first and then while Henry lined up for his, she scanned the other couples at the targets, finding Lily and Jasper at the target to her immediate right. Jasper, like Henry, had removed his waistcoat so that he now only had on his white blouse and gold embroidered vest. He cut a stunning figure, long legs parted slightly in the proper stance, bow raised and arms taut with perfectly controlled strength. The shirt molded to his muscles, showing off his body in a way that seemed all too intimate. Muscles she remembered touching, digging her fingers into as she'd come apart in his arms. Gemma forced herself to look away.

After several rounds the contestants narrowed down to four. Lily and Gemma were against each other on one target and Jasper and Gemma's father were on the other target. Lily took her stance after Gemma fired. She raised her bow rather too quickly and with the faintest glint of mischief in her eyes that Gemma nearly missed, she released her arrow. It zipped through the air at a wide angle and embedded itself in the outermost circle on the target.

"Lily, what are you doing?" Gemma hissed at her friend.

Lily merely shrugged one elegant little shoulder, a hint of a smile upon her lips and then she left for the tea tables. Gemma's father raised his bow, one eye fixed on the target and then he took his shot. He'd always been decent at archery, but like Lily, his shot went wide, wide enough that he missed the target entirely. It sunk into the ground some yards behind it. The white tuft of the arrow's feathers quivered with the force of the shot. With a casual shrug, her father turned, smiled at Lily and left the archery area.

Had her father purposely used too much strength to send the arrow sailing well out of reach of the target? And if he had…why? That would mean Jasper won his round, and now she and Jasper were the only two left.

Devil take it, this was not going to end well for either of them.

Chapter Six

The crowd, which had gathered around the archers at the beginning of the contest, melted away so only Gemma and Jasper remained. She was never more thankful for the apparent disinterest of those people. Being the center of attention had never been something she enjoyed, and knowing she would have to be around Jasper, feeling as unbalanced as she did now…it was best if she wasn't under the scrutiny of others.

"Gemma," Jasper greeted softly. His voice was full of warmth and it reminded her too much of the garden shed and what they'd done there. Her lower body gave a pulsing response, reminding her of just how tender she still was.

"Mr. Holland," she replied quietly, however she couldn't hide the little growl in her voice. After this party was over, she was going to return home, and never set foot in Midhurst again, not if it meant seeing Jasper. She steeled herself against another wretched pang in her heart at James's callous betrayal of her and Jasper's deception.

Thankfully all of the attention was primarily back on James and Arabella. James's voice carried over the air while he told the crowd how he first met Arabella. No one watched Jasper or Gemma when they approached the last target, bows in hand. Gemma resolved to not say another word to him. She would likely be furious at him for the next century. Introducing her to pleasure like that last night in the garden, and then again seducing her today in the garden shed.

She tried not to think about the ramifications of what had happened in the shed on her future. There was little hope now of marriage to anyone. Her husband, if she was fortunate enough to find one, would likely discover she was no longer a maiden.

She shivered as a heavy sense of dread choked her. She gripped her bow hard enough that her knuckles turned white. Why was the world so unfair toward a woman and not a man?

"Would you care to go first Gemma?" Jasper asked.

"You will address me as Miss Haverford," she replied icily.

Jasper glanced over at the distracted crowd before leaning in close to her and stroking her cheek with the back of his hand. Gemma swatted his hand away, avoiding the intensity of his gaze and the way it seemed to bring her right back to that moment in the shed when they'd been connected so deeply, touching everywhere, mouths a breath apart. She hated the fact that she loved the burn that simple touch drew forth on her skin and the almost tangible memories it evoked.

"Wouldn't you say that after what we shared today, we no longer need to be bound by the rules of formality?"

Even though she despised his words, she knew he was right. His hand strayed lower, to tease her waist where she was most ticklish. Shivers shot up her spine. He grinned mischievously, reaching for a more firm grasp, but she resumed her restraint and whacked his hand with the tip of her bow.

"Please Gemma, give me a smile. I know you are angry with me, but I don't want you to be. We were friends once, weren't we? I should like to be friends again." He set his bow on the ground beside his feet.

"Friends?" She planted one hand on her hip and challenged him. "We were never friends, Jasper. You always chased me away when I tried to follow you and James around. You got mad when James tugged on my curls, you left jars of tadpoles on my bedroom window hoping to frighten me when I woke up and saw them wriggling about in the pond water." She almost smiled at the memory.

Tadpoles had been rather fascinating to her, and whenever she'd found a jar, the little green bodies lit by bright sunlight on the open window ledge, she'd pull up a chair and watch the creatures inside the glass. She supposed it was because her father had nurtured in her an appreciation for science. The tadpoles would grow up to be frogs someday, and the thought that they would had captivated her. She had a love of the things that made the world what it was, a place of endless wonder and never ending miracles. Miracles that Jasper had left on her window when he was a boy to try and frighten her. This time a little smile did escape and she blushed.

Jasper cleared his throat and tugged at his cravat with one crooked finger. "Did you ever think that I might be jealous of James? The way you used to look at him, with those big beautiful eyes, and all that ginger colored hair so perfect for tugging on." He reached up as though lost in a dream of days past and curled one lock of her hair about his finger, tugging.

Gemma stared up at him, completely consumed by the look in his eyes and the strange exciting thrills her body had in response to that single little tug of her hair. What would it be like if he fisted his hand completely in her hair and pulled her head back for his kiss? It would be divine...she shook her head, trying desperately to clear her thoughts of such wonderful, no sinful, ideas.

"Then why push me away?" she demanded in a hushed whisper. Was he really jealous of James? Had he liked her much more than he'd pretended to? She couldn't despise a man who had secretly been jealous of his friend because of her. She was still angry and hurt but the seething rage had faded. His actions had been those of a jealous man, not of one full of callous disregard.

He raked a hand through his dark hair, pulling

hard on the strands as though he attempted to control himself. "You were so young Gemma. I knew better than to let myself feel things toward you."

"Young? Jasper, I'm only one year younger than you." He was twenty-six, but she had to admit he had lived more than she had in many ways. She'd been in Midhurst while he'd been out seeing the world, fighting battles, protecting His Majesty's Empire. It made her feel strangely small and insignificant in comparison.

"A boy of fifteen is very different from a girl of fourteen." He stroked his hand down her waist again, toying with the folds of her skirt. Once or twice he gripped it harder and she wondered if he was tempted to pull her closer.

She blew out a very slow breath, trying to still her racing heart. "I suppose you might be right. I knew nothing of boys or men at that age. I confess I still don't understand the male creature. You are a mysterious lot." Her tone came out teasing, and she didn't mind. This frank discussion was good. They needed to speak plainly of this or else she might really be tempted to hate him for the rest of her life and she didn't want to hate Jasper. He was too good in so many ways, even if he had seduced her. But what a sweet seduction it had been. It made her understand why some women were compromised. The temptation to be with someone sometimes outweighed the good sense of one's mind.

"Perhaps we should finish the contest," she suggested and gestured with the bow she still gripped in one hand at the last target.

"Very well." Jasper sighed and retrieved his bow from the ground.

Gemma lined up for her shot, raising the bow and notching her arrow, but he would not leave her be.

"Your stance, while excellent, could still be improved..." He moved to stand behind her, his entire length pressed up against her. The rush of heat that followed made her blush a deep scarlet. She demand he step back, even when his arms came up around hers to better her stance. He released her arms and settled his palms possessively on her waist while he waited patiently for her to take her shot.

"I can't concentrate when you are touching me, Mr. Holland," she said, trying to wiggle her hips to dislodge those warm hands. He tightened his grip and pulled her back against him. It was impossible to ignore the state of his arousal which dug into her lower back. She couldn't help but gasp.

"I can't release you Gemma, you left me in a state of desire that is unseemly for public eyes. Please, stop that wriggling or else I'll be in certain trouble..." he warned.

"It would serve you right, you know, for me to leave you in such a state." She bit the inside of her cheek to hide her smile.

"And I'm sure I quite deserve that, but then there will be all those pesky questions about who left me in that state. You wouldn't want anyone to guess it might be your beauty that inspired such a reaction in me, now would you?" His fingers dug into her waist.

"Threats are beneath you, Mr. Holland."

"Not true." He laughed. "I'd threaten quite a bit to stay close to you."

"Jasper, you mustn't say such things." Gemma tried to step away, but he held fast to her hips. The silent show of his strength sent sparks of energy through her and goose bumps broke out on her skin.

"Ahh! At last, I hate it when you call me Mr. Holland. It seems only when I thoroughly distract you, do I get you to call me Jasper." His chuckle created a warm rush of breath upon the back of her neck, making her tremble at the way it made her feel. Heat pooled inside her lower belly and she tried to exert some control over herself.

She stilled her faint struggling and tried to concentrate on taking her shot. She lifted the bow, pulled back the bowstring so it touched her lips, and let it fly. The arrow went a little to the left of center and she muttered a disappointed curse, which made Jasper laugh.

"Please take your shot Mr. Holland, I beg you." Gemma waved her bow at the target, urging him to go.

"Would you call me Jasper again if I win?" he asked, arching one eyebrow. Half his mouth quirked into a sly smile.

Gemma weighed this consequence against getting some small measure of revenge. She planned to so thoroughly distract him he'd certainly lose.

"If you win...I will do more than call you Jasper." She smiled this time, the same smile she'd seen Lily use to catch Henry when the pair had first met. It was a lure, something Gemma had never wanted to use before. But now she wanted to use it on Jasper, to wound him the way she'd been wounded. So she would string him out, it wasn't as if she had anything else to lose now. James was gone, she'd been compromised, and nothing else mattered.

Its effect on Jasper was clear, his gaze sharpened on her and he furrowed his brow. "Just what sort of extra reward would I be entitled to claim?" he asked, seemingly amused at her sudden willingness to play his game.

"I am sure that whatever your imagination can devise will be suitable. I no longer care about my reputation so don't bother to censor your desires on my account," she snapped.

At her harsh reaction, his lips turned downward and he ducked his head, avoiding her gaze. "Ahh, I see. Perhaps no reward then. We ought to just finish the game." He cleared his throat and all playfulness was gone.

Jasper took his stance. Gemma stood close to him, memorizing the outline of his muscles against his white blouse where the cloth molded to his arms as he raised his bow. Perhaps she could manage some measure of distraction the way he had with her. He poised to release his arrow and Gemma spoke softly near his ear, running a hand from his waist up to his chest while she pressed her body against his from behind.

You've tempted me, now I'll tempt you...

Chapter Seven

"I do believe you've awakened a rather sinful side in me, Mr. Holland…" Gemma said in a husky whisper. The rich sound of it sent a bolt of arousal straight to Jasper's groin and he swallowed a curse.

"Oh?" He tried to sound uninterested as he readied to take his shot. If his aim was true, he would win the game, and although nothing was at stake, he desperately wanted to win. He was prepared to release his arrow when Gemma spoke again.

"After our interlude in the shed, I'm quite resolved to seek that sort of pleasure again and soon. I have you to thank for opening my eyes to the better parts of living," she said with a light tone, one of careless disregard. He knew though that she couldn't possibly mean it…He hadn't made her a jaded woman after just one encounter in a garden shed, had he?

"Perhaps I'll go to London and become someone's mistress. It's all I'm good for these days. Perhaps I'll even consider being your mistress..." She leaned up on her tiptoes and kissed his left ear.

The shock of her words and the lingering kiss sent his arrow disastrously wide, so wide it missed the target by nearly thirty feet and tore straight through the fluffy plumed feather of Lady Greenley's bonnet. Lady Greenley, who'd been conversing with Gemma's mother, screamed when his arrow ripped her bonnet from her head and embedded it in the ground several feet away.

"We're under attack! Sound the alarm!" Lady Greenley shrieked, parasol swinging as she ran toward the tea tables.

Mrs. Haverford's head whipped around in their direction and she glared at him and Gemma.

"She will kill you when she finds out you destroyed her best bonnet," Gemma said with her hands resting firmly on her hips. A little smile twitched her lips.

"And right before she beheads me with that bloody parasol, I will be sure to tell her that I did not act alone, but that you were my accomplice in the bonnet murdering plot," he retorted.

Much to his surprise she started to giggle.

"You would betray me to such a fierce creature like Lady Greenley? You scoundrel!" She laughed heartily. It made something tug deep in his chest and his own heart beat faster. He loved to see her laugh, the way it lit up her eyes and banished all sadness. He never wanted to see tears of defeat glimmering in her gaze ever again. It would break him.

"Come on, this way, before she beheads us!" Jasper grasped her hand and pointed toward the tea tables. Gemma turned to see Lady Greenley had turned back around in her ranting.

"Oh heavens, she knows it's you, Jasper!" Gemma gasped softy.

Lady Greenly moved her focus from the hat stuck firmly in the grass, to where Jasper and Gemma stood. The old matronly lady plucked at her sleeves in a strangely serious manner, like a solider checking his uniform moments before he set out to battle.

Oh dear. Jasper inwardly groaned. Lady Greenley headed for him in strong, quick strides, parasol ready, eyes ablaze with bloody vengeance. He'd faced many a harrowing storm, and battles at sea, yet nothing compared to this one elderly woman with her parasol. The might of the British Empire was built upon women like Lady Greenley.

"You devil, trying to kill an old woman? By God you will rue the day you accepted my invitation to this party!" Lady Greenley shouted in Jasper's direction.

"Perhaps we ought to run for our lives?" Jasper asked casually as though offering her a cup of tea. He was rewarded with a merry glint in her eyes.

"Oh, yes. Fleeing would be wise," Gemma agreed and Jasper tugged her back into the safety of the garden.

He led her down turn after dizzying turn in the hedgerows before finally pulling her behind a tall hedge wall that had some loose leafy branches which they peered through to the other side. Lady Greenley paraded about, hollering for the blaggards to show themselves, her parasol waving like a saber in the air. Gemma started to laugh but Jasper clamped a hand over her mouth, silencing her.

"Shh…we must be silent, fair huntress, else we'll attract the beast's attention…"

She didn't glance his way when he used the nickname she'd told him about so long ago in her letters. He hadn't forgotten, couldn't ever forget what she'd written.

Dearest James,

Can you believe it's almost hunting season here? My father is leading a fox hunt with the local gentleman of Midhurst. Even though he still calls me his Fair Huntress, I can't bear to think of the poor fox. I'll continue to work with my bow instead, much more suited to my namesake…

The image of her, standing tall with a bow, hair whipping about her face from the wind while she prepared to bring down a mighty stag flashed across his mind. It was a sight his dreams couldn't erase. There was so much about her he'd never forget, could never let go of. If only he could have her as his own, his woman, but what if she couldn't forgive him for what he'd done? Deception was the worst sort of betrayal. He'd tricked her in the garden and used her reaction to his body in the shed against her for his own selfish desire to possess what little part of her he could. And even more, he'd deceived her for eleven years with his letters.

For eleven years, she'd been in love with his best friend, not him, and yet he was the one who'd become obsessed with her, the little country gentleman's daughter who'd never set foot outside Midhurst except for her seasons in London. She had become his world in the last decade, and she would never know the truth of how much he couldn't bear the thought of losing her.

Gemma tugged at his hand and he let it go for a brief moment before grabbing it again.

"Should we move further into the garden? Or do you think we're safe from pursuit?" she whispered, turning her head so that her cheek brushed his.

He kept her caged in against the bushes from behind, and loved the feel of her body pressed length to length with his. Savoring these brief moments would be all he'd ever have with her.

"Stay here, if she comes too close, we can go deeper, but for now..." He let a sly grin twist his lips and wrapped his arms around her...

The elderly lady called out to them and moved a little closer to their hiding spot. Jasper pulled her back up against him and Gemma's heart raced. Her body recognized his instinctively, his iron muscled frame, strong as it enclosed her from behind. He moved one hand back up to her mouth, covering it again.

"Shh…I don't want you to make a sound, we mustn't be overheard." He slid his other hand from her waist down to her leg, digging his fingers into the cloth of her gown.

The pressure of his hand on her inner thigh, so close to the tender spot between her legs, made her knees buckle. She remained absolutely still, except for a faint tremor that spread throughout her body. The last thing she wanted was to alert Lady Greenley to their close proximity while in such a compromising position.

Jasper moved his hand closer to her mound, but he stopped just short of it, to powerfully stroke her through the thin fabric of her gown. She let her head fall back to rest against his chest, sucking in breaths as her body throbbed in dark, secret places.

Being held so close to him and wrapped in his arms, enveloped her in his masculine scent. It brought back a rush of images from the garden shed. How she'd loved making love to him, no matter the pain and discomfort, sharing herself with him had been a secret sort of wonder that she feared she might never experience again.

Jasper bent his head and feathered his lips along the slope of her neck in teasing kisses. His hand remained firmly in place, still covering her mouth which prevented the moan that rose in her when he sucked on the tender skin of her throat. It was wicked, letting him muffle her like this and arouse her at the same time. Yet it thrilled her too, the way he seemed to know how to touch her and keep her silent while they were so close to being discovered.

I am wicked, he has made me wicked. It should have shamed her. Perhaps that would come later, but for now she wanted to embrace this wanton side of herself with Jasper. All too soon this party would end and so would her future, but she could cling to him and this sensual dream just a little longer.

A flush of heat flowed through her whole body and she stopped fighting the building pleasure of sensations.

Like an instrument, Jasper strummed her to life at the merest caress of his hands. He tightened his palm on her thigh and rubbed her there, moving closer and closer to where she wanted him to touch her. The pain between her legs doubled, but it was a pain she remembered, a pain of need, not of actual hurt.

That lightning moment of ecstasy in the shed came flooding back, the intensity of their union, the power of their shared gaze and mingled breaths…the stiffness of him embedded deep within her.

Wetness blossomed instantly between her legs and tingles of anticipation danced excitedly up and down her limbs.

"Haverford? Holland? I know you're in here!"

Lady Greenley shouted.

Jasper's breath on her neck quickened and he chuckled softly in between the sensuous dance of his lips on her skin.

Gemma put her right hand on top of Jasper's where he still caressed her inner thigh. He laced his fingers through hers and moved his arm back to her waist, still holding her hand, her fingers locked with his. It was a powerful feeling to help hold his arm around her waist, as though they were dancing without any steps.

Her body hungered for his, in a primal urge that could never change, never stop. She would *always* crave his caress and knowing that terrified her because she would never have Jasper to call her own. He would never be *hers*.

Lady Greenley vanished from sight and whatever had been building between them came to a halt. For a long moment neither of them moved, afraid to break the hushed reverence of their closeness.

With a slow sign of regret, Jasper politely disentangled himself from her and peered through the hedge. She assumed he wanted to be sure Lady Greenley had given up on her prey.

"It's safe to go, I think," he whispered. His face was a tad flushed. He must have been enjoying himself as well.

At least I'm not the only one affected, if only we didn't have to part ways. But they did. He'd made it clear to her that he wouldn't take her as his wife and she couldn't simply let her feelings for James go, even if he had turned out to be different than the man she'd grown to love in her letters. If only she and Jasper—No. She couldn't allow herself to think on what might have been. What choice did that leave either of them? Blasted men! It seemed one couldn't live with them or live without them. It also seemed that one could want a man who'd ruined her on purpose with no intent to marry her. Was she betraying her gender by being so torn between strangling him and kissing him?

Probably, the little chiding voice in her head shot back.

"Shall we?" Jasper offered her his arm.

Gemma studied him for a long moment and then politely shook her head. Brushing out her skirts, she walked ahead of him, leading the way. It was best if they were not seen together. She couldn't bear to think about how much she wanted to be back in his arms, feeling the caress of his lips, the touch of his hands upon her skin. But because that wasn't possible she'd cut herself off from him now.

When at last they emerged from the gardens people were already leaving. Carriages were lining up and horses being brought around for the men who'd ridden to the party.

Gemma slipped into her parent's carriage without being seen or noticed by more than a handful of neighbors who simply waved at her. Throwing herself into the carriage seat, she breathed a sigh of relief that the horrid day was over. She wanted nothing more than to get home and burn the whole stack of letters James had written her.

"Well, Gemma? Did you enjoy the party?" her father asked while he helped her mother into their carriage.

"It was…eventful." What else could she say?

Her father smiled. "Yes it was, wasn't it, what with young Randolph getting engaged. Doesn't surprise me though, even when he was a boy he was leaping headlong into things without thinking properly," her father mused.

"Oh, John hush," her mother warned.

"How do you mean, father?" Gemma leaned forward to better press her father into continuing his suddenly interesting observations.

"Well, that Stevens girl for one. Any man worth his salt can see what sort of creature she is…not a good one, that's for sure. But you take a man like Jasper Holland, well, there's a man with a good head on his shoulders. His time away has only improved him. He's saved up a quaint fortune and now that he's home his estate will have a proper master again. It's been empty too many years since his parents have passed." Her father talked on about other guests and Gemma soon lost interest.

Her mother however watched her with a curious expression. "Gemma, are you well? There is something different about you…"

"Different?" Gemma looked down at herself in concern, wondering if her gown had been ruined or something else was amiss in her appearance.

"Yes, my dear, you look a little flushed again. Are

you coming down with a fever?"

"Fever?" she echoed faintly.

"And your gown...what have you been doing? That muslin is quite wrinkled in places...are those twigs in your hair?" Her mother eyed her worriedly.

Her father patted her mother's knee in reassurance. "Oh, she's fine, Julia, she has color in her cheeks, and a twinkle in her eye. It suits her. I'm sure she's been out gallivanting in the gardens, let her be."

The rest of the ride home, Gemma's parents left her to her thoughts which were focused on Jasper and the stack of letters she meant to burn to ash before the night was over.

"Just a minute, you scoundrel." Lady Greenley's shrill voice stopped Jasper dead in his tracks halfway across the lawn.

Tugging his coat tightly about his shoulders, he pivoted and turned back to face the old matron.

She had her bonnet back on her head, and he winced at the shaft-sized ragged-edge tear where his arrow had pierced part of the thick expensive plumage.

"Lady Greenley," he replied. What did one say to a seasoned old woman who could likely march beside him on a battlefront?

"I know what you were up to today in my garden." Her gray eyes were bright and clear. "Hedges talk, dear boy, and my hedges have told me quite a bit about you and Miss Haverford."

Hedges talking? The woman was mad...utterly mad.

"Lady Greenley, I really don't know what you—"

"Harrumph! Don't try to lie, young pup. I've put up with more cunning men than you in my day. Now, tell me what you mean to do about Haverford," she spoke so plain of Gemma, using her last name like an army general discussing one of the men in her garrison.

"Miss Haverford? I've nothing to do with her." The lie tasted bitter on his tongue.

Before he could even draw a breath, the parasol thumped him hard in the chest and he muttered a foul curse not fit for even the old dragon Lady Greenley's ears.

"Watch your tongue, young man. Now, Haverford. You're desperately in love with her of course, but you think you cannot have her. Why?" She raised a gloved finger, articulating her point. "Because she's always been in love with that half-wit Randolph. Yes, yes, I know all about that. Watched her post those silly letters to him all these years in town. She didn't think I noticed but I did." The old woman smiled.

"Er..." Should he just let the old woman ramble on and maybe try to duck back into the gardens? He could probably sleep in the shed if need be, a tad uncomfortable, but he'd slept in worse conditions at sea.

"And don't think I didn't notice the handwriting

on the letters she received. It changed, you see. I often saw the letters those first few months, the ones from him."

"Him?" Jasper asked.

"Randolph!" Lady Greenley blew out an exasperated breath. "Keep up with me, dear boy. You see Randolph only wrote to her a short time. Someone else started writing back to her, pretending to be him. The penmanship was all wrong. I remarked on it to her, but she said it was because he was on a ship, couldn't write during the swells of the ocean. What rot and nonsense."

Jasper went very still. How could the old woman have figured it out? The changing penmanship when he had taken over writing to Gemma only a year into their service. He'd done his best at first to replicate James's hand, but after a year he'd fully transitioned back to his own handwriting.

"And what has this to do with me, Lady Greenley?" he asked.

The elderly woman fixed a keen-eyed gaze on him, planting the tip of her parasol in the ground and leaning on it. "I think it has *everything* to do with you, my boy. I know you have some silly notion that you can't be as good a man as your father was. But know this, he died with your name on his lips while you were away doing your duty to this country. He was proud of you. We are all proud of you, Holland. Do not think for a moment you aren't worthy of a woman like Haverford, because you are. You wrote to her for nigh on a decade, didn't you? That is something a good man would do, a man who should marry the woman he's madly in love with. Wouldn't you agree?" She tilted her head to the side but he didn't know what to say. He did want Gemma no matter what and had decided he would seduce her, even if it took years to win her heart back from James.

"Better find your tongue, dear boy, then make your way to Haverford's house and beg her forgiveness and ask her to marry you." And with that Lady Greenley left him, alone and confused.

What if it was too soon? She'd only just had James break her heart. With a woman like Gemma, she wouldn't simply turn her love toward another man so quickly. She was too loyal for that. Under other circumstances he would have praised her for such a quality, but now it stood between him and his wooing of her.

He returned to the worry at hand. Would she say yes if he offered for her? He didn't deserve for her to say yes, not after the cavalier way he'd used her for his own pleasure and taken her virtue in a blasted garden shed. He'd been too desperate to show her how good it could be between them. And now he would pay for it, likely by suffering her disgust for the rest of their lives. But…what if he could earn Gemma's forgiveness somehow and prove he could make her happy? Would she ever agree to marry him after all that had passed between them?

Chapter Eight

The almost purple shadows of the early twilight washed the drawing room in soft muted tones as Jasper paced before the fireplace at the Holland family house. With his hands clasped behind his back, he moved with militaristic precision born of years of pacing the decks while he stood early morning watches, eyes straining to catch sight of enemy sails, or to muse on thoughts of home when the waters had been still. This time wasn't too different from then, except now he was debating on what to do about the woman who'd made his last decade worth living.

He couldn't get Gemma out of his head. In the span of one afternoon everything had changed. The woman he'd gown to care for in ten years of letter writing was infinitely more amazing in the flesh. He couldn't bear the thought of never speaking to her again or worse, knowing some other man would hold her, kiss her and make her cry out with pleasure. It was his privilege, no one else's, to make her happy, to show her the world's delights, both in pleasure of mind and body. The question was, could he convince her that he cared for her. If she knew the truth of his letters and James's scheme, she would hate them both forever and his chance would be ruined.

"Sir?" His valet's voice came from the library door, jarring him out of his strategizing.

"Yes?" Jasper turned to face the short aging man.

"It's Mr. Randolph to see you, sir," the man announced, stepping aside to let James pass him into the library before the valet left them alone.

"What a day we've had, eh, Jas?" James grinned.

"Only you, friend. You've gotten engaged to Miss Stevens as you wished. Although it will always puzzle me why you would choose her after you've seen how beautiful and perfect Gemma has turned out. Congratulations to you both," Jasper added hurriedly.

James's gaze moved about the room and he merely waved a hand in the air. "Oh don't play coy with me, Jas. I know a bit of an afterglow when I see it, and our dear green girl is green no longer. She was glowing like a ripe peach. Didn't take you long to pluck the fruit off the vine. How was it?" James chuckled.

Jasper struck James in the jaw with a powerful right hook. James staggered back, lips parted, and panted as he stared at his friend.

James's smile crept back. "Well now, here's an

unexpected turn. Can it be you've fallen head over heels for the innocent country girl?" He touched his bruised lip where a thin line of blood trickled down his chin.

"James, don't force me to show you the door. I'll not tolerate a word against Gemma in jest or otherwise." He warned, and cradled his bruising knuckles. James's half-smile faded and he took a tentative step toward his friend.

"Dear God, it's true. You're out of your mind with love! Cool, calm Jas has become a hot-headed buck in love." James smiled and patted his friend's back good-naturedly.

"I don't love her, you are quite mistaken. She is a sweet girl that's all."

"Sweet? Never in my life have I heard you praise a woman like you have Gemma in these past two days. Before that, when we were at sea I distinctly recall you begging your leave from dinner early nearly once a month to hurry off and answer letters when they came in. I didn't know it was Gemma you were writing to at the time, but now it all makes sense. My good man you are in love with her whether you will acknowledge it or not."

Jasper sank down into the nearest armchair as the truth hit him...he did love Gemma. Lady Greenley and James were right. How it happened...when it happened, he wasn't sure. But seeing her the night before in the gardens, kissing her, making love to her today in the shed had been experiences he would never get out of his mind. Her beauty on the outside shone as brightly as the beauty within, the beauty he'd spent five years growing to love. He did love her. Loved her so much that everything he'd done to her in the past few days to hurt her was killing him inside. He couldn't let James know how much he loved Gemma, not until Gemma was safely his. While he trusted his best friend with many things including his life, he didn't trust him not to try to steal Gemma back.

He couldn't bear to think that Gemma would vanish from his life forever...but how could he confess the secret of the letters to her without incurring her hatred?

"Well, I suppose I ought to go, seeing as you have a lady to woo." James started for the door to leave.

"What are you talking about?" Jasper grunted.

James gave him that indulgent smile parents often give slow-witted children. "Don't you know how these stories go, Jas? You have to ride hard on your fastest horse to the fair lady's house, and climb the rose covered trellis to her bedchamber. When she grants you entrance, you get down on your knees and beg for her love. Then it's a kiss or two and off to her father. It's simple enough." James chuckled.

"Simple? I think I'd rather be facing a fleet of French frigates, with our broadside guns only half-manned..." Jasper groaned, but his friend had already left. Jasper sighed heavily and then called for his valet.

"Yes sir?" The valet waited for his master's instructions.

"Ready my fastest horse," he commanded.

The sun had set a few hours ago and all Gemma wanted to do was lay on her bed and not move. Every bone in her body ached, and she was weary of life. What had happened today with James and Jasper had shattered her to pieces. Eleven years of her life had disappeared today in a blink and her future was uncertain. A tension in her chest made it a little harder to breathe. What was she to do now that she had no plan for her future and no options? A dull throb began to beat like drums just behind her eyes. She would have to get through this. Somehow…

She propped one elbow on her pillow and stared at the small table by her bed. A stack of letters bound in a black satin ribbon sat within arm's reach. Gemma hadn't been able to summon up the courage to burn them yet. Reaching out, she stroked her fingertips over the packet with loving despair.

What harm would it do to read a letter before she burned the lot of them? Slipping one out from the pile, she unfolded the sheets. She scanned the first few lines of one of the early letters and nearly choked. There it was, a reference to her being the fair huntress. She had shared the pet name her father had for her with James and he had often written back to her, calling her the fair huntress.

Jasper had called her a fair huntress today. How had he known to call her that? Perhaps James had shared that with him? It seemed unlikely that he would have shared that detail. It also struck her as odd that the man who she'd written to for the last eleven years, hadn't acted like the man she'd fallen in love with. He'd seemed to be a total stranger, one uncaring of her feelings, and unbelieving of her when she needed his trust the most. That was not the man she loved. So how then did Jasper know what her father called her? Had he stolen James's letters?

The bushes below her window rustled softly and a curious scuffling sound accompanied by a muttered curse echoed up from below the window.

Gemma dropped the letter on her bed and sat up when a man appeared over the edge of her windowsill. He tumbled over the ledge and onto her floor with a grunt.

"Jasper?" She gasped in shock.

He looked like a deranged garden nymph with cuts from rose thorns on his hands and green leaves and twigs knotted in his trousers and shirt. Gemma didn't know whether to laugh or be scandalized that he'd just climbed up to her second story window like a misguided Romeo.

"Jasper, what on earth are you doing here?" she hissed.

He collected himself and flashed her a sheepish grin. He shook his head and twigs and leaves rained down on the floor. "That climb up the trellis was a great deal easier when I was a lad putting tadpoles on your windowsill."

A little breathless laugh escaped her. "I can imagine."

"I'm sorry I didn't use the front door, but I

wanted a minute alone with you. Of course now I cannot remember what on earth I wanted to say since you're so…" He waved a hand down her body.

Glancing down at herself, Gemma blanched. She was barely clothed in just her chemise and she rushed to grab her robe from the chair next to him.

"Don't hide yourself, Gemma, I would bask in your beauty…the way only a lowly sailor can hope to reach the stars of the night sky…" He caught her waist, tugging her gently against him.

Those words…it was from the most recent letter, the one which had sent her the blindfold with the silver stars on it. How could he know what James had written? He knew *too much*. Her letters must have been handed over to him. That would explain how he knew all her heart's desires, all her secrets…

"Jasper…please…" Her body flushed and heated wherever it touched him, but she couldn't want him. She loved James, had loved James. She couldn't love someone else, not so soon.

"Gemma, I had to see you again, there's something I need to tell you." His gaze fell to the pile of letters strewn on her bed, then to her scantily clad appearance. "Lord, you make this so difficult. I'm trying to confess my sins to you, and all I want to do is drag you back into my arms and kiss you until you agree to forgive me."

Confess his sins? Hadn't Jasper done enough to break her heart today?

"You should leave. If my parents find out you've come—"

He dipped her back, catching her in his embrace

to kiss her deeply.

She resisted only a second before softening beneath his hungry mouth. Whenever he kissed her, fire seemed to burn between their lips, a fire she craved like nothing else. This man had the power to bind her with the magic of a kiss and she hated that she *loved* that about him. When at last he released her, he got down on one knee and clasped her hands in his.

Startled by the sudden move, she tried to tug her hands free but he wouldn't release her.

"Marry me, Gemma," he said.

Her eyes sparkled with fresh tears, which she couldn't wipe away because he wouldn't let go of her hands. Even though James had turned out to be so wretched, she couldn't shake off how she'd felt about him for the last eleven years. Those deeper emotions wouldn't vanish like mists beneath the noonday sun. Heartache took time to heal and she hated that she'd been so taken in by James and his sweet words.

"I cannot marry you, not when I am in love someone else," she said.

"You're still in love with James?" he asked, his tone strangely quiet.

She nodded and a pained chuckle escaped her lips. "Silly isn't it? The man I love is not the man I met today, but I can't just let go so easily of what I feel." She was suffering such heartfelt torment her entire body started to shake.

Jasper got up off his knee and settled them both on her bed with her beside him so he could wipe her tears away with his fingertips. "Why do you love him?" His fingers were soft on her skin as he erased the tracks of her tears.

"I shouldn't love him, not anymore, he's not the man I fell in love with. That man, the man who wrote to me, *that* James, is who I love. The last few years… our letters…they mean *everything* to me…I cannot forget that sort of love so soon," she confessed. Despite her desire to not wound Jasper anymore, she couldn't help but wind her arms around his neck and bury her face into his chest. It was so unfair to them both that she wanted the man who wrote the letters as much as she wanted the man whose body held her now. It was impossible to choose between them.

"You love the man who wrote those letters?" he asked.

She looked up at him. Teardrops coated her long dark lashes, making it hard to see through them. She blinked, then hastily dragged a hand over her eyes to clear her lashes. "Yes…" she said.

A tempting, roguish smile curved his lips, as though he had the rest of his life to form that smile and enjoy the way it made her shiver with longing. "Gemma, that's what I came to tell you. *I* wrote those letters. Not James."

Her heart seemed to stop beating for a brief instant, enough that her chest stung with the unexpected pain when it jolted back to life. "What?" She almost croaked out the word, unable to speak more than that.

"The last ten years, I've been the one writing to you. James wanted me to because he didn't have the courage to break off your understanding. But I couldn't either, not when I started writing to you…I fell in love with you, Gemma."

Jasper wrote the letters that had tied her heart into knots? He was the one who'd penned the amusing poems about the seamen and their daily duties. He was the one she'd confessed all her dreams to and he'd shared his back. More pain dug its claws into her heart. Another deception, another pack of lies tore into her, ripping the last bit of control keeping her together.

"You wrote the letters?" Each word came out of her lips in a strained rasp.

"Yes."

"Did you mean any of it? Or was every letter a lie?" When he tried to touch her, she shoved at his hands.

Jasper bowed his head, but his eyes fixed on her. "Yes. Every *bloody* word. I gave you all that I am, Gemma. I did not lie about a single thing. I never even signed the letters as James. It was always 'J' for Jasper. Even from the start I didn't wish to lie to you." He ignored her attempt to retreat and clasped her face in his hands, their lips a breath apart. An unrelenting gleam in his eyes softened her own bleeding heart. He meant what he said, it was in the firm set of his mouth and the intensity of his gaze.

"Please, Gemma." His voice was a husky whisper half ragged with emotion. "You saved me. Your letters saved me time and time again. Let me fight to win you back, tell me I still have a chance to earn your heart back." His eyes brightened with…were those tears she glimpsed?

"You want to fight for me?" She reached up to curl her fingers around his wrists.

He answered with a slow, definite nod. "James is my closest friend. I owed him a debt for a time when he saved my life at sea. That was the only reason I agreed to this wretched plan to trick you and I hate myself for it. Believe me. Better yet, let me prove it to you. Let me show you how much I adore you, how much I love you to distraction. You are first in my life, now and always. Even if you won't give me your heart, you still hold mine in your hands." He brushed his thumbs over her cheeks. His words were a hypnotic spell upon her hurting soul, healing it of all the pain it had suffered in the last few days.

The man she loved wasn't James. He was Jasper. And he *loved* her back. The finality and the utter relief hit her so hard she expelled a breath and had to suck in another when her head spun.

"Gemma? Are you all right?"

Clutching his shoulders, she almost giggled "I never used to get faint until you showed up. What would lady Greenley think of me, swooning like some ninny?"

His warm laugh rumbled deep from his chest. "She'd tell you to stand up straight and snap out of it, Haverford." His tone imitated the old battle axe Lady Greenley.

Gemma laughed harder, only to stifle the sound with her hands. It would be an utter disaster if her parents overheard her and came to check on her.

Sobering again, she looked up at him. There was so much she wanted to ask him, to know about everything that they'd written to each other in the last decade, but she had to be clear about what he had done, and what James had done.

"And the garden? Did you tell me to meet you there and send me the blindfold?" The puzzle pieces seemed to be falling into place…the changing penmanship, the change of tone and interest, the depth of emotion too had changed. James never did like to talk about anything serious, but Jasper had.

With a grim expression, he nodded. "I did send you the blindfold and asked you to meet me in the garden. James told me I had to compromise you so he'd have a reason to break it off when he discovered you'd been with someone else. I hated myself for doing that to you."

"Why didn't he just come to me and tell me from the start he didn't love me?" She leaned into him, eager to feel his heart beat against her cheek.

"Because he's a cur. I should have told him I wouldn't do it, but I was a fool who wanted to help him out. I went to the garden out of loyalty to him, but when I saw you that first time in the garden, God how I wanted you, Gemma. Everything we'd shared over the years, it just came rushing back to me and I couldn't walk away from you." He tilted her chin up so she had to look him in the eye.

"You truly love me?" His warmth against hers fogged up her mind, but she had to be sure of him and his love.

"More than you know," he admitted with an unexpected vulnerability in his eyes that made her love him all the more.

"I climbed a bloody trellis, braving thorny peril for you my fair huntress. Now, give me an answer, one that won't break this poor sailor's heart. Can I yet reach the fair star that shines in my night sky?" His lips teased her cheek and for the briefest second she forget to breathe.

She loved Jasper. The realization made her giddy.

"I...I will marry you Jasper." She turned her head to catch his lips with hers in a sweet, tender kiss, one full of emotion and nothing else between them except that love which had once burned only upon the pages of their letters. Now it burned between their lips.

He brushed her hair back and she caught his hand, seeing the red angry bruises on his knuckles.

"What happened?" she asked, then brushed her lips over his reddened skin.

He frowned a little. "I hit James."

"You *hit* James? What on earth for?" She couldn't imagine the two men coming to blows.

"He was being himself, and I was tired of him besmirching an innocent woman's good name," he said.

She raised his hand to her lips again and lovingly kissed the tender bruises. He'd defended her honor. Such a gentleman rogue...and he was hers.

"You know, if you want to heal my other wounds with your kisses, I was recently attacked by Lady Greenley in several places." His lips curved into a deeply dangerous smile that made Gemma's body flash with tempting heat.

"Oh? And where would that be?" She arched an

eyebrow at him, offering a warm smile to encourage him.

He touched his cheek, she kissed it. He touched his neck and she pressed a kiss there too. He pulled his blouse off and touched his chest. Gemma feathered her lips down from his neck inch by pleasurable inch.

"Anywhere else?" she asked in a low sultry voice.

His eyes darkened and he hissed out a breath, adjusting his trousers. "Well…" He started to touch his thigh when footsteps thudded on the stairs.

"Quick, get down. It's my father!" She shoved him off the bed behind her, ignoring the thump and the stifled groan. At the moment her father knocked on her door, she kicked at Jasper's body by her legs, urging him to slide under her bed.

"Gemma dear? Are you all right? May I come in?" her father asked, his voice a little muffled by the wooden door.

"I'm not entirely decent, papa, but you may peek inside if you wish," she called out.

"I'd like a peek inside too," Jasper's wicked whisper slithered up her bare legs and a warm hand started to slide up her calf.

She kicked out, but Jasper's hand didn't leave.

Her father poked his head in the door and looked at her, a pleasant smile hovering about his lips. "Everything all right dear?"

"Yes, I'm fine, just preparing for bed," she lied.

He studied her with an unreadable gaze and she flushed. It had everything to do with Jasper's lips against the inside of her thigh, just out of her father's sight.

"Well, your mother is turning in for the night. I'll be up a little while longer if you need me." Her father started to leave but paused, and with another little twist of his lips, he spoke again. "Mr. Holland, when you find yourself able to rise from behind my daughter's bed, please come to my study so you and I might discuss Gemma's dowry." And then her father shut the bedroom door leaving them alone again.

Gemma fell back onto the bed mortified, burying her face in her hands.

Jasper leapt to his feet and towered over her where she sat on the bed. He gently shoved her flat on her back and slid his hands underneath her chemise, trying to lift it off her.

"Jasper, what are you doing?" She tried to tug her chemise back down, but he brushed her hands away.

"Your father doesn't expect me for a little while, so let's enjoy the moment," he purred. He kissed her lips while parting her legs and eased himself down onto her.

Gemma giggled when he nibbled on her ear. She loved the way he could be part rough and part gentle as though his need for her was so great, but his love for her tempered him enough to go slower when she needed it.

"You're terrible, you know that?" she said, her breath coming faster now. She let her hands roam over his back, and she grasped his shirt, lifting it up. Bare skin, that's what she wanted. His skin beneath her hands so she could feel every muscle move and twitch while he made love to her.

"You expect me to admire my star from afar? I think not, I've tasted the heaven that is your love and cannot bear to wait another second..." His voice was husky and his eyes dreamily half-closed as he cupped one of her breasts, massaging it gently, expertly, until she panted with the desire to have his mouth there.

Jasper pressed down harder against her, the force of his desire pressed against her now aching core.

How could love making with him be like this? Half passion, half delight, as though being with him was not only about pleasure, but about sheer breathless joy? Who knew love could be this way? That she could be in love with a man and feel so close to him, inside and out as she did now. That they could enjoy each other while being so intimate. It was wondrous. Simply wondrous. Another one of life's miracles she wouldn't take for granted.

"That wouldn't perhaps be Lady Greenley's parasol would it?" She teased and slid her hand underneath him to stroke him through his breeches. She cupped the thick length of him, squeezed hard enough that he growled against her neck and nipped her ear lobe. The tender spot that made her entire body explode with a fiery need that would have her begging soon.

"Good God no, but I promise to use it much better than a parasol..." His rich voice rumbled in a deep throaty chuckle as he freed himself of his pants.

With a little wriggle she got closer and he positioned himself. One thrust and he was in her to the hilt. She whimpered at the stretching and the ghost of pain, but it didn't last long before pleasure overtook it.

Their faces were close, their bodies touching everywhere and something about that realization made her tremble. Every part of her was open to him, not just her body, but her heart.

"Do you promise to love me, forever?" she asked as their bodies rocked together in perfect sync.

He captured her wrists and pinned them onto the bed beside her head, the dominant move making her burn even hotter. He had control of them both now, could do anything he liked to her and because she trusted him, she knew he would only ever give her pleasure.

"I don't have to promise you, Gemma," he murmured against her mouth and thrust into her slowly, gently, as though he had all the time in the world to make love to her.

"What?" Confusion flitted across her passion dazed mind.

He chuckled, slid himself deeper into her, hitting a spot that made her entire body go limp. A climax hit her hard enough that she saw stars.

"Promises can be broken. My love for you? How I feel about you, about us? It's not something that will ever break. You're mine, Gemma Haverford, and I'm never letting you go."

Neither of them spoke. He continued to rock his body against hers, and she rode out the rippling aftershocks of pleasure while watching him come above her. His parted lips, the widening of his eyes, and the smile of bliss that followed.

"God, woman, I'm so glad you're mine." He

whispered it so softly she thought for a moment she'd imagined it.

Cupping his face, she traced his lips with hers, and felt the sting of happy tears in her eyes. "And you're mine. I should have known better than to resist such a temptation."

"Temptation?" He cocked a brow.

"Oh yes, from the moment you touched me in the garden, you've been a wicked temptation, but now you're mine, my wicked rogue."

"Wicked rogue? I rather like that." He flashed her a crooked smile that would have weakened her knees if she had still been standing.

Gemma laughed before finding his lips on hers again. It was beautiful, this passion born of words, consummated with the body and endured by the souls. Every moment was worth the wait.

Wicked Designs

CHAPTER ONE

London, September 1820

Something wasn't right. Emily Parr allowed the elderly coachman to help her into the town coach, and the queer look he gave her made her skin crawl. Peering into the dark interior of the vehicle, she was surprised to find it empty. Uncle Albert was supposed to accompany her to social engagements and if not him, certainly a chaperone. Why then was the coach empty?

She settled into the back seat, her hands clutching her reticule tight enough that the beadwork dug into her palms through her gloves. Perhaps her uncle was meeting with his business partner, Mr. Blankenship. She'd seen Blankenship arrive just before she'd gone upstairs to prepare for the ball. A shudder rippled through her. The man was a lecherous creature with beetle-black eyes and hands that tended to wander too freely whenever he was near her. Emily was not worldly, having only just turned eighteen a few months earlier, but this last year with her uncle had enlightened her to a new side of life and none of it had been good.

Her first London Little Season should have been a wonderful experience. Instead it had begun with the death of her parents at sea and ended with her new life in the dusty tomb of her uncle's townhouse. With an insubstantial library, no pianoforte and no friends, Emily had started to slide into a melancholy haze. It was crucial she make a good match and fast. She had to escape Uncle Albert's world, and the only way she could do that was to legally obtain her father's fortune.

A distant cousin of her mother's held the money in trust. It was a frustrating thing to have a man she'd never met hold the purse strings on her life. Uncle Albert despised the situation as well. As her guardian he was forced to give an accounting to her mother's cousin, which thankfully kept him from delving too deeply into her accounts for his own needs. The small fortune was the best bargaining chip she had to entice potential suitors. Though the money would go to her husband, she hoped to find a man who would respect her enough not to squander what was rightfully hers. But arriving at the ball without a chaperone would damage her chances in husband hunting, it simply wasn't done to show up alone. It spoke lowly of her uncle as well as their financial situation.

As relieved as she was to not have her uncle or Mr. Blankenship escorting her, her stomach still clenched. She recalled the cold way the elderly driver smiled at her just before she'd climbed inside. The slickness of that grin made her feel a little uneasy, like he knew something she didn't and it amused him. It was silly—the old man wasn't a threat. But she couldn't shake the wariness that rippled through her. She would have been thankful for Uncle Albert's presence, even if it meant another lecture on how costly she was to provide for and how kind he'd been in taking her in after her parents' ship was lost.

The driver was engaged to bring her to Chessley House for the ball, and nothing would go wrong. If she kept saying it over and over, she might believe it. Emily focused her thoughts on what tonight would bring, hoping to ease her worry. She would join her new friend, Anne Chessley, as well as Mrs. Judith Pratchet, an old friend of Anne's mother, who'd kindly agreed to sponsor Emily for the Little Season. There was every possibility she would meet a man and catch his interest enough that he would approach her uncle for permission to court her.

Emily almost smiled. Perhaps tonight she would dance with the Earl of Pembroke.

Last night, the handsome earl had smiled at her during their introduction and asked her to dance. Emily had nearly wept with disappointment when she informed him that Mrs. Pratchet had already filled her dance card.

The earl had replied, "Another time, then?" and Emily nodded eagerly, hoping he would remember her.

Perhaps tonight I shall have a spot of luck. She desperately hoped so. Emily wasn't so foolish as to believe she had any real chance of marrying a man like the Earl of Pembroke, but it was nice to be noticed by a man of his standing. Sometimes that attention was noticed by others.

The coach halted sharply a moment later, and she nearly toppled out of her seat, her thoughts interrupted, her daydreams fleeing.

"Ho there, my good man!" a man shouted from nearby.

Emily moved toward the door, but the vehicle rocked as someone climbed onto the driver's seat, and she fell back in her seat again.

"Twenty pounds is yours if you follow those two riders ahead and do as we ask," the newly-arrived man said.

Having regained control of her balance, she flung the coach curtains back. Two riders occupied the darkened street, their backs to her. What was going on? A sense of ill-ease settled deep in her stomach. The coach jerked and moved again. As she had feared, the driver didn't stop at Chessley House. He followed the riders ahead.

What was this? A kidnapping? A robbery? Should she stick her head out of the window and ask them to stop? If robbing her was their intent, asking them what they were doing might be a bad idea… Why would they take her when there were so many other heiresses, ones more lovely than her, having their first come out this year? Surely this wasn't an abduction. Her mind reeled as she struggled to cope with the situation. What would her father have done in this situation? Load a pistol and fight them off. Having no pistol, she'd have to think of something clever. Could these men be reasoned with? *Unlikely.*

Emily worried her bottom lip as she debated her options. She could scream for help, but such a reaction could worsen matters. She could open the door and throw herself out onto the street, but the clatter of hooves behind the coach erased that idea. She'd be lucky to survive the fall if she tried, and the horses behind were too close. She'd likely be killed. Emily fell back against the seat with a shaky sigh, her heart racing. She'd have to wait until the driver stopped.

For what seemed like an hour she kept nervously glancing out the windows to assess what direction the coach was going. By now London was far behind her. Only open country stretched on both sides of the road. A rumble of hooves heralded an approaching rider, and a man astride a sleek black gelding galloped past the window. He was too close and the horse too tall for her to get a good view of him. The moonlight rippled off the horse's shiny coat as it rode past.

She knew by the close proximity of the rider and the determined way he rode in the saddle that he was involved with this business. Who in their right mind, except perhaps that foul old man, Blankenship, would kidnap her? He'd be the sort to engage in such a nefarious activity.

The other evening he'd come to dinner at her uncle's house and when her uncle had turned away for only a second, Blankenship had twined one of this thick, stubby fingers around a lock of her hair, tugging it hard until she'd nearly cried out. He'd whispered horrible things in her ear, nasty things that made her sick as he told her he planned to marry her as soon as her uncle had approved. Emily had stared back at him, stating she'd never marry him. He'd only laughed and said, "We'll see, my sweet. We shall see."

Well, she wouldn't back down. She wasn't some pawn to be captured and held at someone's mercy. They'd have to fight to take her.

Emily looked out the window on the other side to count the riders. Two led the party at the front, mere yards ahead. Another two flanked the coach on either side. One of them rode with a second horse roped to his saddle, likely for the man who rode now with the driver. Not the best of odds. Perhaps she could outsmart them.

The coach slowed, then gently creaked to a stop. Emily took stock of her situation. She fought for composure, each breath slower than the one before. If she panicked, she might not survive. She had to hide. But she could not physically escape *five* men.

Her eyes fell to the seat across from her.

Maybe—

Godric St. Laurent, the twelfth Duke of Essex, leaned back in his saddle watching the abduction he'd orchestrated unfold. Covering his mouth with a gloved hand, he stifled a yawn. Things were going smoothly. In fact, this entire kidnapping bordered on the point of tedious. They'd intercepted the coach ten minutes before it reached Chessley House. No one witnessed the escort of riders or the driver changing his route. Oddly enough, the young woman hadn't shown any signs of resistance or concern from inside the coach. Wouldn't she have made some protestations when she realized what was happening? A thought stopped him dead. Had she somehow slipped out of the coach when they'd slowed on a corner before they'd left town? Surely not, they would have seen her. Most likely she was too terrified to do anything, hence the silence from inside. Not that she had anything to fear, she would not be harmed.

He nodded to his friend Charles who was perched next to the driver. A bag of coins jingled as Charles dropped it into the jarvey's waiting hands.

They had reached the halfway point between London and Godric's ancestral estate. They would go the rest of the way on horseback, with the girl sharing a horse with either him or one of his friends. The driver would return to London with a message for Albert Parr and a wild story that exonerated himself from blame.

"Ashton, stay here with me." Godric waved his friend over while the others rode the horses a good distance away to wait for his signal. Abductions were tricky things, and having only himself and one other man take hold of the girl would be better. She might

LAUREN SMITH

have a fit of hysterics if she saw the other three men too close.

He rode up to the coach, curious to see whether the woman inside matched his memory. He'd seen her once before from a window overlooking the gardens when he'd visited her uncle. She'd been kneeling in the flowerbeds, her dress soiled as she weeded. A job more suited to a servant than a lady of quality. He'd been ready to dismiss her from his mind when she'd turned and glanced about the garden, a smudge of dirt on the tip of her upturned nose. A butterfly from a nearby flower had fluttered above her head. She hadn't noticed it, even as it settled on her long, coiling auburn hair. Something in his chest gave a funny little flip, and his body had stirred with desire. Any other woman so innocent would not have caught his interest, but he'd glimpsed a keenness in her eyes, a hidden intelligence as she dug into the soil. Miss Emily Parr was different. And different was intriguing.

Ashton handed the driver the ransom letter for Parr and took up a position near the front of the coach. Taking hold of the door, Godric opened it up, waiting for the screaming to start.

None came.

"My deepest apologies, Miss Parr—" Still no screaming. "Miss Parr?" Godric thrust his head into the coach.

It was empty. Not even a fire-breathing dragon of a chaperone, not that he'd expected one. His sources had assured him she would be alone tonight.

Godric looked over his shoulder. "Ash? You're sure this is Parr's coach?"

"Of course. Why?" Ashton jumped off his horse, marched over and thrust his head into the empty coach. He was silent a long moment before he withdrew. Ashton put his finger against his lips and motioned to the inside. A tuft of pink muslin peeped out from the wooden seat. He gestured for Godric to step away from the coach.

Ashton lowered his voice. "It seems that our little rabbit chase has turned into a fox hunt. She's hidden in the hollow space of the seat, clever girl."

"Hiding under the seat?" Godric shook his head, bewildered. He didn't know one woman of his acquaintance who would do something so clever. Perhaps Evangeline, but then if anything could be said of that woman, it was that she was far from ordinary. A prickling of excitement coursed through his veins, into his chest. He loved a challenge.

"Let's wait a few minutes and see if she emerges."

Godric looked back at the coach, impatience prickling inside him. "I don't want to wait here all night."

"She'll come out soon enough. Allow me." Ashton walked back to the coach and called out to

Godric in a carrying voice. "Blast and damnation! She must have slipped out before we took charge of the coach. Just leave it. We'll take the driver back to London tomorrow." Ashton shut the door with a loud slam and motioned for Godric to join him.

"Now we wait," Ashton whispered. He indicated that he would guard the left coach door while Godric stationed himself at the right.

Emily listened to the drum of retreating hooves and silently counted to one hundred. Her heart jolted in her chest as she considered what the men would do if they caught her. Highwaymen could be cruel and murderous, especially if their quarry offered little. She had no access to her father's fortune, which left only her body.

Icy dread gripped Emily's spine, paralyzing her limbs. She drew a breath as anxiety spiraled through her.

I must be brave. Fight them until I can fight no more. With trembling hands, she pushed at the roof of the seat, wincing as it popped open. Once she climbed out, she brushed dirt from her gown, noticing some tears from the rough wood on the inside of the seat. But the tears held no importance. All that mattered was survival.

Emily looked out the coach window. Nothing stood out in the darkness. Only the faint glimmer of moonlight touched the road with milky tendrils. Stars winked and flickered overhead, pale lights, distant and cold. A shudder wracked her frame, and Emily hugged herself, wanting so much to be at home. She missed her warm bed and her parents' murmurs from down the hall. It was a comfort she'd taken for granted. But she couldn't afford to think about them, not when she was in danger.

Were the men truly gone? Could it really be this easy?

She opened the coach door, and stepped down onto the dirt road. Strong arms locked about her waist and yanked her backward. The collision with a hard body knocked the breath from her lungs. Terror spiked her blood as she struggled against the arms that held her.

"Good evening, my darling," a low voice murmured.

Emily screamed once, before she bit down on the hand that covered her mouth. She tasted the smooth leather of fine riding gloves.

The man roared and nearly dropped her. "Damn!"

Emily rammed an elbow backwards into her attacker's stomach and began to wrestle free until he grabbed her arm. She swung about, striking him across the face with a balled fist. The man staggered back, leaving her free to dive inside the coach.

If she could get to the other side and run, she might stand a chance. She scrabbled towards the door, but never made it. The devil surged into the coach after her. Turning to face him, she was knocked flat onto her back.

She screamed again as his body settled over hers.

The dim moonlight revealed his bright eyes and strong features.

He caught her flailing wrists, pinning them above her head. "Quiet!"

Emily wanted to rake his eyes out, but the man was relentless. His hips ground against hers and panic drove her to a new level of terror. Her fears of being forcibly taken surfaced as his warm breath fanned over her face and neck. She shrieked, and he reared back away from her, as though the sound confused him.

"I'm not going to hurt you." His voice vibrated with a low growl, ruining any promise his words might carry.

"You're hurting me now!" She yanked her arms uselessly against his hold.

The man eased off her somewhat, and Emily took her chance. She tucked her knees up, and with all the power she could summon, she kicked. Her attacker stumbled out the open door and fell onto his back. Emily barely registered that he was winded before she turned and exited the other side of the coach.

The moment she emerged, another man lunged for her. To escape him, Emily fell back against the side of the coach. Rather than grab her, he held his arms wide to keep her from slipping by him, like he was corralling livestock.

"Easy, easy," he purred.

Emily whipped her head to the left and pleaded with her mind to think, but the man she'd bitten rounded the corner and pounced, pinning her against the coach, his arms caging her in. His solid muscular body towered over her. His jaw clenched as though one move from her would trigger something dark and wild. Emily's breath caught, and her heart pounded violently against her ribs.

The man was panting and angry. The intensity of his eyes mesmerized her, but the second he blinked, the spell broke and she fought with every bit of strength she could muster.

The Story continues in *Wicked Designs*, The League of Rogues Book 1 available wherever books are sold.

OTHER LAUREN SMITH TITLES

Historical
Tempted By A Rogue
The League of Rogues Series
Wicked Designs
His Wicked Seduction
Her Wicked Proposal
The Seduction Series
The Duelist's Seduction

Contemporary
The Surrender Series
The Gilded Cuff
The Gilded Cage
The Gilded Chain

Paranormal
The Bite of Winter
Dark Seductions Series
The Shadows of Stormclyffe Hall
Brotherhood of the Blood Moon Series
Blood Moon on the Rise

ABOUT THE AUTHOR

Amazon best-selling author Lauren Smith is an attorney by day, author by night, who pens adventurous and edgy romance stories by the light of her smart phone flashlight app. She's a native Oklahoman who lives with her three pets: a feisty chinchilla, sophisticated cat and dapper little schnauzer. She's won multiple awards in several romance subgenres including being an Amazon.com Breakthrough Novel Award Quarter-Finalist and a Semi-Finalist for the Mary Wollstonecraft Shelley Award.

Be sure to sign up for her newsletter at www.laurensmithbooks.com and follow her on Facebook at www.facebook.com/LaurenDianaSmith or on twitter at @LSmithAuthor. She loves hearing from readers!

CPSIA information can be obtained at www.ICGtesting.com
Printed in the USA
LVOW06s2116291115

464611LV00003B/87/P

THE
PEASANT WAR
IN GERMANY

By
FREDERICK ENGELS

INTERNATIONAL PUBLISHERS, New York

©, 1926, by International Publishers Co., Inc.

New Edition, 1966

All Rights Reserved

3rd Edition, 2000, 2006

© International Publishers Co., Inc.

This printing 2012

In October 1870 this work was published in book form—*Der deutsche Bauernkrieg von Friedrich Engels*. Zweiter, mit einer Einleitung versehener Abdruck, Leipzig, Verlag der Expedition des *Volksstaat*.

A new, third, authorised edition came out in 1875. For this edition Engels wrote a special addendum to the 1870 Preface, dated July 1, 1874.

In this volume the Preface is printed according to the 1870 Preface verified with the 1875 Edition.

In English the Preface was first published in F. Engels, *The Peasant War in Germany*, International Publishers, New York, 1926.

This edition compiled from vols. 10 and 21 of the MECW, with a new Index. The Twelve Articles, and illustrations are from IP's original editions, 1926 and 1966.

ISBN 10 0-7178-0720-7
ISBN 13 978-0-7178-0720-8

Library of Congress Cataloging-in-Publication Data

Engels, Friedrich, 1820-1895.
    [Deutsche Bauernkrieg. English]
    The peasant war in Germany / by Frederick Engels.
        p. cm.
    Includes bibliographical references and index.
    ISBN 0-7178-0720-7 (alk. paper)
    1. Peasants' War, 1524-1525. 2. Germany--Politics and government--1517-1648. 3. Peasant uprisings--Germany. 4. Reformation--Historiography. 5. Communism and Christianity. I. Title.

DD182 .E513 2000
943'.031--dc21

                                                                                    00-026699

CONTENTS

PREFACE, Frederick Engels   vii

THE PEASANT WAR IN GERMANY

I. The Economic Situation and Social
     Classes in Germany   1

II. The Main Opposition Groups and their
     Programmes; Luther and Muenzer   12

III. Precursors: Peasant Uprisings, 1476-1517   29

IV. Uprising of the Nobility   42

V. The Peasant War in Swabia and Franconia   47

VI. The Peasant War in Thuringia,
     Alsace and Austria   70

VII. Significance of the Peasant War   79

THE TWELVE ARTICLES OF THE PEASANTS   87

NOTES   95

INDEX   105

PEASANT TROOPS ON THE MARCH

Frederick Engels

PREFACE
[TO THE SECOND EDITION
OF *THE PEASANT WAR IN GERMANY*]

The following work was written in London in the summer of 1850, the recent counter-revolution still fresh in mind; it appeared in the 5th and 6th issues of the *Neue Rheinische Zeitung. Politisch-ökonomische Revue,* edited by Karl Marx, Hamburg, 1850. My political friends in Germany desire it to be reprinted, and I accede to their desire, because, to my regret, the work is still timely today.

It makes no claim to providing material derived from independent research. On the contrary, all the material on the peasant risings and on Thomas Münzer is taken from Zimmermann.[a] His book, despite gaps here and there, is still the best compilation of factual data. Moreover, old Zimmermann enjoyed his subject. The same revolutionary instinct, which prompted him throughout the book to champion the oppressed class, made him later one of the best of the extreme Left [129] in Frankfurt.[b]

If, nevertheless, Zimmermann's presentation lacks inner cohesion; if it does not succeed in showing the political and religious controversies of the times as a reflection of the contemporary class struggles; if it sees in these class struggles only oppressors and oppressed, evil folk and good folk, and the ultimate victory of the evil ones; if its exposition of the social conditions which determined both the outbreak and the outcome of the struggle is extremely defective, it was the fault of the time in which the book

---

[a] W. Zimmermann, *Allgemeine Geschichte des grossen Bauernkrieges,* Th. 1-3, Stuttgart, 1841-1843.— *Ed.*

[b] The third edition (1875) further has: "It is true that since then he is said to have aged somewhat."— *Ed.*

came into existence. On the contrary, for its time, it is written quite realistically and is a laudable exception among the German idealist works on history.

My presentation, while sketching the historical course of the struggle only in its bare outlines, attempted to explain the origin of the Peasant War, the position of the various parties that played a part in it, the political and religious theories by which those parties sought to clarify their position in their own minds, and finally the result of the struggle itself as following logically from the historically established social conditions of life of these classes; that is to say, it attempted to demonstrate the political structure of Germany at that time, the revolts against it, and the contemporary political and religious theories not as causes but as results of the stage of development of agriculture, industry, roads and waterways, commerce in commodities and money then obtaining in Germany. This, the only materialist conception of history, originates not with myself but with Marx, and can also be found in his works on the French Revolution of 1848-49, in the same *Revue,* and in *The Eighteenth Brumaire of Louis Bonaparte.*[130]

The parallel between the German Revolution of 1525 and that of 1848-49 was too obvious to be altogether ignored at that time. Nevertheless, despite the uniformity in the course of events, where various local revolts were crushed one after another by one and the same princely army, despite the often ludicrous similarity in the behaviour of the city burghers in both cases, the difference was also clear and distinct.

"Who profited from the Revolution of 1525? The *princes.* Who profited from the Revolution of 1848? The *big* princes, Austria and Prussia. Behind the minor princes of 1525 stood the petty burghers, who chained the princes to themselves by taxes. Behind the big princes of 1850, behind Austria and Prussia, there stand the modern big bourgeois, rapidly getting them under their yoke by means of the national debt. And behind the big bourgeois stand the proletarians." [a]

I regret to have to say that in this paragraph much too much honour was done to the German bourgeoisie. Both in Austria and in Prussia it has indeed had the opportunity of "rapidly getting" the monarchy "under its yoke by means of the national debt", but nowhere did it ever make use of this opportunity.

As a result of the war of 1866 Austria fell into the lap of the bourgeoisie as a gift. But it does not know how to rule, it is

---

[a] F. Engels, *The Peasant War in Germany* (present edition, p. 83).—*Ed.*

powerless and incapable of anything. It can do only one thing: savagely attack the workers as soon as they begin to stir. It still remains at the helm solely because the *Hungarians* need it.

And in Prussia? True, the national debt has increased by leaps and bounds, the deficit has become a permanent feature, state expenditure grows from year to year, the bourgeoisie have a majority in the Chamber and without them taxes cannot be increased nor loans floated. But where is their power over the state? Only a few months ago, when there was again a deficit, the bourgeoisie occupied a most favourable position. By holding out only just *a little,* they could have forced far-reaching concessions. What do they do? They regard it as a sufficient concession that the government *allows them* to lay at its feet close on 9 millions, not just *one* year, oh no, but *every year,* and for all time to come.[131]

I do not want to blame the poor National-Liberals[132] in the Chamber more than they deserve. I know they have been left in the lurch by those who stand behind them, by the mass of the bourgeoisie. This mass does not *want* to rule. It still has 1848 in its bones.

Why the German bourgeoisie exhibits this astonishing cowardice will be discussed later.

In other respects the above statement has been fully confirmed. Beginning with 1850, the more and more definite recession into the background of the small states, which serve now only as levers for Prussian or Austrian intrigues; the increasingly violent struggle between Austria and Prussia for supremacy; finally, the forcible settlement of 1866,[133] under which Austria retains its own provinces, while Prussia subjugates, directly or indirectly, the whole of the North, and the three states of the Southwest[a] are left out in the cold for the time being.

In all this grand performance[134] only the following is of importance for the German working class:

First, that through universal suffrage the workers have got the power of being directly represented in the legislative assembly.

Secondly, that Prussia has set a good example by swallowing three other crowns held by the grace of God.[135] Even the National-Liberals do not believe that *after* this operation it still possesses the same immaculate crown, held by the grace of God, which it formerly ascribed to itself.

Thirdly, that there is now only *one* serious adversary of the revolution in Germany—the Prussian government.

---

[a] Bavaria, Baden, Württemberg.— *Ed.*

And fourthly, that the German-Austrians will now at last have to make up their minds as to which they want to be, Germans or Austrians; whom they prefer to belong to—Germany or their extra-German trans-Leithan appendages.[136] It has been obvious for a long time that they have to give up one or the other, but this has been continually glossed over by the petty-bourgeois democrats.

As regards the other important issues relative to 1866, which since then have been thrashed out *ad nauseam* between the National-Liberals on the one hand, and the People's Party[137] on the other, the history of the next few years should prove that these two standpoints are so bitterly hostile to one another solely because they are the opposite poles of one and the same narrow-mindedness.

The year 1866 has changed almost nothing in the social relations of Germany. The few bourgeois reforms—uniform weights and measures, freedom of movement, freedom of occupation, etc., all within limits acceptable to the bureaucracy— do not even come up to what the bourgeoisie of other West European countries have enjoyed for a long time, and leave the main abuse, the bureaucratic license system, untouched.[138] For the proletariat all laws concerning freedom of movement, the right of naturalisation, the abolition of passports, etc., are anyhow made quite illusory by the common police practices.

What is much more important than the grand performance of 1866 is the growth of German industry and commerce, of railways, telegraphs and ocean steam shipping since 1848. However much this progress lags behind that of England, or even of France, during the same period, it is unprecedented for Germany and has accomplished more in twenty years than was previously done in a whole century. Only now has Germany been drawn, seriously and irrevocably, into *world commerce.* The capital of the industrialists has multiplied rapidly; the social position of the bourgeoisie has risen accordingly. The surest sign of industrial prosperity— *swindling*—has become very widespread and chained counts and dukes to its triumphal chariot. German capital is now constructing Russian and Romanian railways—may it not come to grief!—whereas only fifteen years ago, German railways went begging to English entrepreneurs. How, then, is it possible that the bourgeoisie has not conquered political power as well, that it behaves so cowardly towards the government?

It is the misfortune of the German bourgeoisie to arrive too late, as is the favourite German manner. The period of its florescence is occurring at a time when the bourgeoisie of the other West

European countries is already politically in decline. In England, the bourgeoisie could get its real representative, Bright, into the government only by an extension of the franchise, whose consequences are bound to put an end to all bourgeois rule. In France, where the bourgeoisie as such, as a class in its entirety, held power for only two years, 1849 and 1850, under the republic, it was able to continue its social existence only by abdicating its political power to Louis Bonaparte and the army. And in view of the enormously increased interaction of the three most advanced European countries, it is today no longer possible for the bourgeoisie to settle down to comfortable political rule in Germany after this rule has had its day in England and France.

It is a peculiarity of the bourgeoisie, in contrast to all former ruling classes, that there is a turning point in its development after which every further expansion of its agencies of power, hence primarily of its capital, only tends to make it more and more unfit for political rule. *"Behind the big bourgeois stand the proletarians."* In proportion as the bourgeoisie develops its industry, commerce and means of communication, in the same proportion it increases the numbers of the proletariat. At a certain point—which is not necessarily reached everywhere at the same time or at the same stage of development—it begins to notice that its proletarian double is outgrowing it. From that moment on, it loses the strength required for exclusive political rule; it looks around for allies with whom to share its rule, or to whom to cede it entirely, as circumstances may require.

In Germany this turning point for the bourgeoisie came as early as 1848. To be sure, at that time the German bourgeoisie was less frightened by the German proletariat than by the French. The June 1848 battle in Paris showed the bourgeoisie what it had to expect; the German proletariat was restless enough to prove to it that the seed for the same crop had already been sown on German soil, too; from that day on the edge was taken off all bourgeois political action. The bourgeoisie looked around for allies, sold itself to them regardless of the price—and even today it has not advanced one step.

These allies are all reactionary by nature. There is the monarchy with its army and its bureaucracy; there is the big feudal nobility; there are the small country squires, and there are even the priests. With all of these the bourgeoisie made pacts and bargains, if only to save its dear skin, until in the end it had nothing left to barter.

And the more the proletariat developed, the more it became aware of itself as a class and acted as a class, the more faint-hearted did the bourgeois become. When the astonishingly bad strategy of the Prussians triumphed over the astonishingly worse strategy of the Austrians at Sadowa, it was difficult to say who heaved a deeper sigh of relief—the Prussian bourgeois, who was also defeated at Sadowa, or the Austrian.

In 1870 our big bourgeois are acting exactly the same way as the middle burghers acted in 1525. As to the petty bourgeois, artisans and shopkeepers, they will always be the same. They hope to swindle their way up into the big bourgeoisie; they are afraid of being pushed down into the proletariat. Hovering between fear and hope, they will save their precious skins during the struggle and join the victor when the struggle is over. Such is their nature.

The social and political activity of the proletariat has kept pace with the rise of industry since 1848. The role that the German workers play today in their trade unions, cooperative societies, political associations and at meetings, elections and in the so-called Reichstag, is by itself sufficient proof of the transformation Germany has imperceptibly undergone in the last twenty years. It redounds to the credit of the German workers that *they alone* have succeeded in sending workers and workers' representatives into parliament, whereas neither the French nor the English have so far achieved this.

But even the proletariat has not yet outgrown the parallel of 1525. The class exclusively dependent on wages all its life is still far from being the majority of the German people. It is, therefore, also compelled to seek allies. These can be looked for only among the petty bourgeois, the lumpenproletariat of the cities, the small peasants and the agricultural labourers.

The *petty bourgeois* we have spoken of above. They are extremely unreliable except after a victory has been won, when their shouting in the beer houses knows no bounds. Nevertheless, there are very good elements among them, who join the workers of their own accord.

The *lumpenproletariat,* this scum of depraved elements from all classes, with headquarters in the big cities, is the worst of all the possible allies. This rabble is absolutely venal and absolutely brazen. If the French workers, in every revolution, inscribed on the houses: *Mort aux voleurs!* Death to thieves! and even shot some, they did so not out of reverence for property, but because they rightly considered it necessary above all to keep that gang at bay. Every leader of the workers who uses these scoundrels as guards or relies on them for support proves himself by this action alone a traitor to the movement.

The *small peasants*—for the bigger peasants belong to the bourgeoisie—differ in kind. They are either *feudal peasants* and still have to perform corvée services for their gracious lord. Now that the bourgeoisie has failed in its duty of freeing these people from serfdom, it will not be difficult to convince them that they can expect salvation only from the working class.

Or they are *tenant farmers*. In this case the situation is for the most part the same as in Ireland. Rents are pushed so high that in times of average crops the peasant and his family can barely make ends meet; when the crops are bad he is on the verge of starvation, is unable to pay his rent and is consequently entirely at the mercy of the landowner. The bourgeoisie never does anything for these people, unless it is compelled to. From whom then should they expect salvation if not from the workers?

There remain the peasants who cultivate their *own small plots of land.* In most cases they are so burdened with mortgages that they are as dependent on the usurer as the tenant on the landlord. For them also there remains only a meagre wage, which, moreover, since there are good years and bad years, is highly uncertain. These people can least of all expect anything from the bourgeoisie, because it is precisely the bourgeoisie, the capitalist usurers, who suck the lifeblood out of them. Still, most of these peasants cling to their property, though in reality it does not belong to them but to the usurer. It will have to be brought home to them all the same that they can be freed from the usurer only when a government dependent on the people has transformed all mortgages into debts to the state, and thereby lowered the interest rates. And this can be brought about only by the working class.

Wherever medium-sized and large estates prevail, *farm labourers* form the most numerous class in the countryside. This is the case throughout the North and East of Germany and it is *there* that the industrial workers of the towns find their *most numerous and most natural allies.* In the same way as the capitalist confronts the industrial worker, the landowner or large tenant confronts the farm labourer. The same measures that help the one must also help the other. The industrial workers can free themselves only by transforming the capital of the bourgeois, that is, the raw materials, machines and tools, and the means of subsistence they need to work in production, into the property of society, that is, into their own property, used by them in common. Similarly, the farm labourers can be rescued from their hideous misery only when, primarily, their chief object of labour, the land itself, is withdrawn from the private ownership of the big peasants and the still bigger feudal lords, transformed into public property and cultivated by cooperative associations of agricultural workers on their common account. And here we come to the famous resolution of the International Working Men's Congress in Basle that it is in the interest of society to transform landed property into common, national property.[139] This resolution was adopted mainly for countries where there is large-scale landed property, and, consequently, big estates are operated, with one master and many labourers on them. This state of affairs is still largely predominant in Germany, and therefore, next to England, the resolution was *most timely precisely for Germany*. The agricultural proletariat, the farm labourers—that is the class from which the bulk of the armies of the princes is recruited. It is the class which, thanks to universal suffrage, now sends into parliament the large number of feudal lords and Junkers; but it is also the class nearest to the industrial workers of the towns, which shares their living conditions and is steeped even more in misery than they. This class is impotent because it is split and scattered, but its latent power is so well known to the government and nobility that they let the schools fall into decay deliberately in order to keep it ignorant. It is the immediate and most urgent task of the German labour movement to breathe life into this class and draw it into the movement. The day the mass of the farm labourers will have learned to understand their own interests, a reactionary—feudal, bureaucratic or bourgeois—government will become impossible in Germany.

Written on about February 11, 1870

First published in the second edition of *The Peasant War in Germany*, Leipzig, October 1870

Printed according to the text of the second edition of the book, checked with the preface to the third edition (Leipzig, 1875)

THE PEASANT WAR IN GERMANY[294]

The German people, too, have their revolutionary tradition. There was a time when Germany produced characters that could match the best men in the revolutions of other countries, when the German people displayed an endurance and vigour which would in a more centralised nation have yielded the most magnificent results, and when the German peasants and plebeians were full of ideas and plans that often make their descendants shudder.

In face of the slackening that has now ensued almost everywhere after two years of struggle, it is high time to remind the German people of the clumsy yet powerful and tenacious figures of the Great Peasant War. Three centuries have passed and many a thing has changed; still the Peasant War is not so impossibly far removed from our present struggle, and the opponents who have to be fought are still essentially the same. We shall see the classes and fractions of classes which everywhere betrayed 1848 and 1849 in the role of traitors, though on a lower level of development, already in 1525. In any case, it is no credit to the modern insurrection that the robust vandalism of the Peasant War was seen only here and there in the movement of the past few years—at Odenwald, in the Black Forest, and in Silesia.

I

To begin with, let us briefly review the situation in Germany at the beginning of the sixteenth century.

German industry had made considerable progress in the fourteenth and fifteenth centuries. The local village industry of the feudal type was superseded by the guild system of industry in the towns, which produced for wider circles, and even for remoter markets. The weaving of coarse woollen fabrics and linens had become a permanent and widespread branch of industry, and even finer woollen and linen fabrics and silks were manufactured in Augsburg. Along with the art of weaving especial growth was witnessed in industries which were nurtured by the ecclesiastic and secular luxury of the late medieval epoch and verged on the fine arts: those of the gold- and silver-smith, the sculptor and engraver, etcher and wood-carver, armourer,[a] engraver of medals, wood-turner, etc. A succession of more or less important discoveries, the most prominent of which were the invention of gunpowder * and printing, had contributed substantially to the development of the crafts. Commerce kept pace with industry. By its century-long monopoly of sea navigation the Hanseatic League [295] ensured the elevation of all Northern Germany from medieval barbarism. Even though since the end of the fifteenth century the League had quickly begun to succumb to the competition of the English and Dutch, the great trade route from India to the north still lay through Germany,

* As has now been shown beyond doubt, gunpowder came to the Arabs through India from China, and they brought it through Spain to Europe along with fire-arms.— *Note by Engels to the 1875 edition.*

[a] This word is missing in the 1850 edition.— *Ed.*

1

Vasco da Gama's discoveries notwithstanding, and Augsburg still remained the great market of Italian silks, Indian spices, and all Levantine products. The towns of Upper Germany, particularly Augsburg and Nuremberg, were centres of an opulence and luxury quite remarkable for that time. The production of raw materials had also considerably increased. The German miners of the fifteenth century were the most skilful in the world and the flowering of the towns had also elevated agriculture from its early medieval crudity. Not only had large stretches of land been put to the plough, but dye crops and other imported plants were introduced, whose careful cultivation had favourable influence on farming in general.

Still, the progress of Germany's national production had not kept pace with the progress in other countries. Agriculture lagged far behind that of England and the Netherlands, and industry far behind that of Italy, Flanders and England, while the English, and especially the Dutch, had already begun ousting the Germans from the sea trade. The population was still very sparse. Civilisation existed only here and there, concentrated round the several centres of industry and commerce; but the interests of even these centres were highly divergent, with hardly any point of contact. The trade relations and export markets of the South differed totally from those of the North; the East and the West stood outside almost all traffic. Not a single city was in a position to be the industrial and commercial centre of the whole country, such, for instance, as London had already become for England. All internal communications were almost exclusively confined to coastal and river navigation and to the few large trade routes from Augsburg and Nuremberg via Cologne to the Netherlands, and via Erfurt to the North. Away from the rivers and trade routes there was a number of smaller towns which lay outside the major traffic and continued to vegetate undisturbed in the conditions of the late Middle Ages, needing only few foreign goods and providing few products for export. Of the rural population only the nobility came in contact with wider circles and with new needs; in their relations, the peasant masses never went beyond their immediate locality and its horizons.

While in England and France the rise of commerce and industry had the effect of intertwining the interests of the entire country and thereby brought about political centralisation, Germany had not got any further than grouping interests by provinces, around merely local centres, which led to political division, a division that was soon made all the more final by Germany's exclusion from world commerce. In step with the disintegration of the *purely feudal*

Empire, the bonds of imperial unity became completely dissolved, the major vassals of the Empire became almost independent sovereigns, and the cities of the Empire, on the one hand, and the knights of the Empire, on the other, began entering into alliances either against each other or against the princes or the Emperor. Uncertain of its own position, the imperial government vacillated between the various elements comprising the Empire, and thereby lost more and more authority; in spite of all its intrigues and violence, the attempt at centralisation in the manner of Louis XI was only just able to hold together the Austrian hereditary lands. Who finally won and were bound to win in this confusion, in these countless and interrelated conflicts, were the bearers of centralisation amidst the disunity, the bearers of local and provincial centralisation—the *princes*, at whose side the Emperor himself became more and more of a prince like the others.

In these circumstances, the position of the classes inherited from the Middle Ages had changed considerably, and new classes had emerged beside the old.

The *princes* came from the high nobility. They were already almost independent of the Emperor and possessed most of the sovereign rights. They made war and peace on their own, maintained standing armies, convened Diets, and levied taxes. They had brought a large part of the lesser nobility and most of the towns under their sway, and resorted continuously to all possible means of incorporating in their dominion all the remaining imperial towns and baronial estates. They were centralisers in respect to these towns and estates, while acting as a decentralising force in respect to the imperial power. Internally, their government was already highly autocratic. They convened the estates only when they could not do without them. They imposed taxes and borrowed money whenever it suited them; the right of the estates to ratify taxes was seldom recognised and still more seldom practised. And even when practised, the prince usually had the majority by virtue of the knights and prelates, the two tax-exempted estates that participated in the benefits enjoyed from taxes. The princes' need for money grew with their taste for luxury, the expansion of their courts, the standing armies, and the mounting costs of government. The taxes became ever more oppressive. The towns were mostly protected from them by their privileges, and the full impact of the tax burden fell upon the peasants, the subjects of the princes, as well as upon the serfs, bondsmen and tithe-paying peasants [*Zinsbauern*][a] of their vassal knights. Where direct taxation

---

[a] This word is missing in the 1850 and 1870 editions.—*Ed.*

proved insufficient, indirect taxes were introduced. The most refined devices of the art of finance were called into play to fill the anaemic treasury. When nothing availed, when there was nothing to pawn and no free imperial city was willing to grant any more credit, the princes resorted to currency operations of the basest kind, coined depreciated money, and set high or low compulsory exchange rates at the convenience of their treasuries. Furthermore, trade in urban and other privileges, later forcibly withdrawn only to be resold at a high price, and the use of every attempt at opposition as an excuse for all kinds of extortion and robbery, etc., etc., were common and lucrative sources of income for the princes of the day. Justice, too, was a perpetual and not unimportant merchandise. In brief, the subjects of that time, who, in addition, had to satisfy the private avarice of the princely bailiffs and officials, had a full taste of all the blessings of the "paternal" system of government.

The middle nobility of the medieval feudal hierarchy had almost entirely disappeared; it had either risen to acquire the independence of petty princes, or sunk into the ranks of the lesser nobility. The *lesser nobility,* or *knighthood,* was fast moving towards extinction. Much of it was already totally impoverished and lived in the service of the princes, holding military or civil offices; another part of it was in the vassalage and under the sway of the princes; and a small part was directly subject to the Emperor. The development of military science, the growing importance of the infantry, and the improvement of fire-arms dwarfed the knighthood's military merits as heavy cavalry, and also put an end to the invincibility of its castles. Like the Nuremberg artisans, the knights were made redundant by the progress of industry. The knights' need for money considerably hastened their ruin. The luxury of their palaces, rivalry in the magnificence of tournaments and feasts, the price of armaments and horses—all increased with the development of society,[a] while the sources of income of the knights and barons increased but little, if at all. As time went on, feuds with their attendant plunder and extortion, highway robbery and similar noble occupations became too dangerous. The payments and services of their subjects yielded the knights hardly more than before. To satisfy their growing requirements, the gracious knights had to resort to the same means as the princes. The peasantry was plundered by the nobility with a dexterity that increased every year. The serfs were sucked dry, and the bondsmen were burdened with ever new payments and services on a great variety of pretexts and on all possible occasions. Statute

---

[a] The 1850 and 1870 editions have "civilisation" instead of "society".— *Ed.*

labour, tributes, rents, land-sale taxes, death taxes, protection
-moneys,[296] etc., were raised at will, in spite of all the old agreements.
Justice was denied or sold for money, and when the knight could not
get at the peasant's money in any other way, he threw him into the
tower without further ado and forced him to pay a ransom.

The relations between the lesser nobility and the other estates
were also anything but friendly. The knights bound by vassalage to
the princes strove to become vassals of the Empire, the imperial
knights strove to retain their independence; this led to incessant
conflicts with the princes. The knight regarded the arrogant clergy
of those days as an entirely superfluous estate, and envied them
their large possessions and the wealth held secure by their celibacy
and the church statutes. He was continually at loggerheads with the
towns, he was always in debt to them, he made his living by
plundering their territory, robbing their merchants, and by holding
for ransom prisoners captured in the feuds. And the knights'
struggle with all these estates became the more violent the more the
money question became to them as well a question of life.

The *clergy*, that bearer of the medieval feudal ideology, felt the
influence of historic change just as acutely. Book-printing and the
claims of growing commerce robbed it of its monopoly not only
in reading and writing, but also in higher education. The division of
labour also made inroads into the intellectual realm. The newly
rising juridical estate drove the clergy from a number of the most
influential offices. The clergy was also on its way to becoming largely
superfluous, and demonstrated this by its ever greater laziness and
ignorance. But the more superfluous it became, the more it grew in
numbers, due to the enormous riches that it still continuously
augmented by all possible means.

There were two entirely distinct classes among the clergy. The
clerical feudal hierarchy formed the *aristocratic* class: the bishops and
archbishops, abbots, priors, and other prelates. These high church
dignitaries were either imperial princes or reigned as feudal lords
under the sovereignty of other princes over extensive lands with
numerous serfs and bondsmen. They exploited their dependants as
ruthlessly as the knights and princes, and went at it even more
wantonly. In addition to brute force they applied all the subterfuges
of religion; in addition to the fear of the rack they applied the fear of
ex-communication and denial of absolution; they made use of all the
intrigues of the confessional to wring the last penny from their
subjects or to augment the portion of the church. Forgery of
documents was for these worthies a common and favourite means of
swindling. But although they received tithes from their subjects in

addition to the usual feudal services and quitrents, these incomes were not enough for them. They fabricated miracle-working sacred images and relics, set up sanctifying prayer-houses, and traded in indulgences in order to squeeze more money out of the people, and for quite some time with eminent success.

It was these prelates and their numerous *gendarmerie* of monks, which grew constantly with the spread of political and religious witch-hunts, on whom the priest-hatred not only of the people, but also of the nobility, was concentrated. Being directly subject to the Emperor,[a] they were a nuisance for the princes. The life of luxurious pleasure led by the corpulent bishops and abbots, and their army of monks excited the envy of the nobility, and the more flagrantly it contradicted their preaching, the more it inflamed the people, who had to bear its cost.

The *plebeian* part of the clergy consisted of rural and urban preachers. These stood outside the feudal church hierarchy and had no part in its riches. Their work was less controlled, and, important though it was for the church, it was for the moment far less indispensable than the police services of the barracked monks. They were, therefore, the worse paid by far, and their prebends were mostly very meagre. Of burgher or plebeian origin, they were close enough to the life of the masses to retain their burgher and plebeian sympathies in spite of their clerical status. For them participation in the movements of the time was the rule, whereas for monks it was an exception. They provided the movement with theorists and ideologists, and many of them, representatives of the plebeians and peasants, died on the scaffold as a result. The people's hatred of the clergy turned against them only in isolated cases.

What the Emperor was to the princes and nobility, the *Pope* was to the higher and lower clergy. Where the Emperor received the "general pfennig"[297] or the imperial taxes, the Pope received the universal church taxes, out of which he paid for the luxury of the Roman court. And in no country were these church taxes collected more conscientiously and exactingly than in Germany—thanks to the power and number of the clergy. Particularly the annates,[298] collected on the bestowal of bishoprics. The growing needs led to the invention of new means of raising revenues, such as trade in relics and indulgences, jubilee collections, etc. Large sums of money flowed yearly from Germany to Rome in this way, and the consequent increased oppression not only heightened the hatred for

---

[a] Instead of *reichsunmittelbar* (directly subject to the Emperor) the 1850 edition has *souverän* (sovereign).—*Ed.*

the clergy, but also roused the national sentiments, particularly of the nobility, the then most nationalistic estate.

In the medieval *towns* three distinct groups developed from the original citizenry with the growth of commerce and the handicrafts.

The urban society was headed by the *patriciate*, the so-called *honourables*. They were the richest families. They alone sat in the town council, and held all town offices. Hence, they not only administered but also consumed all the town revenues. Strong by virtue of their wealth and time-honoured aristocratic status recognised by Emperor and Empire, they exploited the town community and the peasants belonging to the town in every possible way. They practised usury in grain and money, seized monopolies of all kinds, gradually deprived the community of all rights to communal use of town forests and meadows and used them exclusively for their own private benefit, exacted arbitrary road-, bridge- and gate-tolls and other imposts, and trafficked in trade, guild, and burgher privileges, and in justice. They treated the peasants of the town precincts with no more consideration than did the nobility and clergy. On the contrary, town bailiffs and village officials, patricians all, added a certain bureaucratic punctiliousness to aristocratic rigidity and avarice in collecting imposts. The town revenues thus collected were administered in a most arbitrary fashion; the accounts in the town books, a mere formality, were neglected and confused in the extreme; embezzlement and deficit were the order of the day. How easy it was at that time for a comparatively small, privileged caste bound by family ties and common interests, to enrich itself enormously out of the town revenues, is easily seen from the many embezzlements and swindles[a] which 1848 brought to light in so many town administrations.

The patricians took pains everywhere to let the rights of the town community fall into disuse, particularly in matters of finance. Only later, when their machinations transcended all bounds, the communities came into motion again to at least gain control over the town administration. In most towns they actually regained their rights, but due to the eternal squabbles between the guilds, the tenacity of the patricians, and the protection the latter enjoyed from the Empire and the governments of the allied towns, the patrician council members soon in effect regained their former undivided dominance, be it by cunning or force. At the beginning of the

---

[a] The 1850 and 1870 editions have *Tripotagen* (knavery) instead of *Schwindeleien* (swindles).— *Ed.*

sixteenth century the communities in all the towns were again in the
opposition.

The town opposition to the patricians broke up into two factions
which took quite distinct stands in the Peasant War.

The *burgher opposition*, forerunners of our present-day liberals,
included the richer and middle burghers, and, depending on local
conditions, a more or less appreciable section of the petty burghers.
Their demands did not overstep purely constitutional limits. They
wanted control over the town administration and a share in
legislative power, to be exercised either by an assembly of the
community itself or by its representatives (big council, community
committee); further restriction of the patrician nepotism and the
oligarchy of a few families which was coming to the fore ever more
distinctly within the patriciate itself. At best, they also demanded
several council seats for burghers from their own midst. This party,
joined here and there by the dissatisfied and impoverished part of
the patriciate, had a large majority in all the ordinary community
assemblies and in the guilds. The adherents of the council and the
more radical part of the opposition together formed only a small
minority among the real *burghers.*

We shall see how this "moderate", "law-abiding", "well-to-do"
and "intelligent" opposition played exactly the same role, with
exactly the same effect, in the movement of the sixteenth century, as
its successor, the constitutional party, played in the movement of
1848 and 1849.[299]

Beyond that, the burgher opposition declaimed zealously against
the clergy, whose idle luxury and loose morals roused its bitter scorn.
It urged measures against the scandalous life of those worthy men. It
demanded the abolition of the clergy's special jurisdiction and tax
exemption, and particularly a reduction in the number of monks.

The *plebeian opposition* consisted of ruined burghers and the mass
of townsmen without civic rights—journeymen, day labourers, and
the numerous precursors of the lumpenproletariat, who existed even
in the lowest stages of urban development. The lumpenproletariat is,
generally speaking, a phenomenon that occurs in a more or less
developed form in all the so far known phases of society. The
number of people without a definite occupation and permanent
domicile increased greatly at that time due to the decay of feudalism
in a society in which every occupation, every sphere of life, was still
fenced in by countless privileges. In all the developed countries
vagabonds had never been so numerous as in the first half of the
sixteenth century. In war time some of these tramps joined the
armies, others begged their way across the countryside, and still

others eked out a meagre living in the towns as day labourers or from whatever other occupation that was not under guild jurisdiction. All three groups played a part in the Peasant War—the first in the armies of princes which overpowered the peasants, the second in the peasant conspiracies and in peasant gangs where its demoralising influence was felt at all times, and the third in the clashes of the urban parties. It will be recalled, however, that a great many, namely those living in the towns, still had a substantial share of sound peasant nature and had not as yet been possessed by the venality and depravity of the present "civilised" lumpenproletariat.

As we see, the plebeian opposition in the towns of that day was a very mixed lot. It brought together the depraved parts of the old feudal and guild society with the undeveloped, budding proletarian elements of the germinating modern bourgeois society. There were impoverished guild burghers, on the one hand, who still clung to the existing burgher system by virtue of their privileges, and the dispossessed peasants and discharged vassals as yet unable to become proletarians, on the other. Between these two groups were the journeymen, who still stood outside official society and whose condition was as close to that of the proletariat as this could be with the contemporary state of industry and the guild privileges; but due to these privileges they were, at the same time, almost all prospective burgher artisans. The party affiliation of this conglomeration was therefore highly uncertain, and varied from locality to locality. Before the Peasant War the plebeian opposition took part in the political struggles not as a party, but as a noisy marauding tagtail of the burgher opposition, a mob that could be bought and sold for a few barrels of wine. The peasant revolts turned it into a party, and even then it remained almost everywhere dependent on the peasants in its demands and actions—a striking proof of how much the town of that time still depended on the countryside. In their independent actions, the plebeians demanded extension of the monopoly in urban handicrafts to the countryside, and had no wish to see a curtailment of town revenues come about through the abolition of feudal burdens within the town precincts, etc.; in brief, they were reactionary in their independent actions, and delivered themselves up to their own petty-bourgeois elements—a typical prelude to the tragicomedy staged in the past three years by the modern petty bourgeoisie under the trade mark of democracy.

Only in Thuringia under the direct influence of Münzer, and in a few other localities under that of his pupils, was the plebeian faction of the towns carried away by the general storm to such an extent that the embryonic proletarian element in it gained the upper hand for a time over all the other factions[a] of the movement. This episode grouped round the magnificent figure of *Thomas Münzer*, was the culmination point and also the briefest episode, of the Peasant War. It stands to reason that the plebeian factions were the quickest to collapse, that they had a predominantly fantastic outlook, and that the expression of their demands was necessarily extremely uncertain; in the existing conditions they found the least firm ground to stand on.

Beneath all these classes, save the last one, was the exploited bulk of the nation, the *peasants*. It was on the peasant that the whole arrangement of social strata reposed: princes, officials, nobles, clergymen, patricians and burghers. No matter whose subject the peasant was—a prince's, an imperial baron's, a bishop's, a monastery's or a town's—he was treated by all as a thing, a beast of burden, and worse. If a serf, he was entirely at the mercy of his master. If a bondsman, the legal levies stipulated in the agreement were enough to crush him; yet they were daily increased. He had to work on his lord's estate most of his time; out of what he earned in his few free hours he had to pay tithes, tributes, the quitrent, princely levies [*Bede*], road (war) tolls, and local and imperial taxes. He could neither marry nor die without paying something to the lord. Besides his statute labour he had to gather litter, pick strawberries and bilberries, collect snail-shells, drive the game in the hunt, and chop wood, etc., for his gracious lord. The right to fish and hunt belonged to the master; the peasant had to look on quietly as his crop was destroyed by wild game. The common pastures and woods of the peasants were almost everywhere forcibly appropriated by the lords. The lord did as he pleased with the peasant's own person, his wife and daughters, just as he did with the peasant's property. He had the right of the first night. He threw the peasant into the tower when he wished, and the rack awaited the peasant there just as surely as the investigating attorney awaits the arrested in our day. He killed the peasant or had him beheaded when he pleased. There was none out of the edifying chapters of the *Carolina*[300] dealing with "ear clipping", "nose cutting", "eye gouging", "chopping of fingers and hands", "beheading", "breaking on the wheel", "burning", "hot irons", "quartering", etc., that the gracious lord and patron would not apply at will. Who would defend the peasant? It was the barons, clergymen, patricians or jurists who sat in the courts, and they knew

---

[a] The 1850 edition has *Faktoren* (agents) instead of *Fraktionen* (factions).—*Ed.*

perfectly well what they were being paid for. After all, every official estate of the Empire lived by sucking the peasants dry.

Though gnashing their teeth under the terrible burden, the peasants were still difficult to rouse to revolt. They were scattered over large areas, and this made collusion between them extremely difficult. The old habit of submission inherited by generation from generation, lack of practice in the use of arms in many regions, and the varying degree of exploitation depending on the personality of the lord, all combined to keep the peasant quiet. For this reason we find so many local peasant insurrections in the Middle Ages but, prior to the Peasant War, not a single general national peasant revolt, at least in Germany. Moreover, the peasants were unable to make revolution on their own as long as they were confronted by the united and organised power of the princes, the nobility and the towns. Their only chance of winning lay in an alliance with other estates. But how could they join with other estates if they were exploited to the same degree by all of them?

As we see, in the early sixteenth century the various estates of the Empire—princes, nobles, prelates, patricians, burghers, plebeians and peasants—formed an extremely confusing mass with their varied and highly conflicting needs. The estates stood in each other's way, and each was continually in overt or covert conflict with all the others. The division of the nation into two large camps, as seen in France at the outbreak of the first Revolution and as witnessed today on a higher level of development in the most advanced countries, was thus a rank impossibility. Anything like it could only come about if the lowest stratum of the nation, the one exploited by all the other estates, the peasants and plebeians, would rise up. The entanglement of interests, views and aspirations of that time will be easily understood from the confusion brought about in the last two years by the present far less complicated structure of the German nation, consisting of the feudal nobility, the bourgeoisie, the petty bourgeoisie, the peasants and the proletariat.

II

The grouping of the then numerous and different estates into bigger entities was made virtually impossible by decentralisation, local and provincial independence, the industrial and commercial isolation of the provinces from each other, and poor communications. It came about only with the general spread of revolutionary political and religious ideas during the Reformation. The various estates that either embraced or opposed those ideas, concentrated the nation—only very laboriously, to be sure, and only approximately—into three large camps: the Catholic or reactionary, the Lutheran bourgeois reformist, and the revolutionary. If we discover little logic in this great division of the nation, and if we find partly the same elements in the first two camps, this is explained by the dissolution of most of the official estates handed down from the Middle Ages, and by the decentralisation which, for the moment, imparted to these estates in different localities opposing tendencies. In recent years we have so often encountered similar facts in Germany that this apparent jumble of estates and classes in the much more complicated environment of the sixteenth century cannot surprise us.

In spite of the latest experiences, German ideology still sees nothing except violent theological bickering in the struggles that brought the Middle Ages to an end. Should the people of that time, say our home-bred historians and political sages, have only come to an understanding concerning divine matters, there would have been no reason whatever for quarrelling over the earthly affairs. These ideologists are so gullible that they accept unquestioningly all the illusions that an epoch makes about itself or that ideologists of an epoch make about that epoch. People of that kind see in, say, the

Revolution of 1789 nothing but a somewhat heated debate over the advantages a constitutional monarchy has over absolutism, in the July Revolution[a] a practical controversy over the untenability of justice "by the grace of God", and in the February Revolution[b] an attempt at solving the problem: "republic or monarchy?", etc. To this day our ideologists have hardly any idea of the *class struggles* fought out in these upheavals, of which the political slogan on the banner is every time a bare expression, although the tidings about them are carried discernibly enough not only from abroad, but also by the rumble and grumble of many thousands of native proletarians.

Even the so-called religious wars of the sixteenth century mainly concerned very positive material class interests; those wars were class wars, too, just as the later internal collisions in England and France. Although the class struggles of those days were clothed in religious shibboleths, and though the interests, requirements, and demands of the various classes were concealed behind a religious screen, this changed nothing at all and is easily explained by the conditions of the times.

The Middle Ages had developed altogether from the raw. They wiped the old civilisation, the old philosophy, politics and jurisprudence off the slate, to begin anew in everything. The only thing they kept from the shattered old world was Christianity and a number of half-ruined towns divested of all civilisation. As a consequence, just as in every primitive stage of development, the clergy obtained a monopoly in intellectual education and education itself became essentially theological. In the hands of the clergy politics and jurisprudence, much like all other sciences, remained mere branches of theology, and were treated in accordance with the principles prevailing in the latter. Church dogmas were also political axioms, and Bible quotations had the validity of law in any court. Even when a special estate of jurists had begun to take shape, jurisprudence long remained under the patronage of theology. This supremacy of theology in the entire realm of intellectual activity was at the same time an inevitable consequence of the fact that the church was the all-embracing synthesis and the most general sanction of the existing feudal order.

It is clear that under the circumstances all the generally voiced attacks against feudalism, above all the attacks against the church, and all revolutionary social and political doctrines were necessarily

---

[a] Of 1830.—*Ed.*
[b] Of 1848.—*Ed.*

also mostly theological heresies. The existing social relations had to be stripped of their halo of sanctity before they could be attacked.

The revolutionary opposition to feudalism was alive throughout the Middle Ages. It took the shape of mysticism,[301] open heresy, or armed insurrection, depending on the conditions of the time. It is well known how much sixteenth-century reformers depended on mysticism. Münzer himself was indebted to it. The heresies gave expression partly to the patriarchal Alpine shepherds' reaction to the feudalism advancing upon them (Waldenses[302]), partly to the opposition of the towns that had outgrown feudalism (the Albigenses,[303] Arnold of Brescia, etc.), and partly to direct peasant insurrections (John Ball and, among others, the Hungarian teacher in Picardy[304]). We can here leave aside the patriarchal heresy of the Waldenses and the Swiss insurrection, which was in form and content a reactionary, purely local attempt at stemming the tide of history. In the two remaining forms of medieval heresy we find already in the twelfth century the precursors of the great antithesis between the burgher and peasant-plebeian oppositions, which caused the defeat of the Peasant War. This antithesis is seen throughout the later Middle Ages.

The town heresies—and those are the actual official heresies of the Middle Ages—were directed primarily against the clergy, whose wealth and political station they attacked. Just as the present-day bourgeoisie demands a *gouvernement à bon marché* (cheap government), the medieval burghers chiefly demanded an *église à bon marché* (cheap church). Reactionary in form like any heresy that sees only degeneration in the further development of church and dogma, the burgher heresy demanded the revival of the simple early Christian Church constitution and abolition of exclusive priesthood. This cheap arrangement would eliminate monks, prelates, and the court in Rome; in short, all the expensive element of the church. The towns, which were republics themselves, albeit under the protection of monarchs, were the first to enunciate in general terms through their attacks upon the Papacy that a republic was the normal form of bourgeois rule. Their hostility to some of the dogmas and church laws is explained partly by the foregoing, and partly by their living conditions. Their bitter opposition to celibacy, for instance, has never been better explained than by Boccaccio. Arnold of Brescia in Italy and Germany, the Albigenses in Southern France, John Wycliffe in England, Hus and the Calixtines[305] in Bohemia, were the principal exponents of this trend. The towns were then already a recognised estate sufficiently capable of fighting secular feudalism with its privileges by force of arms or in the assemblies of the estates.

This explains quite simply why here the opposition to feudalism amounted only to opposition to *ecclesiastical* feudalism.

We also find in Southern France and in England and Bohemia that most of the lesser nobility joined the towns in their struggle against the clergy and in their heresies—which is explained by the dependence of the lesser nobility on the towns, and by their common interests as opposed to the princes and prelates. We shall encounter the same thing in the Peasant War.

The heresy that lent direct expression to peasant and plebeian needs and was almost invariably associated with an insurrection was of a totally different nature. Though it shared all the demands of the burgher heresy in relation to the clergy, the Papacy and the revival of the early Christian Church constitution, it went infinitely further. It demanded the restoration of early Christian equality among members of the community and recognition of this equality also as a prescript for the burgher world. It invoked the "equality of the children of God" to infer civil equality, and partly even equality of property. Equality of nobleman to peasant, of patrician and privileged burgher to the plebeian, abolition of statute labour, quitrents, taxes, privileges, and at least the most crying differences in property—those were the demands advanced with more or less determination as naturally consistent with the early Christian doctrine. At the time when feudalism was at its zenith there was little to choose between this peasant-plebeian heresy of the Albigenses, for example, and the burgher heresy, but in the fourteenth and fifteenth centuries it developed into a clearly distinctive party opinion and usually occupied an independent place alongside the heresy of the burghers. This was so in the case of John Ball, preacher of Wat Tyler's rebellion in England, and the Wycliffe movement, and of the Taborites [306] and the Calixtines in Bohemia. In the case of the Taborites there was even already a republican tendency under the theocratic cloak, a view further developed by the plebeians in Germany in the late fifteenth and early sixteenth centuries.

The fanaticism of mystically-minded sects, the Flagellants and Lollards, [307] etc., which continued the revolutionary tradition in times of suppression, was contiguous with this form of heresy.

At that time the plebeians were the only class that stood outside the existing official society. They had no access to either the feudal or the burgher association. They had neither privileges nor property; they did not even have the kind of heavily-taxed property possessed by the peasant or petty burgher. They were propertyless and rightless in every respect; their living conditions never even brought them into direct contact with the existing institutions, which ignored them completely. They were a living symptom of the decay of the feudal and guild-burgher society, and at the same time the first precursors of the modern bourgeois society.

This explains why even then the plebeian faction could not confine itself to fighting only feudalism and the privileged burghers; why, in fantasy at least, it reached beyond the then scarcely dawning modern bourgeois society; why, an absolutely propertyless faction, it questioned the institutions, views and conceptions common to all societies based on class antagonisms. In this respect, the chiliastic dream-visions[308] of early Christianity offered a very convenient starting point. On the other hand, this sally beyond the present and even the future could be nothing but violent and fantastic, and was bound to slide back at its first practical application to within the narrow limits set by the contemporary situation. The attack on private property and the demand for community of property was bound to dissolve into a primitive organisation of charity; vague Christian equality could at best dissolve into civic "equality before the law"; elimination of all authority would finally end in the establishment of republican governments elected by the people. The anticipation of communism in fantasy became in reality an anticipation of modern bourgeois conditions.

This violent anticipation of coming historical developments, easily explained by the living conditions of the plebeians, is first seen in *Germany*, with *Thomas Münzer* and his party. True, the Taborites had a kind of chiliastic community of property, but that was a purely military measure. Only in the teachings of Münzer did these communist notions express the aspirations of a real section of society. He was the first to formulate them with a certain definiteness, and only after him do we find them in every great popular upheaval, until they gradually merge with the modern proletarian movement; just as the struggles of free peasants in the Middle Ages against the increasing feudal domination merged with the struggles of serfs and bondsmen for the complete abolition of the feudal system.

The first of the three large camps, the *conservative Catholic*, embraced all the elements interested in maintaining the existing conditions, i.e. the imperial authorities, the ecclesiastical and a section of the lay princes, the richer nobility, the prelates and the city patricians, while the camp of *Lutheran* reform, *moderate in the burgher manner*, attracted all the propertied elements of the opposition, the mass of the lesser nobility, the burghers, and even some of the lay princes who hoped to enrich themselves through confiscation of church estates and wanted to seize the opportunity of gaining greater independence from the Empire. As for the peasants and plebeians, they formed a *revolutionary* party whose demands and doctrines were most forcefully set out by Münzer.

Luther and Münzer each fully represented his party by his doctrine, as well as by his character and behaviour.

Between 1517 and 1525 *Luther* changed just as much as the present-day German constitutionalists did between 1846 and 1849, and as every bourgeois party does when, placed for a time at the head of the movement, it is overwhelmed by the plebeian or proletarian party standing behind it.

When in 1517 Luther first opposed the dogmas and statutes of the Catholic Church his opposition was by no means of a definite character. Though it did not overstep the demands of the earlier burgher heresy, it did not and could not rule out any trend which went further. At that early stage it was necessary that all the opposition elements should be united, the most resolute revolutionary energy should be displayed, and the sum of the existing heresies against the Catholic orthodoxy should be represented. In exactly the same way our liberal bourgeoisie of 1847 was still revolutionary, called itself socialist and communist, and clamoured for the emancipation of the working class. Luther's sturdy peasant nature asserted itself in the stormiest fashion in that first period of his activity.

"If the raging madness" (of the Roman churchmen) "were to continue, it seems to me no better counsel and remedy could be found against it than that kings and princes apply force, arm themselves, attack those evil people who have poisoned the entire world, and put an end to this game once and for all, *with arms, not with words*.[a] Since we punish thieves with the sword, murderers with the halter,[b] and heretics with fire, why do we not turn on all those evil teachers of perdition, those popes, cardinals and bishops, and the entire swarm of the Roman Sodom *with arms in hand, and wash our hands in their blood*?"[c]

But this initial revolutionary zeal was short-lived. Luther's lightning struck home. The entire German people was set in motion. On the one hand, peasants and plebeians saw the signal to revolt in his appeals against the clergy, and in his sermon of Christian freedom; on the other, he was joined by the moderate burghers and a large section of the lesser nobility. Even princes were drawn into the maelstrom. The former believed the day had come to settle

---

[a] The last three words are italicised by Engels.— *Ed.*

[b] Luther wrote:"punish thieves with the halter, murderers with the sword".— *Ed.*

[c] *Epitoma responsionis ad Martinum Luther* [1520]. Engels quotes according to W. Zimmermann, *Allgemeine Geschichte des grossen Bauernkrieges*, Th. 1, S. 364-65.— *Ed.*

scores with all their oppressors, the latter only wished to break the
power of the clergy, the dependence upon Rome, to abolish the
Catholic hierarchy and to enrich themselves on the confiscation of
church property. The parties stood aloof from each other, and each
had its spokesmen. Luther had to choose between them. He, the
protégé of the Elector of Saxony,[a] the revered professor of
Wittenberg who had become powerful and famous overnight, the
great man with his coterie of servile creatures and flatterers, did not
hesitate for a single moment. He dropped the popular elements of
the movement and took the side of the burghers, the nobility, and
the princes. His appeals for a war of extermination[b] against Rome
resounded no more. Luther now preached *peaceful progress* and
passive resistance (cf., for example, *An den Adel teutscher Nation,* 1520,
etc.). Invited by Hutten to visit him and Sickingen in the castle of
Ebern, where the nobility conspired against the clergy and the
princes, Luther replied:

"I do not wish the Gospel *defended by force and bloodshed.* The World was conquered
by the Word, the Church is maintained by the Word, the Word will also put the
Church back into its own, and Antichrist, who gained his own without violence, will
fall without violence."[c]

From this reversal or, to be more exact, from this more definite
explication of Luther's policy sprang that bartering and haggling
over institutions and dogmas to be retained or reformed, that
disgusting diplomatising, conciliating, intriguing and compromising,
which resulted in the Confession of Augsburg, the finally impor-
tuned articles of a reformed burgher church.[309] It was quite the same
kind of petty bargaining as was recently repeated in political form *ad
nauseam* at the German national assemblies, agreement assemblies,
chambers of revision, and Erfurt parliament.   The philistine nature
of the official Reformation was most distinctly on display at these
negotiations.

There were good reasons for Luther, henceforth the recognised
representative of the burgher reform, to preach lawful progress.
The bulk of the towns espoused the cause of moderate reform, the
lesser nobility became more and more devoted to it, and a section of
the princes joined in, while another section vacillated. Success was as

---

[a] Frederick III.— *Ed.*
[b] The 1850 edition has *Vertilgungsrufe* (appeals for extermination) instead of
Aufrufe zum Vertilgungskampfe (appeals for a war of extermination).— *Ed.*
[c] A passage from Luther's letter to Hutten quoted in his letter to Spalatin dated
January 16, 1521. Intalicised by Engels. (See W. Zimmermann, op. cit., Th. 1, S.
366.)— *Ed.*

good as won, at least in a large part of Germany. The remaining regions could not in the long run withstand the pressure of moderate opposition in the event of continued peaceful development. On the other hand, any violent upheaval was bound to bring the moderate party into conflict with the extremist plebeian and peasant party, to alienate the princes, the nobility, and many towns from the movement, leaving the alternative of either the burgher party being overshadowed by the peasants and plebeians or all the parties to the movement being crushed by a Catholic restoration. We have seen examples enough of late of how, after gaining the slightest victory, bourgeois parties sought to steer a lawful course between the Scylla of revolution and the Charybdis of restoration.

Since in the social and political conditions of that time the results of every change were bound to benefit the princes and inevitably increased their power, it came about that the burgher reform fell the more completely under the control of the reformed princes, the more sharply it broke away from the plebeian and peasant elements. Luther himself became more and more their vassal, and the people knew perfectly well what they were doing when they accused him of having become just another flunkey of the princes, and when they stoned him in Orlamünde.

When the Peasant War broke out, and this in regions where the nobility and the princes were mostly Catholic, Luther tried to strike a mediatory pose. He resolutely attacked the authorities. He said it was their oppression that was to blame for the rebellion, that it was not the peasants but God himself who had risen against them. Yet, on the other hand, he said, the revolt was ungodly and contrary to the Gospel. In the end he advised both parties to yield and reach an amicable understanding.[a]

But in spite of these well-meaning mediatory offers, the revolt spread swiftly and even involved Protestant regions dominated by Lutheran princes, lords and towns, rapidly outgrowing the "circumspect" burgher reform. The most determined faction of the insurgents under Münzer made its headquarters in Luther's immediate proximity in Thuringia. A few more successes and the whole of Germany would be in flames, Luther surrounded and perhaps piked as a traitor, and the burgher reform swept away by the tide of a peasant-plebeian revolution. This was no time for circumspection. All the old animosities were forgotten in the face of the revolution. Compared with the hordes of peasants, the servants

---

[a] M. Luther, *Ermanunge zum fride auff die zwelff artikel der Bawrschafft ynn Schwaben,* Wittemberg, 1525.— *Ed.*

of the Roman Sodom were innocent lambs, sweet-tempered children of God. Burgher and prince, noble and clergyman, Luther and the Pope, all joined hands "against the murderous and plundering peasant hordes".[a]

"They must be *knocked to pieces, strangled* and *stabbed, covertly* and *overtly*, by everyone who can, just as one must kill a *mad dog!*" Luther cried. "Therefore, dear sirs, help here, save there, stab, knock, strangle them everyone who can, and should you lose your life, bless you, no better death can you ever attain." There should be no false mercy for the peasant. Whoever hath pity on those whom God pities not, whom He wishes punished and destroyed, belongs among the rebels himself. Later the peasants themselves would learn to thank God when they had to give up one cow in order to enjoy the other in peace, and the princes would learn through the upheaval the spirit of the mob that must be ruled by force only.[b] "The wise man says: *cibus, onus et virga asino.*[c] The peasants must have nothing but chaff. They do not hearken to the Word, and are foolish, so they must hearken to the rod and the gun, and that serves them right. We must pray for them that they obey. Where they do not there should be little mercy. *Let the guns roar among them,* or else they will do it a thousand times worse."[d]

Our late socialist and philanthropic bourgeoisie said the same things when the proletariat claimed its share of the fruits of victory after the March events.

Luther had put a powerful tool into the hands of the plebeian movement by translating the Bible. Through the Bible he contrasted the feudalised Christianity of his day with the moderate Christianity of the first centuries, and the decaying feudal society with a picture of a society that knew nothing of the ramified and artificial feudal hierarchy. The peasants had made extensive use of this instrument against the princes, the nobility, and the clergy. Now Luther turned it against the peasants, extracting from the Bible such a veritable hymn to the God-ordained authorities as no bootlicker of absolute monarchy had ever been able to match. Princedom by the grace of God, resigned obedience, even serfdom, were sanctioned with the aid of the Bible. Not the peasant revolt alone, but Luther's own mutiny against religious and lay authority were thereby disavowed; not only the popular movement, but the burgher movement as well, were betrayed to the princes.

---

[a] Part of the title of the pamphlet: M. Luther, *Wyder die mördische unnd reubischenn Rottenn der Paurenn* [Wittemberg, 1525]. The passage that follows is quoted according to the text given by W. Zimmermann (op. cit., Th. 3, S. 370). Italics by Engels.— *Ed.*

[b] An indirect quotation from M. Luther, *Ein Sendbrief von dem harten Büchlein wider die Bauern* [1525].— *Ed.*

[c] Latin for "food, pack, and lash to the ass".— *Ed.*

[d] *M. Luthers Schreiben an Johann Rühel,* May 30, 1525. Italics by Engels. Quoted according to W. Zimmermann, op. cit., Th. 3, S. 714.— *Ed.*

Need we name the bourgeois who recently provided examples of the same disavowal of their own past?

Let us now compare the plebeian revolutionary, *Münzer*, with Luther, the burgher reformer.

Thomas Münzer was born in *Stolberg*, in the Harz, somewhere around 1498.[311] His father is said to have died on the scaffold, a victim of the obduracy of the Count of Stolberg. In his fifteenth year Münzer organised a secret union at the Halle school against the Archbishop of Magdeburg[a] and the Roman Church in general. His learning in the theology of his time brought him an early doctor's degree and the position of chaplain in a Halle nunnery. Here he treated the church dogmas and rites with the greatest contempt. At mass he omitted the words of the transubstantiation and, as Luther said, devoured the almighty gods unconsecrated.[b] The medieval mystics, and particularly the chiliastic works of Joachim the Calabrese, were the main subject of his studies. The millennium and the Day of Judgment of the degenerated church and corrupted world propounded and described by that mystic seemed to Münzer imminently close, what with the Reformation and the general unrest of his time. He preached in his neighbourhood with great success. In 1520 he went to Zwickau as the first evangelist preacher. There he found one of those fanatical chiliastic sects that continued their existence on the quiet in many localities, whose momentary humility and detachment concealed the increasingly rampant opposition to the prevailing conditions of the lowest strata of society, and who were now, with the unrest growing, coming into the light of day ever more boldly and persistently. It was the sect of the Anabaptists[312] headed by Niklas *Storch*. They preached the approach of the Day of Judgment and of the millennium; they had "visions, transports, and the spirit of prophecy" and soon came into conflict with the Council of Zwickau. Münzer defended them, though he never joined them unconditionally and would much rather have brought them under his own influence. The Council took drastic measures against them; they had to leave the town, and Münzer with them. This was at the close of 1521.

He went to Prague and sought to gain a foothold there by joining the remnants of the Hussite movement. But all that he accomplished with his proclamation[c] was that he had to flee from Bohemia as well.

---

[a] Ernst.— *Ed.*

[b] *M. Luther's Schrift von der Winkelmesse.* (See W. Zimmermann, op. cit., Th. 2, S. 55.)— *Ed.*

[c] Th. Müntzer, *Ankündigung mit eigner Hand geschrieben, und in Prag 1521 angeschlagen wider die Papisten.* (See W. Zimmermann, op. cit., Th. 2, S. 64-67.)— *Ed.*

In 1522 he became preacher at Allstedt in Thuringia. The first thing he did here was to reform the cult. Even before Luther dared to go so far, he entirely abolished the Latin language and ordered the entire Bible, and not only the prescribed Sunday Gospels and epistles, to be read to the people. At the same time, he organised propaganda in his locality. People flocked to him from all directions, and Allstedt soon became the centre of the popular anti-priest movement of all Thuringia.

Münzer was as yet more theologian than anything else. He still directed his attacks almost exclusively against the priests. He did not, however, preach quiet debate and peaceful progress as Luther did at that time, but continued Luther's earlier violent sermons, calling upon the princes of Saxony and the people to rise in arms against the Roman priests.

"Does not Christ say, 'I came not to send peace, but a sword'? What must you" (the princes of Saxony) "do with that sword? Only one thing if you wish to be the servants of God, and that is to drive out and destroy the evil ones who stand in the way of the Gospel. Christ ordered very earnestly (Luke 19:27): 'bring hither mine enemies and slay them before me'.... Do not shallowly pretend that the power of God will do it without the aid of your sword, for then it would rust in its sheath. Those who stand in the way of God's revelation must be destroyed mercilessly, as Ezekiel, Cyrus, Josiah, Daniel and Elijah destroyed the priests of Baal, else the Christian Church will never come back to its source. We must uproot the weeds in God's vineyard at harvest time. God said in the Fifth Book of Moses, 7, 'thou shalt not show mercy unto the idolaters, but ye shall destroy their altars, and break down their images and burn them with fire that I shall not be wroth at you'." [a]

But these appeals to the princes were of no avail, while revolutionary sentiments among the people grew day by day. Münzer, whose ideas became ever sharper and ever more bold, now resolutely broke away from the burgher Reformation, and henceforth also became an out-and-out political agitator.

His philosophico-theological doctrine attacked all the main points not only of Catholicism, but of Christianity generally. In the form of Christianity he preached a kind of pantheism, which curiously resembled modern speculative contemplation[313] and at times even approached atheism. He repudiated the Bible both as the only and as the infallible revelation. The real and living revelation, he said, was reason, a revelation that has existed at all times and still exists among all peoples. To hold up the Bible against reason, he maintained, was to kill the spirit with the letter, for the Holy Spirit of which the Bible speaks is not something that exists outside us—the Holy Spirit is our

---

[a] Th. Müntzer, *Die Fürstenpredigt. Auslegung des andern vnterschyds Danielis dess propheten gepredigt auffm schlos zu Alstet vor den tetigen thewren Herzcogen vnd vorstehern zu Sachssen durch Thomä Müntzer diener des wordt gottes,* Alstedt, MDXXIIII.— *Ed.*

reason. Faith is nothing but reason come alive in man, and pagans
could therefore also have faith. Through this faith, through reason
come to life, man became godlike and blessed. Heaven is, therefore,
nothing of another world and is to be sought in this life. It is the
mission of believers to establish this Heaven, the kingdom of God,
here on earth. Just as there is no Heaven in the beyond, there is also
no Hell and no damnation. Similarly, there is no devil but man's evil
lusts and greed. Christ was a man as we are, a prophet and a teacher,
and his supper is a plain meal of commemoration wherein bread and
wine are consumed without any mystic garnish.

Münzer preached these doctrines mostly concealed in the same
Christian phraseology behind which the present-day philosophy has
had to hide for some time. But the arch-heretical fundamental idea is
easily discerned in all his writings, and he obviously took the biblical
cloak much less in earnest than many a disciple of Hegel does in
modern times. Yet three hundred years separate Münzer from
modern philosophy.

Münzer's political doctrine was very closely aligned to these
revolutionary religious conceptions, and overstepped the directly
prevailing social and political conditions in much the same way as his
theology overstepped the conceptions current in his time. As
Münzer's religious philosophy approached atheism, so his political
programme approached communism, and even on the eve of the
February Revolution more than one present-day communist sect
lacked as comprehensive a theoretical arsenal as was "Münzer's" in
the sixteenth century. This programme, which was less a compilation
of the demands of the plebeians of that day than a brilliant
anticipation of the conditions for the emancipation of the proletarian
element that had scarcely begun to develop among the plebeians—this programme demanded the immediate establishment
of the kingdom of God on Earth, of the prophesied millennium, by
restoring the church to its original status and abolishing all the
institutions that conflicted with the purportedly early Christian but
in fact very novel church. By the kingdom of God Münzer meant a
society with no class differences, no private property and no state
authority independent of, and foreign to, the members of society. All
the existing authorities, insofar as they refused to submit and join
the revolution, were to be overthrown, all work and all property
shared in common, and complete equality introduced. A union was
to be established to realise all this, and not only throughout
Germany, but throughout Christendom. Princes and lords would be
invited to join, but should they refuse the union was to take up arms
and overthrow or kill them at the first opportunity.

Münzer set to work at once to organise the union. His sermons became still more militant and revolutionary. He thundered forth against the princes, the nobility and the patricians with a passion that equalled the fervour of his attacks upon the clergy. He depicted the prevailing oppression in burning colours and countered it with his dream-vision of the millennium of social republican equality. Also, he published one revolutionary pamphlet after another, and sent emissaries in all directions, while personally organising the union in Allstedt and its vicinity.

The first fruit of this propaganda was the destruction of St. Mary's Chapel in Mellerbach near Allstedt, according to the command of the Bible (Deut. 7 [5], 6): "Ye shall destroy their altars, and break down their images ... and burn their graven images with fire for thou art an holy people." The princes of Saxony came in person to Allstedt to quell the unrest and bid Münzer come to the castle. There he delivered a sermon the like of which they had not heard from Luther, whom Münzer described as "that easy-living flesh of Wittenberg".[a] Münzer maintained that ungodly rulers, especially priests and monks who treated the Gospel as heresy, should be killed, and referred to the New Testament for confirmation. The ungodly had no right to live save by the mercy of the elect. Should the princes not exterminate the ungodly, God would take their sword from them, *because the entire community had the power of the sword.* The princes and lords are the prime movers of usury, thievery and robbery; they take all creatures into their private possession—the fish in the water, the birds in the air, and the plants in the soil. And then they preach to the poor the commandment, "Thou shalt not steal," while they themselves take everything they find, and rob and oppress the peasant and the artisan. If, however, one of the latter commits the slightest transgression, he has to hang, and Dr. Lügner says to all this: Amen.

"The masters themselves are to blame that the poor man becomes their enemy. If they do not remove the causes of the upheaval, how can things go well in the long run? Oh, dear sirs, how the Lord will smite these old pots with an iron rod! But for saying so, I am regarded a rebel. So be it!" (Cf. Zimmermann's *Bauernkrieg*, Th. 2, S. 75.)[b]

---

[a] This phrase is part of the title of Th. Münzer's pamphlet directed against Luther, *Hochverursachte Schutzrede vnd antwwort / wider das Gaistlosse Sanfft lebende fleysch zu Wittenberg....* Thomas Müntzer Alstedter... Anno MDXXIIII. (In this pamphlet Münzer refers to Luther as Dr. Lügner, the German for Dr. Liar.)—*Ed.*

[b] This quotation from Münzer's speeches (see the above-quoted *Hochverursachte Schutzrede...* and *Die Fürstenpredigt...*) is given according to Zimmermann's book.—*Ed.*

Münzer had the sermon printed. Duke Johann of Saxony punished his Allstedt printer with banishment, and ordered all Münzer's writings to be censored from then on by the ducal government in Weimar. But Münzer paid no heed to this order. He hastened to publish a highly inciting paper[a] in the imperial city of Mühlhausen, wherein he called on the people

"to widen the hole so that all the world may see and understand who our great personages are that have blasphemously turned our Lord into a painted manikin".

It ended with the following words:

"All the world must suffer a big jolt. There will be such a game that the ungodly will be thrown off their seats, and the downtrodden will rise."

Thomas Münzer, "the man with the hammer", wrote the following motto on the title page:

"Beware, I have put my words into thy mouth[b] that thou mayest uproot, destroy, scatter and overthrow, and that thou mayest build and plant. A wall of iron against the kings, princes, priests, and against the people hath been erected. Let them fight, for victory will wondrously lead to the perdition of the strong and godless tyrants."

Münzer's breach with Luther and his party had taken place long before. Luther had had to accept some of the church reforms which Münzer had introduced without consulting him. He watched Münzer's activities with a moderate reformer's nettled mistrust of a more energetic, ambitious party. Already in the spring of 1524, in a letter to Melanchthon, that model of a zealous stick-in-the-mud philistine, Münzer wrote that he and Luther did not understand the movement at all. He said they sought to choke it by the letter of the Bible, and that their doctrine was worm-eaten.

"Dear brethren," he wrote, "cease your waiting and hesitation. It is time, for summer is at the door. Keep not friendship with the ungodly who hinder the Word from working its full force. Flatter not your princes, or you will perish with them. Ye tender scholars, be not wroth, for I can do nothing else."[c]

Luther had more than once challenged Münzer to an open debate. The latter, however, always ready to take up the battle before the people, had not the least desire to let himself in for a theological

---

[a] *Aussgetrückte emplössung des falschen Glaubens der ungetrewen welt...* Jere. am. 23. Cap. Thomas Müntzer mit dem Hammer. Mülhausen, MDXXIIII. (W. Zimmermann, op. cit., Th. 2, S. 77-78.)— *Ed.*

[b] In the 1850 edition there follows a phrase missing in the 1870 and 1875 editions: "I have put you over the people and over the empires."— *Ed.*

[c] From Münzer's letter to Melanchthon of March 27, 1522. (Zimmermann erroneously dated it March 29, 1524.)— *Ed.*

squabble before the partisan public of Wittenberg University. He did not wish "to bring the testimony of the Spirit exclusively before the high school of learning".[a] If Luther were sincere, he should use his influence to stop the chicaneries against his, Münzer's, printer, and lift the censorship so that their controversy might be freely fought in the press.

But now, when Münzer's above-mentioned revolutionary brochure appeared, Luther denounced him publicly. In his published *Brieff an die Fürsten zu Sachsen von dem auffrurischen geyst* he declared Münzer to be an instrument of Satan and called upon the princes to intervene and drive the instigators of the turmoil out of the country, since they did not confine themselves to preaching their evil doctrine but also incited to insurrection, to violent action against the authorities.

On August 1, Münzer was compelled to appear before the princes in the castle of Weimar on the charge of incitement to mutiny. Highly compromising facts had been obtained against him; they were on the scent of his secret union; his hand was detected in the societies of the miners and the peasants. He was threatened with banishment. No sooner had he returned to Allstedt than he learned that Duke George of Saxony demanded his extradition.Union letters in his handwriting had been intercepted, wherein he called George's subjects to armed resistance against the enemies of the Gospel. Had he not left the town, the Council would have extradited him.

In the meantime, the growing unrest among the peasants and plebeians had made it incomparably easier for Münzer to carry on his propaganda. In the Anabaptists he found invaluable agents for this purpose. This sect, which had no definite and positive dogmas, held together only by its common opposition to all ruling classes and by the common symbol of the second baptism, ascetic in its mode of living, untiring, fanatical and intrepid in carrying on propaganda, had grouped itself more and more closely around Münzer. Made homeless by persecutions, its members wandered all over Germany and carried word everywhere of the new teaching, in which Münzer had made their own demands and wishes clear to them. Countless Anabaptists were put on the rack, burned at the stake or otherwise executed, but the courage and endurance of these emissaries was unshakable, and the success of their activities amid the people's rapidly growing unrest was enormous. Thus, after his flight from Thuringia, Münzer found the ground prepared wherever he went.

---

[a] Th. Müntzer, *Aussgetrückte emplössung des falschen Glaubens der ungetrewen welt...*, quoted according to W. Zimmermann, op. cit., Th. 2, S. 77.— Ed.

Near Nuremberg, where Münzer went first,[314] a peasant revolt had been nipped in the bud hardly a month before. Münzer conducted his propaganda surreptitiously; soon people appeared who defended his most audacious theological ideas on the non-obligatory nature of the Bible and the meaninglessness of sacraments, who declared Christ a mere human and the power of the lay authorities ungodly. "There is Satan stalking, the Spirit of Allstedt!" Luther exclaimed.[a] In Nuremberg Münzer printed his reply to Luther.[b] He accused him of flattering the princes and supporting the reactionary party by his insipid moderation. But the people would free themselves all the same, he wrote, and it would go with Dr. Luther as with a captive fox.—The Council ordered the paper confiscated, and Münzer had to leave Nuremberg.

Now he went across Swabia to Alsace, then to Switzerland, and then back to the Upper Black Forest, where an insurrection had broken out several months before, largely precipitated by his Anabaptist emissaries. This propaganda tour of Münzer's had doubtless substantially contributed to the establishment of the people's party, to the clear definition of its demands and to the final general outbreak of the insurrection in April 1525. It was through this tour that the dual effect of Münzer's activities became particularly apparent—on the one hand, on the people, whom he addressed in the only language they could then comprehend, that of religious prophecy; and, on the other hand, on the initiated to whom he could disclose his ultimate aims. Even before his journey he had assembled in Thuringia a circle of resolute men from among the people and the lesser clergy, whom he had put at the head of the secret society. Now he became the soul of the entire revolutionary movement in Southwestern Germany, organised ties from Saxony and Thuringia through Franconia and Swabia up to Alsace and the Swiss border, and counted such South German agitators as Hubmaier of Waldshut, Konrad Grebel of Zurich, Franz Rabmann of Griessen, Schappeler of Memmingen, Jakob Wehe of Leipheim, and Dr. Mantel in Stuttgart, who were mostly revolutionary priests, among his disciples and the heads of the union. He himself stayed mostly in Griessen on the Schaffhausen border, journeying from there across the Hegau, Klettgau, etc. The bloody reprisals by the alarmed princes and lords everywhere against this new plebeian

---

[a] From Luther's letter to Johannes Briessmann, dated February 4, 1525. Quoted according to Zimmermann, op. cit., Th. 2, S. 81.—*Ed.*

[b] Th. Müntzer, *Hochverursachte Schutzrede vnd antwwort/wider das Gaistlosse Sanfft lebende fleysch zu Wittenberg...—Ed.*

heresy contributed not a little to fanning the spirit of rebellion and consolidating the ranks of the union. In this way Münzer conducted his agitation for about five months in Upper Germany and returned to Thuringia when the culmination of the conspiracy was near at hand, because he wished to lead the movement himself. There we shall find him later.

We shall see how truly the character and behaviour of the two party leaders reflected the attitude of their respective parties, how Luther's indecision and fear of the movement, which was assuming serious proportions, and his cowardly servility to the princes fully corresponded to the hesitant and ambiguous policy of the burghers, and how Münzer's revolutionary energy and resolution was reproduced among the most advanced section of the plebeians and peasants. The only difference was that while Luther confined himself to expressing the ideas and wishes of the majority of his class and thereby won very cheap popularity among it, Münzer, on the contrary, went far beyond the immediate ideas and demands of the plebeians and peasants, and organised a party of the élite of the then existing revolutionary elements, which, inasmuch as it shared his ideas and energy, always remained only a small minority of the insurgent masses.

Secret Identity Stamp
of the Peasants

III

The first signs of a budding revolutionary spirit appeared among the German peasants about fifty years after the suppression of the Hussite movement.*

In 1476 the first peasant conspiracy occurred in the bishopric of Würzburg, a land impoverished by the Hussite wars, "by bad government, manifold taxes, payments, feuds, enmity, war, fire, murder, prison and the like",[a] and continually and shamelessly plundered by bishops, priests and the nobility. A young shepherd and musician, *Hans Böheim of Niklashausen,* also called the Drum-Beater and *Hans the Piper,* suddenly appeared as a prophet in the Tauber valley. He declared that he had had a vision of the Virgin Mary, that she had commanded him to burn his drum, to stop serving the dance and sinful sensuality, and to exhort the people to penance. Everyone should purge himself of sin and the vain lusts of the world, forsake all ornaments and finery, and make a pilgrimage to the Madonna of Niklashausen to obtain forgiveness.

Already here, with the first precursor of the movement, we find the asceticism typical of all medieval uprisings tinged with religion and, in modern times, of the early stages of every proletarian movement. This ascetic austerity of morals, this demand to forsake all joys of life and all entertainments, opposes the ruling classes with

---

* In our chronology we are following the data given by Zimmermann, upon which we are obliged to rely in the absence of adequate sources abroad and which are quite satisfactory for the purposes of the present work.— *Note by Engels to the 1850 edition.* (In the 1870 and 1875 editions this note was omitted since Engels pointed out in the Preface that he was using Zimmermann's data.— *Ed.*)

[a] Engels quotes an extract from a 15th-century manuscript preserved in the Würzburg archive. See W. Zimmermann, *Allgemeine Geschichte des grossen Bauern-krieges,* Th. 1, S. 118.— *Ed.*

29

the principle of Spartan equality, on the one hand, and is, on the other, a necessary stage of transition without which the lowest stratum of society can never set itself in motion. In order to develop its revolutionary energy, to become conscious of its own hostile attitude towards all other elements of society, to concentrate itself as a class, it must begin by stripping itself of everything that could reconcile it with the existing social system; it must renounce the few pleasures that make its wretched existence in the least tolerable for the moment, and of which even the severest oppression could not deprive it. This *plebeian and proletarian asceticism* differs both in its wild fanatical form and in its essence from the bourgeois asceticism of the Lutheran burgher morality and of the English Puritans (as distinct from the Independents [315] and the more radical sects), whose entire secret amounts to *bourgeois thrift*. It stands to reason, however, that this plebeian-proletarian asceticism gradually sheds its revolutionary nature when the development of modern productive forces infinitely multiplies the luxuries, thus rendering Spartan equality superfluous, and when the position of the proletariat in society, and thereby the proletariat itself, become more revolutionary. This asceticism disappears gradually from among the masses, and in the sects, which relied upon it, it degenerates either directly into bourgeois parsimony or into a high-sounding virtuousness which, in practice, degenerates to a philistine or guild-artisan meanness. Besides, renunciation of pleasures need hardly be preached to the proletariat for the simple reason that it has almost nothing more to renounce.

Hans the Piper's call to penitence found a ready response; all the prophets of rebellion began with this call, and, indeed, only a violent exertion, a sudden renunciation of all this habitual mode of existence could set this disunited and widely scattered peasant species, raised in blind submission, into motion. The pilgrimages to Niklashausen began and rapidly increased, and the more massive the stream of pilgrims, the more openly the young rebel spoke out his plans. The Madonna of Niklashausen had told him, he preached, that henceforth there should be neither king nor prince, neither papal nor any other ecclesiastic or lay authority. Each should be a brother to the other and win his bread by the toil of his own hands, and none should have more than his neighbour. All tributes, rents, services, tolls, taxes and other payments and duties should be for ever abolished, and forest, water and pasture should everywhere be free.

The people received this new gospel with joy. The fame of the prophet, "the message of our Lady", spread far and wide; pilgrim throngs flocked to him from Odenwald, from the Main, Kocher and

Jagst, even from Bavaria and Swabia, and from the Rhine. Miracles said to have been performed by the Piper were recounted; people fell to their knees before him, praying to him as to a saint, and then fought for tufts from his cap for relics or amulets. In vain did the priests speak against him, denouncing his visions as the devil's delusions and his miracles as diabolic swindles. The mass of the believers increased precipitously, a revolutionary sect began to take shape, the Sunday sermons of the rebel shepherd drew gatherings of 40,000 and more to Niklashausen.

Hans the Piper preached to the masses for a number of months, but he did not intend to confine himself to preaching. He had secret connections with the pastor of Niklashausen and with two knights, Kunz von Thunfeld and his son, who held to the new teaching and were to become the military leaders of the planned insurrection. Finally, on the Sunday before the day of St. Kilian, when his power appeared to be great enough, the shepherd gave the signal.

"And now go home," he closed his sermon, "and weigh in your mind what our holiest Lady has announced to you, and on the coming Saturday leave your wives and children and old men at home, and you, men, come back to Niklashausen on the day of St. Margaret, which is next Saturday; and bring your brothers and friends, as many as they may be. Do not come with pilgrim's staves, however, but with armour and arms, a candle in one hand, and a sword, pike or halberd in the other, and the Holy Virgin will then tell you what she wishes you to do."[a]

But before the peasants arrived in their numbers, the bishop's[b] horsemen seized the rebel prophet at night and brought him to the castle of Würzburg. On the appointed day almost 34,000 armed peasants appeared, but the news of the Piper's detention crushed them. Most of them went home, while the initiated kept about 16,000 together, with whom they marched to the castle under the leadership of Kunz von Thunfeld and his son Michael. The bishop persuaded them with promises to turn back, but no sooner had they begun to disperse than they were attacked by the bishop's horsemen and many of them taken captive. Two were decapitated, and Hans the Piper was burned at the stake. Kunz von Thunfeld escaped and was allowed to return only after ceding all his estates to the bishopric. The pilgrimages to Niklashausen continued for some time, but were finally also suppressed.

After this initial attempt, Germany remained quiet for some time. Only towards the close of the century were there any new peasant revolts and conspiracies.

---

[a] From a free rendering of the sermon as given by W. Zimmermann (op. cit., Th. 1, S. 121-22).—*Ed.*

[b] Rudolf II von Scherenberg.—*Ed.*

We shall pass over the Dutch peasant revolt of 1491 and 1492, which was suppressed by Duke Albrecht of Saxony in the battle of Heemskerk, the simultaneous peasant revolt in the Abbey of Kempten in Upper Swabia, and the Frisian revolt under Sjoerd Aylva, about 1497,[a] which was also suppressed by Albrecht of Saxony. These revolts were partly too far from the scene of the Peasant War proper, and partly uprisings of hitherto free peasants against the attempt to force feudalism upon them. We pass on to the two great conspiracies which laid the ground for the Peasant War: the *Bundschuh* and the *Poor Konrad.*

The same famine that had precipitated the peasant revolt in the Netherlands, brought about a secret alliance of peasants and plebeians in Alsace in 1493; people of the purely burgher opposition took part in it, and it even enjoyed some sympathy among the lesser nobility. The seat of the alliance was in the region of Schlettstadt, Sulz, Dambach, Rosheim, Scherweiler, etc., etc. The conspirators demanded plunder and extermination of Jews, whose usury then, as now, fleeced the peasants of Alsace, proclamation of a jubilee year, whereby all debts would expire, repeal of duties, tolls and other imposts, abolition of the ecclesiastical and Rottweil (imperial) court, the right of the estates to ratify taxes, reduction of the priests' prebend to fifty or sixty guilders, abolition of the auricular confession, and self-elected courts for every community. When they were strong enough the conspirators planned to overpower the stronghold of Schlettstadt, to confiscate the treasuries of the monasteries and of the town, and from there to arouse the whole of Alsace. The banner of the Union, which was to be unfurled at the start of the uprising, depicted a peasant's clog with a long leather thong, the so-called *Bundschuh,* which served peasant conspiracies as an emblem and name in the following twenty years.

The conspirators were wont to hold their meetings at night on the lonesome Hunger Hill. Initiation into the Bundschuh involved the most mysterious of ceremonies and the severest threats of punishment for betrayal. But the affair got abroad about Easter Week of 1493, the time appointed for the attack on Schlettstadt. The authorities stepped in immediately. Many of the conspirators were arrested and tortured, some were quartered or decapitated, and others had their hands or fingers cut off and were driven out of the country. A great many fled to Switzerland.

---

[a] The Frisian peasant revolt occurred in 1500. Engels gives the date 1497 as in Zimmermann.— *Ed.*

The Bundschuh, however, was far from crushed by this first blow. On the contrary, it continued in secret and the numerous fugitives scattered all over Switzerland and South Germany became as many emissaries. Finding the same oppression and, consequently, the same inclination to revolt everywhere they went, they propagated the Bundschuh in the whole of the present-day Baden. The tenacity and stamina with which the peasants of Upper Germany conspired for about thirty years after 1493, with which they surmounted all the obstacles arising from their scattered way of life on the road to a larger, more centralised organisation, and with which they renewed their conspiracies over and over after countless dispersions, defeats, and executions of their leaders, until an opportunity came at last for a mass uprising—this tenacity is truly admirable.

In 1502 there were signs of a secret movement among the peasants of the bishopric of Speyer, which at that time also included the locality of Bruchsal. The Bundschuh had reorganised itself there with really considerable success. About 7,000 men belonged to the society, whose centre was in Untergrombach, between Bruchsal and Weingarten, and whose ramifications reached down the Rhine to the Main, and up to the Margraviate of Baden. Its articles said: neither rent nor tithe, neither tax nor toll are to be paid any longer to the princes, the nobility, or the clergy; serfdom is to be abolished; the monasteries and other *church estates are to be confiscated and divided among the people, and no other ruler is to be recognised save the Emperor.*

Here we find for the first time expressed by peasants the two demands—secularising church estates in favour of the people, and a united and indivisible German monarchy—which will henceforth be advocated regularly by the more advanced peasants and plebeians, until Thomas Münzer changes *distribution* of church estates to *confiscation* and conversion into *community of property,* and a united German *Empire* to a united and indivisible *republic.*

The revived Bundschuh, like the old, had its own secret meeting place, its oath of silence, its initiation ceremonies, and its union banner with the legend, "Nothing but God's Justice!" Its plan of action was similar to that of the Alsatian union. Bruchsal, most of whose inhabitants belonged to the Bundschuh, was to be captured and a Bundschuh army organised there and sent into the surrounding principalities as an itinerant meeting point.

The plan was betrayed by a clergyman who had learned of it from one of the conspirators in the confessional. The authorities instantly took countermeasures. How widespread the Bundschuh had become is evident from the terror that seized the various imperial estates in Alsace and the Swabian League.[316] Troops were concentrated, and mass arrests were made. Emperor Maximilian, "last of the knights", issued bloodthirsty punitive decrees against the unheard-of peasant undertaking. Throngs of peasants assembled here and there and offered armed resistance, but the isolated peasant troops could not hold out for long. Some of the conspirators were executed, others escaped, but secrecy was so well preserved that, in their own localities and in the possessions of the neighbouring lords, the majority, even the leaders, remained unharmed.

After this new defeat there followed a long period of apparent calm in the class struggle. But work went on underground. In the first years of the sixteenth century *Poor Konrad* appeared in Swabia, evidently with the support of the scattered members of the Bundschuh. In the Black Forest the Bundschuh continued in small isolated groups until, ten years later, an energetic peasant leader succeeded in gathering the various threads into a major conspiracy. Both conspiracies became public one after the other in the restless years of 1513-15, in which the Swiss, Hungarian and Slovenian peasants rose simultaneously in a series of major insurrections.

The man who revived the Upper Rhine Bundschuh was *Joss Fritz* of Untergrombach, a fugitive of the conspiracy of 1502, a former soldier, and in all respects an outstanding figure. After his flight he stayed in various localities between Lake Constance and the Black Forest, and finally settled in Lehen near Freiburg in Breisgau, where he even became a forester. Most interesting facts are contained in the court records about the manner in which he reorganised the Bundschuh from that vantage point and how ingeniously he recruited people of different kinds. The diplomatic talent and tireless perseverance of this model conspirator helped him enrol a great number of people of various classes into the Bundschuh —knights, priests, burghers, plebeians and peasants, and it appears almost certain that he even organised several more or less sharply divided grades of the conspiracy. All serviceable elements were utilised with the greatest circumspection and skill. Apart from the more initiated emissaries who traversed the country in various disguises, vagrants and beggars were employed for subordinate missions. Joss stood in direct contact with the beggar kings, and through them held the numerous vagabond population in the palm of his hand. The beggar kings played a considerable role in his conspiracy. They were very bizarre figures: one roamed the country with a girl whose seemingly wounded feet were his pretext for begging; he had more than eight insignia on his hat—the Fourteen Deliverers, St. Ottilie, Our Mother in Heaven, etc.—and, besides, wore a long red beard and carried a big knotty stick with a dagger and pike. Another, who begged in the name of St. Velten, had spices and wormseeds for sale, and wore a long iron-coloured coat, a red barret with the insignia of the Infant of Trient attached to it, a sword at his side, and many knives and a dagger in his girdle. Others had bleeding wounds, which they deliberately did not allow to heal, and their attire was also picturesque. There were at least ten of them, and for the price of two thousand guilders they were simultaneously to set aflame Alsace, the Margraviate of Baden, and Breisgau, and to put themselves, with at least 2,000 of their kind, under the command of Georg Schneider, a former captain of the mercenaries, on the day of the Zabern parish fair in Rosen, in order to take possession of that town. A courier service from station to station was established by members of the Bundschuh, and Joss Fritz and his chief emissary, Stoffel of Freiburg, rode continually from place to place to hold nocturnal military reviews of the neophytes. The court records offer ample evidence of the spread of the Bundschuh in the Upper Rhine and Black Forest regions. They contain countless names and descriptions of members from the various localities of that region—most of them journeymen, then peasants and innkeepers, a few nobles, priests (like the one from Lehen), and breadless mercenaries. This composition of the Bundschuh is evidence of the more developed character of the society under Joss Fritz. The urban plebeian element was asserting itself more and more. The ramifications of the conspiracy spread throughout Alsace, the present-day Baden, up to Württemberg and the Main. From time to time large gatherings were held on secluded mountains such as the Kniebis, etc., to discuss the affairs of the Union. The meetings of the chiefs, in which local members and delegates of remoter localities often participated, took place on the Hartmatte near Lehen, and it was there that the fourteen articles of the Bundschuh were adopted. The articles agreed upon were: no master besides the Emperor and (according to some) the Pope; abolition of the Rottweil imperial court and restriction of the church court to religious affairs; abolition of interest after it had been paid for so long that it equalled the capital; top interest rate of five per cent; freedom of hunting, fishing, pasture, and woodcutting; restriction of priests each to one prebend; confiscation of church estates and monastery treasures for the Bundschuh war chest; abolition of all inequitable taxes and tolls; eternal peace in all Christendom; determined action against all opponents of the Bundschuh; Bundschuh taxes; seizure of a strong town, such as Freiburg, to serve as Bundschuh headquarters; negotiations with the Emperor as soon as the Bundschuh troops are gathered, and with Switzerland in case the Emperor declines. It was evident that, on the one hand, the demands of the peasants and plebeians were becoming more definite and firm, and that, on the other, concessions had had equally to be made to the moderate and timid.

The blow was to be struck about autumn 1513. Only a Bundschuh banner was lacking, and Joss Fritz went to Heilbronn to have it painted. Besides all sorts of emblems and pictures, it bore the peasant's clog emblem and the legend, "God Help Thy Divine Justice". While he was away a premature attempt was made to overwhelm Freiburg, which was discovered. Some indiscretions in the conduct of propaganda put the Council of Freiburg and the Margrave of Baden[a] on the right scent, and the betrayal by two conspirators completed the series of disclosures. The Margrave, the Council of Freiburg, and the imperial government at Ensisheim[317] instantly sent spies and soldiers; some Bundschuh members were arrested, tortured and executed. But again the majority escaped, Joss Fritz among them. This time the Swiss Government sternly persecuted the fugitives, and even executed many of them. However, it had just as little success as its neighbours in preventing the greater part of the fugitives from remaining continually in the vicinity of their former homes and even returning to them after some time. The Alsace Government in Ensisheim behaved more brutally than the others. It ordered very many to be decapitated, broken on the wheel, and quartered. Joss Fritz himself kept mainly to the Swiss bank of the Rhine, but often crossed to the Black Forest, without ever being apprehended.

Why this time the Swiss made common cause with the neighbouring governments against the Bundschuh is made apparent by the peasant revolt that broke out the following year, 1514, in Berne, Solothurn and Lucerne,[b] resulting in a purge of the aristocratic governments and the patriciate generally. The peasants also won certain privileges for themselves. The success of the local Swiss revolts was due to the simple fact that there was even less centralisation in Switzerland than in Germany. In 1525 the peasants managed to dispose of their local lords everywhere, but succumbed to the organised armies of the princes, and it was these latter that Switzerland did not have.

Simultaneously with the Bundschuh in Baden, and apparently in direct association with it, a second conspiracy was formed in Württemberg. Documents indicate that it had existed since 1503, but

---

[a] Christoph I.— *Ed.*
[b] Its first outbreaks began in 1513.— *Ed.*

since the name Bundschuh became too dangerous after the setback of the Untergrombach conspirators, it adopted the name Poor Konrad. Its main seat was the valley of the Rems at the foot of the mountain of Hohenstaufen. Its existence had been no secret for a long time, at least to the people. The merciless oppression of Duke Ulrich's government coupled with several famine years, which contributed greatly to the outbreak of the movements of 1513 and 1514, had increased the number of conspirators. The newly imposed taxes on wine, meat and bread, and a capital tax of one pfennig yearly on every guilder, provoked the uprising. The town of Schorndorf, where the heads of the complot met in the house of a cutler named Kaspar Pregizer, was to be seized first. In the spring of 1514, the rebellion broke out. Three thousand—and according to some, five thousand—peasants gathered before the town, but were persuaded by the amicable promises of the Duke's officers to withdraw. Duke Ulrich, who had agreed to abolish the new taxes, arrived posthaste with eighty horsemen to find everything quiet in consequence of the promise. He promised to convene a Diet to examine all complaints. But the chiefs of the society knew very well that Ulrich sought only to keep the people quiet until he recruited and concentrated enough troops to be able to break his word and collect the taxes by force. From Kaspar Pregizer's house, "Poor Konrad's chancery", they issued a call for a society congress, and sent emissaries in all directions. The success of the first uprising in the Rems valley had everywhere stimulated the movement among the people. The appeals and the emissaries found a favourable response everywhere, and the congress held in Untertürkheim on May 28 was attended by a large number of representatives from all parts of Württemberg. It was decided to proceed at once with propaganda and to strike in the Rems valley at the first opportunity, in order to spread the uprising from that point in every direction. While Bantelhans of Dettingen, a former soldier, and Singerhans of Würtingen, an esteemed peasant, were bringing the Swabian Jura into the society, the uprising broke out on every side. Though Singerhans was attacked and seized, the towns of Backnang, Winnenden, and Markgröningen fell into the hands of the peasants who had joined forces with the plebeians, and the entire area from Weinsberg to Blaubeuren, and from there to the border of Baden, was in open revolt. Ulrich was compelled to yield. However, while calling the Diet for June 25, he wrote to the surrounding princes and free towns asking for aid against the uprising, which, he said, threatened all princes, authorities and nobles in the Empire, and which "bore an uncommon resemblance to the Bundschuh".

In the meantime, the Diet, i.e. the deputies of the towns, and many delegates of the peasants who also demanded seats in the Diet, came together as early as June 18 in Stuttgart. The prelates had not yet arrived. The knights had not even been invited. The city opposition of Stuttgart, as well as two threatening peasant throngs at Leonberg and in the Rems valley, supported the demands of the peasants. Their delegates were admitted, and it was decided to depose and punish the three hated councillors of the Duke—Lamparter, Thumb and Lorcher—and appoint for the Duke a council of four knights, four burghers and four peasants, to grant him a fixed civil allowance, and to confiscate the monasteries and endowments in favour of the state treasury.

Duke Ulrich countered these revolutionary decisions with a coup d'état. On June 21 he rode with his knights and councillors to Tübingen, where he was followed by the prelates, ordered the burghers to come there as well, which they did, and there continued the Diet without the peasants. The burghers, confronted with military terror, betrayed their peasant allies. On July 8 the Tübingen agreement came about, saddling the country with almost a million of the Duke's debts, laying some restrictions on the Duke which he never observed, and disposing of the peasants with a few meagre general phrases and a very definite penal law against insurrection and association. Naturally, nothing was said any more about peasant representation in the Diet. The peasantry cried treason, but the Duke, who had acquired new credit after his debts were taken over by the estates, soon gathered troops, and his neighbours, particularly the Elector Palatine,[a] also sent him military aid. The Tübingen agreement was thus accepted all over the country towards the end of July, and a new oath was taken. Only in the Rems valley Poor Konrad offered resistance. The Duke, who again rode there in person, barely escaped with his life. A peasant camp was set up on the mountain of Kappel. But as the affair dragged on, most of the insurgents dispersed for lack of food, and the rest also went home after an ambiguous agreement with some of the Diet deputies. In the meantime, Ulrich, his army strengthened with companies willingly placed at his service by the towns, which, having attained their demands, turned fanatically against the peasants, attacked the Rems valley in spite of the agreement and plundered its towns and villages. Sixteen hundred peasants were taken prisoner, sixteen of them instantly decapitated, and most of the others made to pay heavy fines into Ulrich's treasury. Many remained in prison for a long

---

[a] Ludwig V.— *Ed.*

time. Strict penal laws were enacted against a revival of the society, against all gatherings of peasants, and the nobility of Swabia formed a special league for the suppression of all attempts at insurrection.—The top leaders of Poor Konrad had meanwhile succeeded in escaping to Switzerland, whence after a few years they returned home, most of them singly.

At the time of the Württemberg movement, signs of new Bundschuh activity were observed in Breisgau and in the Margraviate of Baden. In June, an insurrection was attempted near Bühl, but it was quickly throttled by Margrave Philip, and its leader, Gugel-Bastian, was seized in Freiburg and beheaded.

In the spring of the same year, 1514, a general peasant war broke out in *Hungary*. A crusade against the Turks was preached, and freedom was promised as usual to the serfs and bondsmen who would join it. About 60,000 gathered under the command of Georg Dózsa, a Szekler,[318] who had distinguished himself in previous Turkish wars and attained nobility. The Hungarian knights and magnates, however, looked with disfavour upon the crusade, which threatened to deprive them of their property and bondsmen. They overtook isolated peasant groups, took back their serfs by force and maltreated them. When this reached the ears of the army of crusaders the fury of the oppressed peasants broke loose. Two of the most enthusiastic advocates of the crusade, Laurentius and Barnabás, fanned the hatred against the nobility in the army by their revolutionary speeches. Dózsa himself was as angered with the treacherous nobility as his troops. The army of crusaders became an army of revolution and Dózsa put himself at the head of the new movement.

He camped with his peasants in the Rákos field near Pest. Clashes with men of the noblemen's party in the surrounding villages and the suburbs of Pest opened the hostilities. It soon came to skirmishes, and then to Sicilian Vespers [319] for all the noblemen who fell into the hands of the peasants, and to destruction by fire of all the castles in the vicinity. The court made its threats in vain. After the first acts of popular justice against the nobility had been accomplished under the walls of the capital, Dózsa proceeded with further operations. He divided his army into five columns. Two were sent to the mountains of Upper Hungary to rouse the populace and exterminate the nobility. The third, under Ambros Száleresi, a citizen of Pest, remained on the Rákos to watch the capital, while the fourth and fifth were led by Dózsa and his brother Gregor against Szegedin.[a]

---

[a] The Hungarian name is Szeged.— *Ed.*

In the meantime, the nobility gathered in Pest, and summoned to its aid Johann Zápolya, the voivode of Transylvania. Joined by the burghers of Budapest, the nobility attacked and annihilated the army on the Rákos, after Száleresi and the burgher elements in the peasant force had gone over to the enemy. A host of prisoners was executed in the most cruel fashion, and the rest sent home minus their noses and ears.

Dózsa failed at Szegedin and marched on Csanád, which he captured on defeating an army of noblemen under István Batory and Bishop Csáky. He took bloody revenge on the prisoners, among them the bishop and the royal Chancellor Teleki, for the Rákos atrocities. In Csanád he proclaimed a republic, abolished the nobility, declared general equality and sovereignty of the people, and then marched against Temesvár,[a] to which Bátory had fled. But while he besieged this fortress for two months and was reinforced by a new army under Anton Hosszú, his two army columns in Upper Hungary were defeated by the nobility in several battles. Johann Zápolya with his Transylvanian army advanced against him, attacked and dispersed the peasants. Dózsa was taken prisoner and roasted alive on a red-hot throne. His flesh was eaten by his own people, this being the condition on which their lives were spared. The dispersed peasants, reassembled by Laurentius and Hosszú, were again defeated, and those who fell into enemy hands were either impaled or hanged. The peasants' corpses hung in thousands along the roads or on the edges of gutted villages. About 60,000, it is said, either fell in battle or were massacred. The nobility saw to it that at the next Diet serfdom was again recognised as the law of the land.

The peasant revolt in the "Wendish mark", that is, Carinthia, Carniola and Styria, which broke out at about the same time, reposed on a Bundschuh-like conspiracy that had taken shape and precipitated a rising in this region—wrung dry by the nobility and imperial officials, ravaged by Turkish invasions, and plagued by famines—as far back as 1503. Already in 1513, the Slovenian and German peasants of this region once more raised the battle standard of the *Stara Prawa* (The Old Rights). If they allowed themselves to be placated that year, and if in 1514, when they gathered anew in larger masses, they were again persuaded to go home by Emperor Maximilian's explicit promise to restore the Old Rights, the war of revenge of the perpetually deceived people broke out with redoubled vigour in the spring of 1515. Just as in Hungary, castles

---

[a] The Romanian name is Timişoara.— *Ed.*

and monasteries were destroyed everywhere, and the captured nobles were tried by peasant juries and decapitated. In Styria and Carinthia the Emperor's captain, Dietrichstein, soon succeeded in crushing the revolt. In Carniola it was only suppressed by a sudden onslaught on Rain (autumn of 1516) and the subsequent countless Austrian atrocities, which duplicated the infamies of the Hungarian nobility.

It is clear why, after this series of decisive defeats and the mass atrocities of the nobility, the German peasants long remained quiet. Yet conspiracies and local uprisings did not cease altogether. Already in 1516 most of the fugitives of the Bundschuh and the Poor Konrad returned to Swabia and the Upper Rhine, and in 1517 the Bundschuh was again in full action in the Black Forest. Joss Fritz himself, still hiding the old Bundschuh banner of 1513 on his chest, again travelled the length and breadth of the Black Forest and developed energetic activity. The conspiracy was revived. Just as four years before, gatherings were held on the Kniebis. However, the secret was discovered, the authorities learned of the matter, and took action. Many conspirators were captured and executed. The most active and intelligent were compelled to flee, among them Joss Fritz, who, though he again evaded capture, seems to have died soon thereafter in Switzerland, for he is not heard of again.

FOOT AND MOUNTED REVOLUTIONARY PEASANTS

IV

At the time when the fourth Bundschuh conspiracy was suppressed in the Black Forest, Luther in Wittenberg gave the signal for the movement that was to draw all the estates into the vortex and shake the whole Empire. The theses of the Augustinian from Thuringia[320] had the effect of a match held to a powder keg. The multifold and conflicting aspirations of the knights and burghers, peasants and plebeians, princes craving for sovereignty, and the lesser clergy, the clandestine mystic sects and the scholarly, satirical and burlesque[321] literary opposition, found in Luther's theses a momentarily general and common expression, and fell in with them with astounding rapidity. Formed overnight, this alliance of all the dissident elements, however brief its duration, suddenly revealed the enormous power of the movement, and drove it forward very rapidly.

However, precisely this rapid growth of the movement was also very quickly bound to develop the seeds of discord that lay concealed in it. At least, it was bound to tear asunder the constituent parts of that agitated mass which, by their very place in life, were directly opposed to each other, and to return them to their normal, hostile state. This polarisation of the motley opposition at two centres of attraction was observed in the very first years of the Reformation. The nobility and the burghers grouped themselves unconditionally around Luther. Peasants and plebeians, as yet failing to see in Luther a direct enemy, formed as before a separate revolutionary party of the opposition. Yet the movement became much more general, more far-reaching, than it had been before Luther, which made sharp contradictions and an open conflict between the two parties inevitable. This direct antithesis soon became apparent. While

Luther and Münzer attacked each other in the press and from the pulpit, the armies of princes, knights and towns that for the most part consisted of Lutherans or elements at least gravitating towards Lutherism, attacked the throngs of peasants and plebeians.

How strongly the interests and requirements of the various elements behind the Reformation diverged is seen from the attempt of the nobility to compel the princes and the clergy to meet their demands even before the Peasant War.

We have already examined the situation of the German nobility early in the sixteenth century. It was on the point of losing its independence to the ever more powerful lay and clerical princes. It saw at the same time that the decline of imperial power, the Empire breaking up into a number of sovereign principalities, was keeping pace with its own decline. It thought that its own collapse meant the collapse of the Germans as a nation. Furthermore, the nobility, and particularly that section of it which owed allegiance to the Empire, was the estate that by virtue of its military profession and its attitude towards the princes, directly represented the Empire and imperial rule. It was the most national of the estates, and the mightier the imperial power, the weaker and less numerous the princes and the stronger the unity of Germany, the more powerful became the nobility. This was the reason for the general discontent of the knighthood with Germany's pitiful political situation, with the weakness of the Empire in foreign affairs which increased as the imperial family added to the Empire one inherited province after another, with the intrigues of foreign powers inside Germany, and with the plots of German princes and foreign countries against imperial rule. The demands of the nobility, therefore, had to be above all concentrated on the demand for an imperial reform whose victims were to be the princes and the higher clergy. *Ulrich von Hutten*, the theorist of the German nobility, took it upon himself to formulate the demand for reforms together with *Franz von Sickingen*, the nobility's military and diplomatic representative.

The imperial reform demanded on behalf of the nobility was conceived by Hutten in very clear and radical terms. Hutten demanded nothing short of eliminating all princes, secularising all church principalities and estates, and establishing a *noblemen's democracy* headed by a monarch, much like the late Polish republic in its best days. Hutten and Sickingen hoped to make the Empire united, free and powerful again through the rule of the nobility, a predominantly military class, elimination of princes, those bearers of disunity, annihilation of the power of the priests, and Germany's liberation from the dominance of Rome.

Founded on serfdom, this noblemen's democracy as fashioned in Poland and, in somewhat modified form, in the early centuries of the states conquered by the Germanic tribes, is one of the most primitive forms of society and quite normally matures into a highly developed feudal hierarchy, a considerably higher stage. Such a pure type of noblemen's democracy was therefore impossible in the sixteenth century.[a] It was impossible if only because of the important and powerful German towns. On the other hand, an alliance of the lesser nobility and the towns that in England brought about the transformation of the monarchy of feudal estates into a bourgeois-constitutional monarchy, was also out of the question. In Germany the old nobility still survived, while in England it had been exterminated in the Wars of the Roses[322] down to twenty-eight families, and replaced by a new nobility of bourgeois extraction and with bourgeois tendencies; in Germany serfdom was still rampant and the nobility drew its income from *feudal* sources, while in England serfdom had been virtually abolished and the nobles had become ordinary bourgeois landowners with a *bourgeois* source of income—the rent. Finally, the centralisation of absolute monarchy which we saw in France and which continuously developed since Louis XI in the conflict between the nobility and the burghers was impossible in Germany if only because the conditions for national centralisation were totally absent or existed in a very rudimentary form.

Under the circumstances, the further Hutten went in putting his ideal into practice, the more concessions he was compelled to make, and the more indefinite became the outlines of his imperial reform. The nobility was not strong enough to carry out the reform on its own. This was evident from its increasing weakness as compared with the princes. Allies were needed, and these could only be found in the towns, among the peasants and the influential theorists of the Reformation movement. But the towns knew the nobility too well to trust it, and rejected every offer of alliance. The peasants rightly considered the nobility, which exploited and maltreated them, as their bitterest enemy, while the theorists of the Reformation held either with the burghers, the princes, or the peasants. What advantages, indeed, could the nobility promise the burghers and the peasants from an imperial reform that was mainly intended to aggrandise the nobility? Under the circumstances Hutten had no other choice but to say little or nothing in his propaganda about the future relations between the nobility, the towns and the peasants. He

---

[a] The 1850 edition has "in sixteenth-century Germany".—*Ed.*

put all blame on the princes, the priests, and the dependence upon Rome, and showed the burghers that it was in their interests to remain at least neutral in the coming struggle between the nobility and the princes. He said nothing of abolishing serfdom or the services imposed upon the peasants by the nobility.

The attitude of the German nobility towards the peasants was at that time exactly the same as that of the Polish nobility towards its peasants in the insurrections of 1830-46.[a] As in the modern Polish uprisings,[323] the movement in Germany could be sustained only through an alliance of all the opposition parties, particularly the nobility and the peasants. Yet it was just this alliance that was *impossible* in both cases. The nobility deemed it unnecessary to give up its political privileges and its feudal rights vis-à-vis the peasants, while the revolutionary peasants would not be drawn by vague and general prospects into an alliance with the nobility, the estate which oppressed them the most. The nobility could no more win over the peasants in Germany in 1522 than it could in Poland in 1830. Only total abolition of serfdom, bondage and all the privileges of the nobility could have induced the rural population to side with the nobility. But like every privileged estate the nobility had not the slightest desire voluntarily to give up its privileges, its highly exclusive position, and most of its sources of income.

Thus, when the struggle finally broke out the nobles had to face the princes alone. And it came as no surprise that the princes, who had for two centuries been cutting the ground from under the nobility, gained another easy victory.

The course[b] of the struggle is well known. In 1522 Hutten and Sickingen, who was already recognised as the political and military chief of the Middle-German nobility, organised in Landau a union of the Rhenish, Swabian and Franconian nobility for a term of six years, ostensibly for self-defence. Sickingen assembled an army, partly on his own, and partly with the neighbouring knights, organised recruitment and reinforcements in Franconia, along the Lower Rhine, in the Netherlands and Westphalia, and in September 1522 opened hostilities by declaring a feud against the Elector-Archbishop of Trier.[c] However, while he was stationed near Trier, his reinforcements were cut off by a swift intervention of the princes. The Landgrave of Hesse and the Elector Palatine[d] came to Trier's

---

[a] The 1850 and 1870 editions have *Insurrektionen seit 1830* (insurrections since 1830) instead of *Insurrektionen 1830-46* (insurrections of 1830-46).— Ed.

[b] The 1850 edition has *Versuch* (attempt) instead of *Verlauf* (course).— Ed.

[c] Richard.— Ed.

[d] Philip I and Ludwig V.— Ed.

aid and Sickingen was compelled to retreat to his castle of Landstuhl. In spite of all Hutten's efforts and those of his other friends, the united nobility, intimidated by the concerted and swift moves of the princes, left Sickingen in the lurch. Sickingen was mortally wounded, surrendered Landstuhl, and died soon after. Hutten had to flee to Switzerland, where he died a few months later on the Isle of Ufnau in the Lake of Zurich.

This defeat and the death of the two leaders broke the power of the nobility as a body independent of the princes. From then on the nobility acted only in the service and under the leadership of the princes. The Peasant War, which broke out soon after, compelled the nobles to seek the direct or indirect protection of the princes. Also, it proved that the German nobility would rather continue exploiting the peasants under the dominance of the princes than overthrow the princes and priests in an open alliance with *emancipated* peasants.

ARMED FRANCONIAN PEASANTS

From a drawing by Albrecht Dürer

V

Not a year passed since Luther's declaration of war against the Catholic hierarchy set in motion all the opposition elements in Germany without the peasants again and again bringing forward their demands. Between 1518 and 1523 one local peasant revolt followed another in the Black Forest and in Upper Swabia, and after the spring of 1524 revolts became systematic. In April 1524 the peasants of the Abbey of Marchthal refused to do statute labour and to pay tributes; in May the peasants of St. Blasien refused to make serf payments; in June the peasants of Steinheim, near Memmingen, announced that they would pay neither tithes nor other duties; in July and August the peasants of Thurgau revolted and were quelled partly by the mediation of Zurich and partly by the brutality of the Confederacy, which executed many of them. Finally, a more determined uprising, which may be regarded as the direct *beginning of the Peasant War*, took place in the Landgraviate of Stühlingen.

The peasants of Stühlingen suddenly refused to deliver anything to the Landgrave, assembled in strong numbers, and on August 24, 1524, moved towards Waldshut under the command of *Hans Müller of Bulgenbach.* Here they founded an evangelist fraternity jointly with the burghers. The latter joined the organisation the more willingly because they were at odds with the government of the Austrian Forelands[324] over the religious persecution of their preacher, Balthasar *Hubmaier,* Thomas Münzer's friend and disciple. A weekly tax of three kreutzers was imposed by the Union—an enormous figure, considering the value of money at that time. Emissaries were sent to Alsace, the Moselle, the entire Upper Rhine and Franconia to bring peasants everywhere into the Union. The Union announced that its purpose was to abolish feudal rule, destroy all castles and monasteries and to eliminate all lords except the Emperor. The *German tricolour*[325] was the banner of the Union.

The uprising gained momentum rapidly in all of what is now Upper Baden. Panic seized the nobility of Upper Swabia, whose armed forces were almost all in Italy, making war against Francis I of France. They had no choice but to drag out the affair by means of negotiations and, in the meanwhile, to collect money and recruit troops until strong enough to punish the peasants for their audacity with "fire and destruction, plunder and carnage".[a] There began that systematic betrayal, that continuous deceit and malice, which were typical of the nobility and the princes throughout the Peasant War and which were their strongest weapon against the decentralised peasants whom it was hard to organise. The Swabian League, consisting of the princes, the nobility and the imperial cities of South-West Germany, put itself between the warring forces, but did not guarantee the peasants any real concessions. The latter remained in motion. From September 30 to the middle of October Hans Müller of Bulgenbach marched through the Black Forest to Urach and Furtwangen, increased his troops to 3,500 men and took up positions near Ewattingen (in the vicinity of Stühlingen). The nobility had no more than 1,700 men at their disposal, and even those were divided. They had to seek an armistice, which was, indeed, concluded in the camp at Ewattingen. The peasants were promised an amicable settlement either directly between the parties concerned or through arbitrators, and an investigation of their grievances by the provincial court at Stockach. The troops of the nobility and of the peasants dispersed.

The peasants worked out sixteen articles which they would press for in the court at Stockach. The articles were very moderate, and went no further than abolition of hunting rights, statute labour, oppressive taxes and the privileges of lords in general, and protection against arbitrary imprisonment and biassed, arbitrary courts.

But no sooner had the peasants gone home than the nobility demanded the restoration of all controversial tributes pending the court decision. Naturally, the peasants refused and referred the lords to the court. The conflict flared up anew, the peasants reassembled and the princes and lords concentrated their troops. This time the movement spread farther beyond Breisgau and deep into Württemberg. The troops under *Georg Truchsess* of Waldburg, the Alba of the Peasant War, watched the manoeuvres of the

---

[a] Cited from the ultimatum tendered by Georg Truchsess, commander of the punitive army of the Swabian League, to the peasants of Hegau on February 15, 1525. (See W. Zimmermann, *Allgemeine Geschichte des grossen Bauernkrieges*, Th. 2, S. 33-34.)—*Ed.*

peasants, attacked their contingents one by one, but did not dare to attack the main force. In the meantime, Georg Truchsess negotiated with the peasant chiefs and reached agreements here and there.

By the end of December proceedings began at the Stockach provincial court. The peasants objected to the court being composed entirely of noblemen. An imperial edict[326] was read to them in reply. The proceedings were drawn out, and in the meantime the nobility, the princes and the Swabian League armed themselves. Archduke Ferdinand who ruled Württemberg,[a] the Black Forest of Baden and Southern Alsace in addition to the hereditary lands which still belong to Austria, called for the utmost severity against the rebel peasants. They were to be captured, tortured and mercilessly slain in whatever manner was the most convenient, their possessions were to be burned and devastated, and their wives and children driven off the land. This shows how the princes and lords observed the armistice and what they meant by amicable arbitration and investigation of grievances. Archduke Ferdinand, to whom the house of Welser, of Augsburg, advanced money,[327] armed himself in all haste. The Swabian League ordered money and a contingent of troops to be raised in three phases.

These above rebellions coincided with the five months of Thomas Münzer's presence in Upper Baden.[328] Although there are no direct proofs of the influence he had on the outbreak and course of the movement, it is completely established indirectly. The more resolute peasant revolutionaries were mostly his disciples, and put forward his ideas. The twelve articles and the *Letter of Articles* of Upper Baden peasants are ascribed to him by all his contemporaries, although beyond any doubt he had no part in composing at least the former. When still on his way back to Thuringia he addressed a decidedly revolutionary manifesto to the insurgent peasants.[329]

Duke Ulrich, exiled from Württemberg in 1519, conspired meanwhile to regain his land with the aid of the peasants. In fact, he had been trying to utilise the revolutionary party ever since he was exiled, and had supported it continuously. His name was associated with most of the local disturbances between 1520 and 1524 in the Black Forest and in Württemberg. Now he was arming for an attack on Württemberg from his castle, Hohentwiel. However, he too was only being used by the peasants, had no influence over them and, even less, their trust.

---

[a] After Duke Ulrich was banished in 1519.— *Ed.*

The winter passed but nothing decisive was undertaken by either side. The princely masters went into hiding. The peasant revolt was gathering momentum. In January 1525 the entire country between the Danube, the Rhine and the Lech was in great ferment, and in February the storm broke.

While the *Black Forest and Hegau Troop* under Hans Müller of Bulgenbach was conspiring with Ulrich of Württemberg and shared in a part of his unsuccessful march on Stuttgart (February and March 1525), the peasants in Ried, above the Ulm, rose on February 9, assembled in a camp near Baltringen protected on all sides by marshes, hoisted the *red flag*, and formed the *Baltringen Troop* under the leadership of Ulrich Schmid. This troop was 10,000 to 12,000 strong.

On February 25, the 7,000-strong *Upper Allgäu Troop* assembled at Schussen, stimulated by the rumour that an armed force was marching against the discontented elements who had appeared in this locality as everywhere else. The people of Kempten, who had been at odds with their archbishop[a] all winter, assembled the next day and joined the peasants. The towns of Memmingen and Kaufbeuren joined the movement after laying down their conditions; yet the ambiguous attitude of the towns to this struggle was already apparent. On March 7 twelve articles were adopted in Memmingen for all the peasants of Upper Allgäu.

Tidings from the Allgäu peasants prompted the formation of a *Lake Troop* under Eitel Hans on Lake Constance. It also grew very quickly and established its headquarters in Bermatingen.

Similarly, early in March the peasants rose in Lower Allgäu, in the region of Ochsenhausen and Schellenberg, in Zeil and Waldburg, the estates of Truchsess. This *Lower Allgäu Troop*, which consisted of 7,000 men, had its camp near Wurzach.

These four troops accepted all the Memmingen articles, incidentally more moderate even than the Hegau articles because they showed a remarkable lack of determination in points relating to the attitude of the armed troops towards the nobility and the governments. Such determination as was shown appeared only in the course of the war, after the peasants had experienced the behaviour of their enemies.

At the same time, a sixth troop formed on the Danube. Peasants from the entire region, from Ulm to Donauwörth, from the valleys of the Iller, Roth and Biber, came to Leipheim and set up camp there. Every able-bodied man from fifteen localities had come, while

---

[a] Sebastian von Breitenstein.— *Ed.*

reinforcements were drawn from 117. The leader of the *Leipheim* -*Troop* was Ulrich Schön, and its preacher was Jakob Wehe, the pastor of Leipheim.

Thus, in the beginning of March there were 30,000 to 40,000 insurgent Upper Swabian peasants under arms in six camps. The peasant troops were a mixed lot. Münzer's revolutionary party was in the minority everywhere. Yet it formed the backbone of all the peasant camps. The bulk of the peasants were always ready to come to terms with the lords wherever they were promised the concessions they had hoped to gain by their menacing attitude. As the uprising dragged on and the princes' armies drew nearer, they became war-weary and most of those who still had something to lose went home. Moreover, a vagabond mass of the lumpenproletariat had joined the troops and this undermined their discipline and demoralised the peasants, because the vagabonds came and went as they pleased. This alone explains why the peasants at first remained everywhere on the defensive, why their morale deteriorated in the camps and why, aside from their tactical shortcomings and the shortage of good leaders, they were no match for the armies of the princes.

While the troops were still assembling, Duke Ulrich invaded Württemberg from Hohentwiel with recruited detachments and a few Hegau peasants. The Swabian League would have been lost if the peasants had used the opportunity to attack the troops of Truchsess von Waldburg from the other flank. But because of the defensive attitude of the peasantry, Truchsess soon succeeded in concluding an armistice with the Baltringen, Allgäu and Lake peasants, starting negotiations and fixing Judica Sunday (April 2)[330] as the day on which the whole affair was to be settled. This gave him a chance to march against Duke Ulrich, to occupy Stuttgart and compel him to abandon Württemberg again on March 17. Then he turned against the peasants, but the mercenaries in his own army revolted and refused to march against them. Truchsess succeeded in placating the mutineers and moved towards Ulm, where new reinforcements were being formed. He left an observation post at Kirchheim near Teck.

The Swabian League, its hands at last free and its first contingents gathered, now threw off its mask, declaring itself

"determined to end with arms in hand and with the aid of God that which the peasants have wilfully undertaken".[a]

***

[a] From the decision made at a conference of League authorities at Ulm in March 1525. (It is recorded in a document from the Ulm archive and quoted by Zimmermann, op. cit., Th. 2, S. 167.)—*Ed.*

The peasants had meanwhile faithfully observed the armistice. They had drawn up their demands, the famous *Twelve Articles*, for the negotiations on Judica Sunday. They demanded the right to elect and depose clergymen through the communities; abolition of the small tithe and utilisation of the great tithe,³³¹ after subtraction of the pastors' salaries, for public purposes; abolition of serfdom, death tolls, fishing and hunting rights; restriction of excessive statute labour, taxes and rents; restitution of forests, pastures and privileges forcibly withdrawn from communities and individuals, and an end to arbitrary justice and administration. Clearly, the moderate conciliatory party still had the upper hand among the peasant troops. The revolutionary party had formulated its programme earlier in the *Letter of Articles*. It was an open letter to all peasant communities, calling on them to join the "Christian Alliance and Brotherhood" for the purpose of removing all burdens either through goodwill, "which was unlikely", or by force, and threatening all shirkers with "lay excommunication", i. e. with expulsion from society and ostracism by members of the league. All castles, monasteries and priests' endowments were also to be placed under lay anathema, the letter said, unless the nobility, the priests and monks relinquished them of their own accord, moved into ordinary houses like other people, and joined the Christian Alliance.—This radical manifesto, obviously composed *before* the spring insurrection of 1525, thus speaks above all of revolution, of complete victory over the still reigning classes, while the "lay excommunication" is designed for the oppressors and traitors who were to be killed, for the castles that were to be burned, and the monasteries and endowments that were to be confiscated and whose treasures were to be turned into cash.

But before the peasants came to present their Twelve Articles to the appointed courts of arbitration, they learned that the Swabian League had violated the armistice and that its troops were approaching. Instantly, they took countermeasures. A general meeting of all Allgäu, Baltringen and Lake peasants was held at Gaisbeuren. The four troops were combined and reorganised into four new columns. A decision was taken to confiscate the church estates, to sell their treasures in favour of the war chest, and to burn the castles. Thus alongside the official Twelve Articles, the *Letter of Articles* became the statute of warfare, and Judica Sunday, the day designated for the conclusion of peace, became the date of a *general uprising*.

The mounting unrest everywhere, continuous local conflicts between peasants and nobility, tidings of the uprising in the Black Forest, which had been brewing in the preceding six months, and of its spread to the Danube and the Lech, are enough to explain the rapid succession of peasant revolts in two-thirds of Germany. But that the individual[a] revolts broke out simultaneously proves that there were men at the head of the movement who organised them through Anabaptist and other emissaries. Already in the second half of March disorders broke out in Württemberg, in the lower reaches of the Neckar, in Odenwald, and in Lower and Middle Franconia. However, April 2, Judica Sunday, was named everywhere beforehand as the day of the general uprising, and everywhere the decisive blow, the revolt *en masse,* was delivered in the first week of April. The Allgäu, Hegau and Lake peasants also sounded the bells on April 1 and called mass meetings to summon all able-bodied men to their camp; they opened hostilities against the castles and monasteries simultaneously with the Baltringen peasants.

In *Franconia,* where the movement had six centres, the insurrection broke out everywhere in the first days of April. At about the same time two peasant camps were formed near *Nördlingen,* with whose aid the revolutionary party of the town under *Anton Forner* gained the upper hand, appointed Forner town mayor, and consummated a union between the town and the peasants. In the region of *Ansbach* the peasants revolted everywhere between April 1 and 7, and from here the uprising spread as far as Bavaria. In the region of *Rothenburg* the peasants had been under arms since March 22. In the town of Rothenburg the rule of the honourables was overthrown by the petty burghers and the plebeians under *Stephan von Menzingen* on March 27, but since peasant dues were the chief source of revenue for the town, the new government also vacillated and acted ambiguously towards the peasants. A general uprising of the peasants and the townships broke out early in April in the Grand Chapter of *Würzburg,*[332] and in the bishopric of *Bamberg* a general insurrection compelled the bishop[b] to yield in five days. And a strong *Bildhausen peasant camp* formed in the North, on the border of Thuringia.

In *Odenwald,* where *Wendel Hipler,* nobleman and former chancellor of the Counts von Hohenlohe, and *Georg Metzler,* an innkeeper from Ballenberg near Krautheim, headed the revolutionary party, the storm broke out already on March 26. The peasants marched from all directions towards the Tauber. The two thousand men of the Rothenburg camp joined them as well. Georg Metzler took

---

[a] The 1850 and 1870 editions have *partiellen* (partial) instead of *einzelnen* (individual).— *Ed.*

[b] Weigand von Redwitz.— *Ed.*

command and after the arrival of all reinforcements marched on
April 4 to the monastery of Schönthal on the Jagst, where he was
joined by the *peasants of the Neckar valley.* The latter, led by *Jäcklein
Rohrbach,* an innkeeper from Böckingen near Heilbronn, had begun
their insurrection in Flein, Sontheim, etc., on Judica Sunday, while
Wendel Hipler took Öhringen by surprise with a number of
conspirators and drew the peasants in the vicinity into the movement. In Schönthal the two peasant columns combined into the
Gay Troop, accepted the Twelve Articles and made a few raids on
castles and monasteries. The Gay Troop was about 8,000 strong and
had cannon and 3,000 muskets. *Florian Geyer,* a Franconian knight,
joined the force and formed the Black Troop, a select corps
recruited mainly from the Rothenburg and Öhringen army reserve.

The Württemberg magistrate in Neckarsulm, Count Ludwig von
Helfenstein, opened the hostilities. He ordered all captured peasants
to be executed on the spot. The Gay Troop marched to meet him.
The peasants were embittered by the massacres and by news of the
defeat of the Leipheim Troop, of Jakob Wehe's execution, and the
Truchsess atrocities. Von Helfenstein, who had moved into Weinsberg, was attacked there. The castle was stormed by Florian Geyer,
the town seized in a prolonged battle and Count Ludwig taken
prisoner along with several knights. On the following day, April 17,
Jäcklein Rohrbach and the most resolute members of the troop held
court over the prisoners and made fourteen of them, with von
Helfenstein at their head, run the gauntlet, this being the most
humiliating death they could think of. The capture of Weinsberg
and Jäcklein's terroristic revenge on von Helfenstein did not fail to
have their effect on the nobility. The Counts von Löwenstein joined
the peasant alliance. The Counts von Hohenlohe, who had joined
previously but had given no aid, immediately sent the desired
cannon and powder.

The chiefs debated among themselves whether they should make
Götz von Berlichingen their commander, "since he could bring to
them the nobility". The proposal found sympathy, but Florian
Geyer, who saw the seeds of reaction in this mood of the peasants
and their chiefs, separated from the Gay Troop and marched on his
own with his Black Troop, first through the Neckar and then the
Würzburg region, everywhere destroying castles and the lairs of the
priesthood.

The rest of the troops marched first of all against Heilbronn. In
this powerful free imperial town the patriciate was, as almost
everywhere, confronted by a burgher and revolutionary opposition.
In secret agreement with the peasants, the latter opened the gates to

Georg Metzler and Jäcklein Rohrbach on April 17 during a disturbance. The peasant chiefs and their people took possession of the town, which was then admitted to their brotherhood and delivered 1,200 guilders in cash and a squad of volunteers. Only the possessions of the clergy and the Teutonic Order[333] were pillaged. On April 22, the peasants moved out, leaving a small garrison. Heilbronn was to become the centre of the various troops, the latter actually sending delegates and conferring over joint actions and the common demands of the peasantry. But the burgher opposition and the patricians, who had joined forces after the peasant invasion, regained the upper hand in the town, preventing decisive steps and waiting only for the approach of the princes' troops to openly betray the peasants.

The peasants marched toward Odenwald. Götz von Berlichingen, who had a few days before offered himself to the Elector Palatine,[a] then to the peasantry, and then again to the Elector, was to join the Evangelist Fraternity on April 24 and assume supreme command of the Gay *Bright* Troop (as distinct from the *Black* Troop of Florian Geyer). At the same time, however, he was the prisoner of the peasants, who mistrusted him and bound him to a council of chiefs, without whose approval he could undertake nothing. Götz and Metzler marched with the bulk of the peasants across Buchen to Amorbach, where, during their stay from April 30 to May 5, they roused the entire Mainz region. The nobility was everywhere compelled to join in, and its castles were thus spared. Only the monasteries were burned and pillaged. The troop had become visibly demoralised. The most energetic men had gone away with Florian Geyer or with Jäcklein Rohrbach who, after the capture of Heilbronn, also separated from the troop, apparently because he, the judge of Count von Helfenstein, could no longer remain with a body that was inclined towards reconciliation with the nobility. This gravitation towards reaching an understanding with the nobility was in itself a sign of demoralisation. Soon Wendel Hipler proposed a very sound reorganisation of the troop. He suggested that the mercenaries, who had been offering their services daily, should be taken on. He also suggested that the troop should no longer be renewed monthly through the arrival of fresh contingents and the dismissal of old ones, and that the men under arms, who had received a certain amount of military training, should be retained. But a community meeting rejected both proposals. The peasants had already become volatile and viewed the war as little more than

---

[a] Ludwig V.— *Ed.*

pillage, where the competition of the mercenaries held no advantage for them and where they wanted to be free to go home as soon as their pockets were filled. In Amorbach matters came to a point where Hans Berlin, a Heilbronn councillor, induced the chiefs and troop councillors to accept a Declaration of the Twelve Articles,[334] a document wherein the remaining arrowheads of the Twelve Articles were blunted and words of humble supplication were put into the mouths of the peasants. But this was too much for the peasants; they rejected the Declaration with a display of vehemence and insisted upon the original Articles.

In the meantime, a decisive change had taken place in the Würzburg area. The bishop,[a] who had withdrawn to fortified Frauenberg near Würzburg after the first peasant uprising early in April and had vainly sent messages in all directions asking for aid, was finally compelled to make temporary concessions. On May 2 a Diet opened in which the peasants were represented, but letters proving the bishop's treacherous moves were intercepted before any results could be achieved. The Diet broke up at once, and hostilities began between the insurgent townsmen and peasants, on the one hand, and the bishop's forces, on the other. The bishop escaped to Heidelberg on May 5, and on the following day Florian Geyer with his Black Troop entered Würzburg, and with him came *the Franconian Tauber Troop*, which consisted of the peasants of Mergentheim, Rothenburg and Ansbach. On May 7 Götz von Berlichingen arrived with his Gay Bright Troop, and the siege of Frauenberg began.

In Limburg and the Ellwangen and Hall regions another contingent was formed by the end of March, and in early April that of Gaildorf, or the *Common Gay Troop*. It showed considerable violence, roused the entire region, burned down many monasteries and castles, including the castle of Hohenstaufen, compelled all the peasants to join it, and forced the nobles, and even the cup-bearers of Limburg, to enter the Christian Brotherhood. Early in May it invaded Württemberg, but was compelled to withdraw. As in 1848 the separatism of the German system of small states obstructed joint action by the revolutionaries of the various states. The Gaildorf Troop, restricted to a small area, was naturally bound to disperse when all resistance within that area was broken. It concluded an agreement with the town of Gmünd and went home, leaving only 500 under arms.

---

[a] Konrad III.— *Ed.*

In the *Palatinate* peasant troops were formed on either bank of the Rhine by the end of April. They destroyed many castles and monasteries, and on May 1 took Neustadt on the Haardt after the Bruchrain peasants had crossed the river on the previous day and forced Speyer to conclude an agreement. Marshal von Habern at the head of the Elector's small force was powerless against them, and on May 10 the Elector was compelled to come to an agreement with the insurgent peasants, guaranteeing them redress of grievances through a Diet.

Finally, in *Württemberg* the revolt had already broken out early in some localities. The peasants of the Urach Jura formed a union against priests and lords already in February and the peasants of Blaubeuren, Urach, Münsingen, Balingen and Rosenfeld revolted at the end of March. The Württemberg region was invaded by the Gaildorf Troop at Göppingen, by Jäcklein Rohrbach at Brackenheim and by the remnants of the beaten Leipheim Troop at Pfullingen, inciting the rural population to revolt. There were also serious disturbances in other localities. Already on April 6 Pfullingen surrendered to the peasants. The Austrian Archduke's[a] government was driven to the wall. It had no money and only few troops. The cities and castles were in a bad state and had neither garrisons nor munition. Even Asperg was practically defenseless.

The government's attempt to call out the town reserves against the peasants caused its instant defeat. On April 16 the Bottwar[b] reserves refused to obey orders. Instead of marching to Stuttgart, they turned to Wunnenstein near Bottwar, where they formed the nucleus of a camp of burghers and peasants whose number increased rapidly. The rebellion in Zabergäu broke out on the same day. The Maulbronn monastery was pillaged and a few more monasteries and castles were laid waste. Reinforcements marched from neighbouring Bruchrain to join the local peasants.

The Wunnenstein troop was under the command of *Matern Feuerbacher*, a Bottwar town councillor. He was a leader of the burgher opposition, but was so strongly compromised that he was compelled to go with the peasants. However, he remained at all times very moderate, prevented the implementation of the *Letter of Articles* against the castles, and sought everywhere to reconcile the peasants with the moderate burgherdom. He prevented the amalgamation of the Württemberg peasants with the Gay Bright Troop, and later likewise prevailed on the Gaildorf Troop to withdraw from

---

[a] Ferdinand I.— *Ed.*

[b] Or Gross b ottwar.— *Ed.*

Württemberg. On April 19 he was deposed for his burgher
tendencies but again made commander the next day. He was
indispensable, and even when Jäcklein Rohrbach arrived with 200
determined men to join the Württemberg peasants on April 22, he
had no choice but to leave Feuerbacher in command and confined
himself to rigid supervision of his actions.

On April 18 the government attempted to negotiate with the
peasants stationed at Wunnenstein. The peasants insisted on the
Twelve Articles, but naturally the government's representatives
could not accept them. The troop set itself in motion. On April 20 it
reached Lauffen, where, for the last time, it turned down the
proposals of the government delegates. On April 22 the troop,
numbering 6,000, appeared in Bietigheim and threatened Stuttgart.
Most members of the Stuttgart Council had fled and a citizens'
committee took over the administration. Among the citizenry there
was the same division as everywhere else into parties of the
honourables, the burgher opposition, and the revolutionary
plebeians. On April 25 the latter opened the gates to the peasants
and Stuttgart was instantly taken. Here the organisation of the *Gay
Christian Troop*, as the Württemberg insurgents now called themselves, was completed and the rules of pay, division of booty,
maintenance, etc., were rigidly defined. A detachment of Stutt-
garters under Theus Gerber joined the troop.

On April 29 Feuerbacher marched with all his men against the
Gaildorfers who had entered Württemberg region at Schorndorf.
He drew the entire area into his alliance and thereby prevailed on
the Gaildorfers to withdraw. In this way he prevented Rohrbach's
revolutionary element in his troop from joining hands with the
reckless Gaildorfers and thus being dangerously strengthened.
Upon receiving news of Truchsess' approach, he left Schorndorf to
meet him, and on May 1 made camp near Kirchheim unter Teck.

We have herewith traced the origin and development of the
uprising in the part of Germany that should be regarded as the
territory of the first group of peasant armies. Before we proceed to
the other groups (Thuringia and Hesse, Alsace, Austria and the
Alps) we must give an account of the military operations of
Truchsess, in which he, alone in the beginning and later supported
by various princes and townships, annihilated this first group of
insurgents.

We left Truchsess near Ulm, where he had come late in March
after leaving an observation corps in Kirchheim unter Teck under
the command of Dietrich Spät. Truchsess' corps, which, including
the League reinforcements concentrated in Ulm, had not quite

10,000 men, of whom 7,200 were infantry, was the only army available for an offensive war against the peasants. Reinforcements came to Ulm very slowly, due partly to the difficulties of recruiting in insurgent localities, partly to the governments' lack of money, and partly to the fact that the few available troops were everywhere more than indispensable for manning the fortresses and castles. We have already taken note of the small number of troops at the disposal of the princes and towns outside the Swabian League. Everything therefore depended upon Georg Truchsess and his League army.

Truchsess turned first against the *Baltringen Troop*, which had in the meantime begun to destroy castles and monasteries in the vicinity of Ried. The peasants, who withdrew at the approach of the League troops, were outflanked and driven out of the marshes, crossed the Danube and plunged into the ravines and forests of the Swabian Jura. In this region the cannon and cavalry which formed the backbone of the League army were of little avail against them, and Truchsess did not pursue them farther. He marched against the Leipheim Troop which had 5,000 men stationed at Leipheim, 4,000 in the Mindel valley, and 6,000 at Illertissen. The Leipheim Troop was fomenting rebellion in the entire region, destroying monasteries and castles, and preparing to march against Ulm with all its three columns. It seems that a certain degree of demoralisation had set in among the peasants here as well, undermining their military morale, for Jakob Wehe tried at the very outset to negotiate with Truchsess. The latter, however, backed by a sufficient military force, declined to negotiate and on April 4 attacked and routed the main troop at Leipheim. Jakob Wehe, Ulrich Schön and two other peasant leaders were captured and beheaded; Leipheim capitulated, and several expeditions to the adjacent countryside subdued the entire region.

A new mutiny of mercenaries, who demanded plunder and additional pay, delayed Truchsess again until April 10, when he marched south-west against the *Baltringen Troop* which had, in the meantime, invaded his estates, Waldburg, Zeil and Wolfegg, and besieged his castles. Here, too, he found the peasants disunited, and defeated them on April 11 and 12 successively in several battles, which completely disrupted the Baltringen Troop. Its remnants withdrew under the command of priest Florian and joined the *Lake Troop*. Truchsess now turned against the latter. The Lake Troop, which had not merely roved through the countryside all this time, but had also drawn the towns of Buchhorn (Friedrichshafen) and Wollmatingen into the brotherhood, held a big military council in the monastery of Salem on April 13 and decided to move against Truchsess. Alarm bells were sounded at once, and 10,000 men joined by the defeated Baltringen Troop assembled in the Bermatingen camp. On April 15 they stood their ground in a battle with Truchsess, who did not want to risk his army in a decisive battle and preferred to negotiate, strengthened in this purpose by news of the approach of the Allgäu and Hegau troops. On April 17 he therefore concluded an agreement with the Lake and Baltringen peasants in Weingarten. On the face of it, the agreement was quite favourable for the peasants, and they accepted it without hesitation. Ultimately, he also prevailed on the delegates of the Upper and Lower Allgäu peasants to accept this agreement, and marched towards Württemberg.

Here Truchsess' cunning saved him from certain defeat. Had he not succeeded in fooling the weak, dull-witted, and for the most part already demoralised peasants and their mostly incapable, timid and venal leaders, he and his small army would have been enveloped by four columns of at least 25,000 to 30,000 men, and would have faced inevitable disaster. It was his enemies' narrow-mindedness, always unavoidable when peasants gather in a mass, that enabled him to dispose of them at the very moment when they could have ended the war with one blow, at least in Swabia and Franconia. The Lake peasants observed the agreement, which naturally was turned against them in due course, so rigidly that they later took up arms against their allies, the Hegau peasants. Although the Allgäu peasants, drawn into the betrayal by their leaders, soon renounced the agreement, Truchsess was by then out of danger.

Though not bound by the Weingarten agreement, the Hegau peasants soon gave a new display of the infinite parochial bigotry and stubborn provincialism that proved the undoing of the entire Peasant War. When, after futile negotiations with them, Truchsess marched off to Württemberg, they followed him and were continually on his flank, but it did not occur to them to unite with the Württemberg Gay Christian Troop, and this because previously the peasants of Württemberg and the Neckar valley had refused them assistance. When Truchsess had marched far enough from their home country, they simply turned back and marched on Freiburg.

We left the Württemberg peasants under the command of Matern Feuerbacher at Kirchheim unter Teck, from where the observation corps left by Truchsess under the command of Dietrich Spät had withdrawn towards Urach. After an unsuccessful attempt to take Urach, Feuerbacher turned towards Nürtingen and sent messages to all insurgent troops in the vicinity to assist him in the decisive battle. And considerable reinforcements did come from both the Württemberg lowlands and from Gäu. The Gäu peasants, who had joined the remnants of the Leipheim Troop that had withdrawn to West Württemberg and roused the valleys of the Upper Neckar and Nagold up to Böblingen and Leonberg, came in two strong columns to join Feuerbacher at Nürtingen on May 5. Truchsess stumbled upon the united troop at Böblingen. Its number, its artillery and position perplexed him. As was his custom, he at once began to negotiate and concluded an armistice with the peasants. But no sooner had he thus secured his position than he attacked them on May 12 *during the armistice* and forced a decisive battle on them. The peasants offered long and courageous resistance until Böblingen finally surrendered to Truchsess owing to betrayal by the burghers. The peasants' left wing, deprived of its base of support, was forced back and outflanked. This decided the issue. The poorly disciplined peasants were thrown into confusion and fled in disorder; those who were not killed or captured by League horsemen threw away their weapons and hurried home. The Gay Christian Troop, and with it the whole Württemberg insurrection, were crushed. Theus Gerber fled to Esslingen and Feuerbacher to Switzerland, while Jäcklein Rohrbach was taken prisoner and dragged in chains to Neckargartach, where he was bound to a stake, surrounded with firewood and roasted to death on a slow fire, while Truchsess, carousing with his knights, gloated over this knightly spectacle.

From Neckargartach Truchsess supported the operations of the Elector Palatine by invading Kraichgau. On receiving word of Truchsess' success, the Elector, who meanwhile had gathered an army, immediately broke his agreement with the peasants, attacked Bruchrain on May 23, captured and burned Malsch in spite of its vigorous resistance, pillaged a number of villages, and garrisoned Bruchsal. At the same time Truchsess attacked Eppingen and captured the chief of the local movement, Anton Eisenhut, whom the Elector immediately executed along with a dozen other peasant leaders. Bruchrain and Kraichgau were thus subdued and compelled to pay an indemnity of about 40,000 guilders. Both armies, that of Truchsess—reduced to 6,000 men in the preceding battles—and that of the Elector (6,500 men), united and moved against the Odenwalders.

Word of the Böblingen defeat spread terror everywhere among the insurgents. The free imperial cities which had come under the heavy hand of the peasants, heaved a sigh of relief. The city of Heilbronn was the first to seek reconciliation with the Swabian League. In Heilbronn the peasants' chancellory and delegates of the various troops deliberated over the proposals they would make to the

Emperor[a] and the Empire in the name of all the insurgent peasants. These negotiations, whose outcome was to apply to all Germany, revealed again that none of the estates, including the peasants, was sufficiently developed to alter the situation in Germany according to its own lights. It was obvious at once that the support of the nobility and particularly of the burghers had to be gained for this purpose. *Wendel Hipler* took charge of the negotiations. Of all the leaders of the movement he had the best grasp on the existing situation. He was not a far-seeing revolutionary like Münzer, nor a peasant representative like Metzler or Rohrbach; his extensive experience and his practical knowledge of the attitude of the various estates towards each other prevented him from representing any one of the estates involved in the movement in opposition to the others. Just as Münzer, a representative of the budding proletariat, a class which then stood totally outside the official organisation of society, was driven to anticipate communism, Wendel Hipler, the representative of what may be described as the cross-section of the nation's progressive elements, anticipated *modern bourgeois society*. The principles he represented and the demands he made were not really immediately practicable. They were the somewhat idealised and inevitable result of the dissolution of feudal society. And the peasants, having set themselves to drafting legislation for the whole Empire, were compelled to accept them. In Heilbronn, therefore, the centralisation demanded by the peasants assumed a more definite form which was, however, worlds removed from the peasants' own idea. For instance, it was much more clearly expressed in the demands for a standard currency, standard weights and measures, abolition of internal customs, etc., that is, in demands that were far more in the interest of townsmen than in that of the peasants. Concessions were made to the nobility that substantially approached the modern system of redemption and that would in the long run transform feudal into bourgeois landownership. In short, since the peasants' demands were composed as an "imperial reform", they necessarily complied with the definitive interests rather than the immediate demands of the burghers.

While this imperial reform was still being debated in Heilbronn, the author of the Declaration of the Twelve Articles, Hans Berlin, was already on his way to meet Truchsess and negotiate the surrender of the township on behalf of the honourables and burghers. Reactionary movements within the town supported this betrayal, and Wendel Hipler was obliged to flee with the peasants.

---

[a] Charles V.— *Ed.*

He went to Weinsberg, where he attempted to assemble the rem-
-nants of the Württemberg Troop and the small mobile unit of
Gaildorfers. But the approach of the Elector Palatine and Truchsess drove him from there as well, and he was compelled to go to
Würzburg to rouse the Gay Bright Troop into action. In the meantime, the armies of the League and the Elector subdued the
entire Neckar region, compelled the peasants to renew their oath of
allegiance, burned many villages, and slayed or hanged all runaway
peasants who fell into their hands. Weinsberg was burned to avenge
the execution of von Helfenstein.

The peasant troops assembled near Würzburg had in the
meantime laid siege to Frauenberg, and on May 15, before even a
breach was made in the wall of the fortress, they bravely but
unsuccessfully attempted to storm it. Four hundred of the best men,
mostly of Florian Geyer's Troop, were left behind in the ditches,
dead or wounded. Two days later, on May 17, Wendel Hipler
arrived and ordered a military council. He proposed to leave only
4,000 men at Frauenberg, and to encamp with the main force of
about 20,000 men at Krautheim on the Jagst under the very nose of
Truchsess, so that all reinforcements might be concentrated there. It
was an excellent plan. Only by keeping the masses together and
securing numerical superiority could the peasants hope to defeat the
princely army, which now numbered about 13,000 men. The
demoralisation and discouragement of the peasants, however, was
too far gone to contemplate any energetic action. Besides, Götz von
Berlichingen, who soon turned traitor, may have helped to hold the
troop in check, and Hipler's plan was thus never executed. Instead,
the forces were split up as usual. Not until May 23 did the Gay Bright
Troop go into action after the Franconians promised to follow
without delay. On May 26 the Ansbach detachments encamped in
Würzburg were induced to return home on receiving word that
their Margrave[a] had opened hostilities against the peasants. The
rest of the besieging army, along with Florian Geyer's Black
Troop, occupied positions at Heidingsfeld in the vicinity of Würzburg.

On May 24 the Gay Bright Troop, not really ready for battle,
arrived in Krautheim. Many learned here that in their absence their
villages had sworn allegiance to Truchsess, and used this as a pretext
to go home. The troop moved on to Neckarsulm, and on May 28
started negotiations with Truchsess. At the same time messengers

---

[a] Casimir, Margrave of Brandenburg, who was in possession of Ansbach and
Bayreuth.— *Ed.*

were sent to the peasants of Franconia, Alsace and Black Forest-Hegau to ask for reinforcements as quickly as possible. From Neckarsulm Götz [von Berlichingen] marched back to Öhringen. The troop steadily melted away. Götz von Berlichingen also disappeared during the march. He had gone home, having previously negotiated with Truchsess through his old brother-in-arms, Dietrich Spät, on going over to the other side. At Öhringen a false rumour of the enemy's approach threw the perplexed and discouraged peasantry into panic. The troop dispersed in utter confusion, and it was with difficulty that Metzler and Wendel Hipler succeeded in keeping together about 2,000 men, whom they again led toward Krautheim. In the meantime, the Franconian army of 5,000 men had come, but due to a side march through Löwenstein towards Öhringen, ordered by Götz with obviously treacherous intents, it missed the Gay Troop and moved towards Neckarsulm. This town, occupied by several detachments of the Gay Bright Troop, was besieged by Truchsess. The Franconians arrived at night and saw the fires of the League camp, but their leaders had not the courage to venture an attack and retreated to Krautheim where they at last found the remainder of the Gay Bright Troop. In the absence of aid, Neckarsulm surrendered to the League force on May 29. At once Truchsess had thirteen peasants executed and set out against the other peasant troops, burning and ravaging, pillaging and murdering along the way. His route through the valleys of the Neckar, Kocher and Jagst was marked with ruins and the corpses of peasants hanging on trees.

At Krautheim the League army encountered the peasants who had been forced by a flanking movement by Truchsess to withdraw towards Königshofen on the Tauber. Here they took up their position, 8,000 strong and with 32 cannon. Truchsess approached them behind the cover of hills and forests. He sent out columns to envelop them, and on June 2 attacked in such greatly superior force and with so much energy that they were defeated and dispersed in spite of the stubborn resistance of several of their troops that lasted into the night. As everywhere, it was the League horsemen, the "Peasants' Death", who were mainly instrumental in annihilating the insurgent army, charging down upon the peasants who were shaken by artillery and musket fire and lance attacks, breaking their ranks completely and slaying them one by one. The fate of 300 Königshofen burghers who had joined the peasant army serves as an illustration of the warfare led by Truchsess and his horsemen. All but fifteen of them were killed in the battle and four of the survivors were subsequently beheaded.

Having thus settled with the peasants of Odenwald, the Neckar valley and Lower Franconia, Truchsess subdued the whole region in a series of punitive expeditions, burning down whole villages and executing countless people. Then he marched against Würzburg. On the way he learned that the second Franconian Troop under Florian Geyer and Gregor von Burgbernheim was stationed at Sulzdorf, and instantly turned against it.

After his unsuccessful storming of Frauenberg, Florian Geyer had mainly devoted himself to negotiating with the princes and towns, especially with Rothenburg and Margrave Casimir of Ansbach, urging them to join the peasant brotherhood. But the negotiations were brought to an abrupt end by the news of the Königshofen defeat. His troop was joined by that of Ansbach under Gregor von Burgbernheim. The Ansbach troop had only recently been formed. Margrave Casimir had managed to keep in check the peasant revolt in his possessions in true Hohenzollern style, partly with promises and partly by means of a threatening mass of troops. He maintained complete neutrality towards all outside troops as long as they did not recruit Ansbach subjects, and tried to direct the hatred of the peasants mainly against the church endowments, through whose ultimate confiscation he hoped to enrich himself. In the meantime he kept arming and biding his time. As soon as he learned of the Böblingen battle he opened hostilities against his rebellious peasants, pillaging and burning their villages and hanging or otherwise killing many of them. But the peasants rallied quickly and defeated him at Windsheim under the command of Gregor von Burgbernheim on May 29. The call of the hard-pressed Odenwald peasants reached them as they were still pursuing him, and they headed at once for Heidingsfeld and from there, with Florian Geyer, again towards Würzburg (June 2). With no word arriving from the Odenwald troop, they left behind 5,000 peasants in Würzburg and with 4,000—the rest having deserted—they followed the others. Made complacent by false news of the outcome of the Königshofen battle, they were attacked by Truchsess at *Sulzdorf* and completely defeated. Truchsess' horsemen and mercenaries staged a terrible bloodbath. Florian Geyer rallied the remainder of his Black Troop, 600 in number, and fought his way to the village of Ingolstadt. Two hundred occupied the church and churchyard, and 400 took the castle. The Elector Palatine's forces pursued Geyer, and a column of 1,200 men captured the village and set fire to the church. Those who did not perish in the flames were slaughtered. The Elector's troops then breached the dilapidated castle wall and attempted to storm the fortress. Turned back twice by the peasants, who had taken cover behind an inner wall, they shot up the inner wall as well, and tried a third assault, which was successful. Half of Geyer's men were massacred, but Geyer managed to escape with the other 200. Their hiding place, however, was discovered on the following day (Whit-Monday). The Elector Palatine's soldiers surrounded the woods in which they lay hidden, and slaughtered all of them. Only seventeen prisoners were taken during those two days. Again Florian Geyer fought his way out of the encirclement with a few of his most intrepid fighters and set out to join the Gaildorf peasants, who had again assembled a body of about 7,000 men. But upon his arrival he found them mostly dispersed by the crushing news from every side. He made a last attempt to assemble the peasants dispersed in the woods, but was surprised by enemy forces at Hall on June 9 and laid down his life fighting.

Truchsess, who had sent word to besieged Frauenberg on the heels of the Königshofen victory, now marched towards Würzburg. The Council came to a secret understanding with him, so that on the night of June 7 the League army was allowed to surround the city where 5,000 peasants were stationed, and the following morning marched with sheathed swords through the gates opened by the Council. This betrayal of the Würzburg "honourables" caused the last troop of the Franconian peasants to be disarmed and all its leaders to be arrested. Truchsess immediately ordered 81 of them decapitated. The various Franconian princes arrived in Würzburg one after the other, and among them the Bishop of Würzburg himself,[a] the Bishop of Bamberg[b] and the Margrave of Brandenburg-Ansbach. The gracious lords distributed the roles among themselves. Truchsess marched with the Bishop of Bamberg, who presently broke the agreement concluded with his peasants and opened his land to the fierce and murderous hordes of the League army. Margrave Casimir devastated his own land. Deiningen was burned and numerous villages were pillaged or gutted. In every town the Margrave held a bloodthirsty court. He ordered eighteen rebels beheaded in Neustadt on the Aisch and in Bergel forty-three suffered the same fate. From there he went to Rothenburg where the honourables had already made a counter-revolution and arrested Stephan von Menzingen. The Rothenburg petty burghers and plebeians now had to pay heavily for behaving so ambiguously towards the peasants, refusing them all help until the very last, insisting in their local narrow-minded egotism on the suppression of

---

[a] Konrad III.— *Ed.*
[b] Weigand von Redwitz.— *Ed.*

countryside crafts in favour of the city guilds, and only unwillingly giving up the city revenues flowing in from the feudal services of the peasants. The Margrave ordered sixteen of them executed, Menzingen naturally first of all.—The Bishop of Würzburg marched through his region in a similar manner, pillaging, ravaging and burning everything on his way. He had 256 rebels decapitated on this triumphal march, and upon returning to Würzburg crowned his handiwork by beheading another thirteen Würzburg rebels.

In the Mainz region the viceregent, Bishop Wilhelm von Strassburg, restored order without resistance. He executed only four men. Rheingau, which had also been in revolt but where everybody had long since come home, was eventually invaded by Frowin von Hutten, a cousin of Ulrich, and fully "pacified" by the execution of twelve ringleaders. Frankfurt, which also experienced considerable revolutionary unrest, was held in check first by the conciliatory attitude of the Council and later by recruited troops. In the Rhenish Palatinate about 8,000 peasants had assembled anew after the Elector's breach of faith, and had again burned monasteries and castles, but the Archbishop of Trier[a] came to the aid of Marshal von Habern and made short work of them on June 23 at Pfeddersheim. A series of atrocities (eighty-two were executed in Pfeddersheim alone) and the capture of Weissenburg on July 7 put an end to the insurrection.

Of all the peasant troops only two were still unvanquished: the Hegau-Black Forest Troop and that of Allgäu. Archduke Ferdinand had tried intriguing against both. Just as Margrave Casimir and other princes sought to utilise the insurrection to annex church lands and principalities, Ferdinand wished to use it for the aggrandisement of the House of Austria. He had negotiated with the Allgäu commander, Walter Bach, and with the Hegau commander, Hans Müller of Bulgenbach, in the hope of prevailing on the peasants to declare allegiance to Austria, but though both chiefs were venal they could not talk their troops into anything more than an armistice between the Allgäu Troop and the Archduke, and neutrality towards Austria.

Retreating from the Württemberg region, the *peasants of Hegau* destroyed a number of castles and gathered reinforcements in the provinces of the Margraviate of Baden. On May 13 they marched on Freiburg, bombarded it from May 18, and entered it triumphantly when the town surrendered on May 23. From there they moved

---

[a] Richard von Greifenklau.—*Ed.*

towards Stockach and Radolfzell, and waged a long but unsuccessful
small war against the garrisons of those towns. Together with the
nobility and other surrounding towns, the latter appealed to the
Lake peasants for help in accordance with the Weingarten agreement. The former rebels of the Lake Troop rose, 5,000 strong,
against their confederates. These peasants were so narrow-minded
and short-sighted that only 600 refused to fight, expressing their
wish to join the Hegau peasants, for which they were massacred.
Meanwhile, persuaded by Hans Müller of Bulgenbach, who had sold
himself to the enemy, the Hegau peasants lifted their siege, and
when thereupon Hans Müller ran away, most of them dispersed.
The remainder entrenched themselves on the Hilzingen Steep,
where they were beaten and annihilated on July 16 by troops that
had in the meantime become available. The Swiss cities negotiated an
agreement on behalf of the Hegau peasants, which, however, did not
prevent the other side from capturing and beheading Hans Müller
in Laufenburg, his betrayal notwithstanding. In Breisgau the town of
Freiburg also deserted the peasant union (July 17) and sent troops
against the peasants, but due to the weakness of the princely force an
agreement was reached here as elsewhere, known as the agreement
of Offenburg [335] (September 18), which also applied to Sundgau. The
eight Black Forest groups and the Klettgau peasants, who were not
as yet disarmed, were again compelled to rebel by the tyranny of
Count von Sulz, and were defeated in October. On November 13 the
Black Forest peasants were forced to conclude an agreement, [336] and
Waldshut, the last bulwark of the insurrection in the Upper Rhine,
fell on December 6.

After Truchsess' departure the *Allgäu peasants* renewed their
campaign against the monasteries and castles and wreaked vengeance for the ravages caused by the League army. They were confronted by few troops, who risked only insignificant isolated skirmishes and never followed them into the woods. In June, a
movement against the honourables broke out in Memmingen, which
had hitherto been more or less neutral. This movement was defeated
only due to the accidental presence in the vicinity of some League
troops, who came in time to aid the honourables. Schappeler,
preacher and leader of the plebeian movement, took refuge in
St. Gallen. The peasants appeared before the town and were about to
begin shooting breaches in its wall when they learned that Truchsess
was approaching from Würzburg. On June 27 they set out against
him in two columns across Babenhausen and Obergünzburg.
Archduke Ferdinand again attempted to win the peasants for the
House of Austria. On the strength of the armistice concluded with

them, he demanded of Truchsess to march no farther against them. The Swabian League, however, ordered Truchsess to attack, but to refrain from pillaging and burning. But Truchsess was too clever to relinquish his prime and most effective weapon even if he were able to hold in check the mercenaries whom he had led from Lake Constance to the Main, from one atrocity to another. The peasants, numbering about 23,000, took up battle positions across the Iller and Leubas. Truchsess opposed them with 11,000 men. The positions of both armies were very strong. The cavalry was ineffective due to the terrain, and if the Truchsess mercenaries were superior to the peasants in organisation, ammunition and discipline, the Allgäu peasants had in their ranks a host of former soldiers and experienced commanders, and many well-manned cannon. On July 19 the League army opened fire, which was continued on both sides through July 20, but with no result. On July 21 Georg von Frundsberg joined Truchsess with 3,000 mercenaries. He knew many of the peasant commanders, for they had served under him in the Italian military expeditions, and entered into negotiations with them. Treason succeeded where military resources proved insufficient. Walter Bach and several other commanders and artillerymen sold out. They set fire to the powder stores of the peasants and induced the troop to attempt an enveloping movement, but as soon as the peasants left their strong positions they ran into an ambush engineered by Truchsess in collusion with Bach and the other traitors. The peasants' ability to defend themselves was impaired since their traitorous commanders had left them under the pretext of reconnoitring and were already on their way to Switzerland. Thus, two of the peasant columns were routed, while a third, under Knopf of Leubas, was able to withdraw in good order. It resumed its position on the mountain of Kollen near Kempten, where it was surrounded by Truchsess. But the latter did not dare attack the peasants; he cut off their supply routes and tried to demoralise them by burning about 200 villages in the vicinity. Hunger and the sight of their burning homes finally brought the peasants to their knees (July 25). More than twenty were immediately executed. Knopf of Leubas, the only leader of this troop who did not betray his banner, fled to Bregenz. There he was captured and hanged after a long imprisonment.

This brought the Peasant War in Swabia and Franconia to an end.

Directly after the outbreak of the first movement in Swabia, *Thomas Münzer* again hurried to *Thuringia*, and in late February or early March stayed in the free imperial town of *Mühlhausen*, where his party was stronger than elsewhere. He held the threads of the whole movement and knew that a storm was brewing in South Germany. So he set out to turn Thuringia into the centre of the movement in North Germany. He found the soil extremely fertile. Thuringia itself, the main scene of the Reformation movement, was in great ferment. The misery of the downtrodden peasants and the prevailing revolutionary, religious and political doctrines had also made a general uprising imminent in the neighbouring provinces of Hesse and Saxony, and in the Harz region. In Mühlhausen itself the bulk of the petty burgherdom was won over to Münzer's extreme standpoint and could hardly wait to assert its superiority over the arrogant honourables. To prevent premature action, Münzer was compelled to act as a moderator, but his disciple, Pfeifer, who held the reins of the movement there, had committed himself so greatly that he could not hold back the outbreak, and as early as March 17, 1525, before the general uprising in South Germany, Mühlhausen made its revolution. The old patrician Council was overthrown and the government handed over to the newly elected "eternal council", with Münzer as president.[337]

The worst thing that can befall the leader of an extreme party is to be compelled to assume power at a time when the movement is not yet ripe for the domination of the class he represents and for the measures this domination implies. What he *can* do depends not on his will but on the degree of antagonism between the various classes, and on the level of development of the material means of existence, of the conditions of production and commerce upon which the degree of intensity of the class contradictions always reposes. What he *ought* to do, what his party demands of him, again depends not on him, but also not on the degree of development of the class struggle and its conditions. He is bound to the doctrines and demands hitherto propounded which, again, do not follow from the class relations of the moment, or from the more or less accidental level of production and commerce, but from his more or less penetrating insight into the general result of the social [a] and political movement. Thus, he necessarily finds himself in an unsolvable dilemma. What he *can* do contradicts all his previous actions and principles and the immediate interests of his party, and what he *ought* to do cannot be done. In a word, he is compelled to represent not his party or his class, but the class for whose domination the movement is then ripe. In the interests of the movement he is compelled to advance the interests of an alien class, and to feed his own class with talk and promises, and with the asseveration that the interests of that alien class are their own interests. He who is put into this awkward position is irrevocably lost. We have seen examples of this in recent times, and need only recall the position in the last French Provisional Government of the representatives of the proletariat,[338] though they themselves represented only a very low stage of development of the proletariat. He who can still speculate with official posts after the experiences of the February government—to say nothing of our own noble German provisional governments and imperial regencies[339]—is either foolish beyond measure or belongs to the extreme revolutionary party at best in word only.

Münzer's position at the head of the "eternal council" of Mühlhausen was indeed much more precarious than that of any modern revolutionary regent. Not only the movement of his time, but also the age, were not ripe for the ideas of which he himself had only a faint notion. The class which he represented was still in its birth throes. It was far from developed enough to assume leadership over, and to transform,[b] society. The social changes of his fancy had little root in the then existing economic conditions. What is more, these conditions were paving the way for a social system that was diametrically opposite to what he envisioned. Nevertheless, he was still committed to his early sermons of Christian equality and evangelical community of property, and was compelled at least to

---

[a] The 1850 edition has "industrial" instead of "social".— *Ed.*
[b] The words "and to transform" are missing in the 1850 edition.— *Ed.*

attempt their realisation. Community of property, the equal
obligation of all to work, and abolition of all authority were
proclaimed. But in reality Mühlhausen remained a republican
imperial city with a somewhat democratised constitution, a senate
elected by universal suffrage and controlled by a forum, and with a
hastily improvised system of care for the poor. The social upheaval
that so horrified its Protestant burgher contemporaries actually
never went beyond a feeble, unconscious and premature attempt to
establish the bourgeois [*bürgerliche*] society of a later period.

Münzer himself seems to have sensed the chasm between his
theories and the surrounding realities, a chasm that he must have felt
the more keenly, the more his visionary aspirations were distorted in
the crude minds of his mass of followers. He devoted himself to
extending and organising the movement with a zeal rare even for
him. He wrote letters and sent messengers and emissaries in all
directions. His writings and sermons breathed a revolutionary fanaticism astonishing even when compared with his former works.
The naive youthful humour of Münzer's revolutionary[a] pamphlets
was totally gone. The placid explicative language of the thinker
typical of his earlier years was gone too. Münzer became a positive
prophet of the revolution. He untiringly fanned hatred against the
ruling classes, he stimulated the wildest passions, and used only the
forceful language that the religious and nationalist delirium had put
into the mouths of the Old Testament prophets. The style he now
had to adopt reflected the educational level of the public he sought
to influence.

The example of Mühlhausen and Münzer's propaganda had a rapid
and far-reaching effect. In *Thuringia, Eichsfeld,* the *Harz,* the *duchies
of Saxony,* in *Hesse* and *Fulda,* in *Upper Franconia* and in *Vogtland,* the
peasants arose, assembled in troops, and set fire to castles and
monasteries. Münzer was recognised as the leader of more or less the
entire movement, and Mühlhausen remained its centre, while a
purely burgher movement won in Erfurt and the ruling party there
kept acting ambiguously towards the peasants.

The princes in Thuringia were at first just as perplexed and
helpless against the peasants as they had been in Franconia and
Swabia. Only in the last days of April did the Landgrave of Hesse
succeed in assembling a corps. It was the same Landgrave Philip
whose piety is praised so much by the Protestant and bourgeois
histories of the Reformation, and of whose infamies against the

[a] The 1850 edition has "prerevolutionary" instead of "revolutionary".—*Ed.*

peasants we shall presently have a word to say. By a series of swift movements and decisive actions, Landgrave Philip quickly subdued the major part of his land, called up new contingents, and then marched into the region belonging to the Abbot of Fulda,[a] who had hitherto been his feudal lord. On May 3 he defeated the Fulda peasant troop at Frauenberg, subdued the whole land, and seized the opportunity not only for freeing himself from the sovereignty of the Abbot, but also for making the Abbey of Fulda a vassalage of Hesse, naturally pending its subsequent secularisation. He then took Eisenach and Langensalza, and advanced against Mühlhausen, the headquarters of the rebellion, jointly with the ducal Saxon troops. Münzer assembled his forces, comprising some 8,000 men and several cannon, at Frankenhausen. The Thuringian troop had little of the fighting power which a part of the Upper Swabian and Franconian troops had developed in their struggle with Truchsess. It was poorly armed and badly disciplined; it had few ex-soldiers in its ranks and lacked sorely in leadership. It appears Münzer himself had not the slightest military knowledge. All the same, the princes thought it best to use the same tactics against him that so often helped Truchsess to victory: breach of faith. They launched negotiations on May 16, concluded an armistice, and then suddenly attacked the peasants before the armistice had elapsed.

Münzer had stationed his people on a mountain still called Schlachtberg,[b] behind a barricade of wagons. Discouragement was spreading rapidly among his men. The princes promised them indulgence if they delivered Münzer alive. Münzer called a general assembly to debate the princes' proposals. A knight and a priest spoke in favour of surrender. Münzer had them both brought inside the circle and decapitated. This act of terrorist energy, jubilantly received by resolute revolutionaries, instilled a certain order among the troop, but most of the men would still have gone away without resistance had it not been noticed that the princes' mercenaries, who had encircled the mountain, were approaching in closed columns in spite of the armistice. A front was hurriedly formed behind the wagons, but already shells and bullets were showering upon the half-defenseless peasants unaccustomed to battle, and the mercenaries had reached the barricade. After a brief resistance the line of wagons was breached, the peasant cannon captured, and the peasants dispersed. They fled in wild disorder to fall into the hands

---

[a] Johann Henneberg.— *Ed.*
[b] Mount Battle.— *Ed.*

of the enveloping columns and the cavalry, who loosened an appalling massacre. Out of 8,000 peasants over 5,000 were slaughtered. The survivors went to Frankenhausen, and the princes' cavalry came hot on their heels. The city was captured. Münzer, wounded in the head, was discovered in a house and taken prisoner. On May 25 Mühlhausen also surrendered. Pfeifer, who had remained there, escaped, but was captured in the region of Eisenach.

Münzer was put on the rack in the presence of the princes, and then decapitated. He went to his death with the courage he had shown throughout his life. He was twenty-eight at the most when executed. Pfeifer was also beheaded, and many others besides. In Fulda Philip of Hesse, that holy man, opened his bloody court. He and the Saxon princes had many killed by the sword, among them in Eisenach, 24; in Langensalza, 41; after the battle of Frankenhausen, 300; in Mühlhausen, more than 100; at Görmar, 26; at Tüngeda, 50; at Sangerhausen, 12; in Leipzig, 8, not to speak of mutilations and more moderate measures, pillaging and burning of villages and towns.

Mühlhausen was compelled to give up its imperial liberty, and was incorporated in the Saxon lands just as the Abbey of Fulda was incorporated in the Landgraviate of Hesse.

The princes now marched through the forest of Thuringia, where Franconian peasants of the Bildhausen camp had joined the Thuringians and had burned many castles. A battle took place outside Meiningen. The peasants were beaten and withdrew towards the town, which suddenly closed its gates to them and threatened to attack them from the rear. Thrown into confusion by its allies' betrayal, the troop surrendered to the princes and ran off in all directions while the negotiations were still under way. The Bildhausen camp had long since dispersed, and after the troop's defeat the remaining insurgents in Saxony, Hesse, Thuringia and Upper Franconia were annihilated.

In *Alsace* the rebellion broke out later than on the right bank of the Rhine. The peasants of the Bishopric of Strassburg rose up as late as the middle of April. Soon after, there was an uprising of peasants in Upper Alsace and Sundgau. On April 18 a contingent of Lower Alsace peasants pillaged the monastery of Altdorf. Other troops formed near Ebersheim and Barr, as well as in the Willer and Urbis valleys. These soon amalgamated into a large Lower Alsace troop and seized towns and hamlets and destroyed monasteries. Everywhere, one out of every three men was called to serve in the troop. The troop's Twelve Articles were much more radical than those of the Swabians and Franconians.[340]

While early in May one column of Lower Alsatians concentrated near St. Hippolite and after a futile attempt to take that town occupied Bercken on May 10, Rappoltsweiler on May 13, and Reichenweier on May 14 by an understanding with their citizens, a second column under Erasmus Gerber moved in for a surprise attack on Strassburg. The attempt failed, and the column now turned towards the Vosges, destroyed the monastery of Mauersmünster and besieged Zabern, which surrendered on May 13. From here it moved towards the Lorraine frontier and roused the adjacent section of the duchy, and at the same time fortified the mountain passes. Big camps were formed at Herbitzheim on the Saar and at Neuburg. Nearly 4,000 German-Lorraine peasants entrenched themselves at Saargemünd. Finally, two advanced troops, the Kolben troop in the Vosges at Stürzelbronn and the Kleeburg troop at Weissenburg, covered the front and the right flank, while the left flank hugged the Upper Alsatians.

The latter, on the march since April 20, had forced Sulz into the peasant brotherhood on May 10, Gebweiler on May 12, and Sennheim and its vicinity on May 15. Though the Austrian Government and the surrounding imperial towns lost no time to join forces against them, they were too weak to offer serious resistance, not to speak of attacking. Thus, the whole of Alsace, with the exception of a few towns, fell into the hands of the insurgents by the middle of May.

But the army that was to break the mischievous spirit of the Alsatians was already approaching. It was the *French* who here restored the power of the nobility. On May 6 Duke Anton of Lorraine marched with an army of 30,000, among them the flower of the French nobility and Spanish, Piedmontese, Lombardic, Greek and Albanian auxiliaries. On May 16 at Lützelstein he engaged 4,000 peasants, whom he defeated without effort, and on May 17 he forced Zabern, which was occupied by the peasants, to surrender. But even while the Lorrainers were entering the city and the peasants were being disarmed, the terms of the surrender were violated. The defenseless peasants were attacked by the mercenaries and most of them slain. The remaining Lower Alsace columns disbanded, and Duke Anton marched on to engage the Upper Alsatians. The latter, who had refused to reinforce the Lower Alsatians at Zabern, were now attacked at Scherweiler by the entire force of Lorrainers. They put up a plucky fight, but the enormous numerical superiority of 30,000 against 7,000, and betrayal by a number of knights, especially that of the magistrate of Reichenweier, reduced their daring to nought. They were beaten and dispersed to the last man. The Duke now proceeded to subdue the whole of Alsace with the usual cruelty. Only Sundgau was spared his presence. By threatening to call him into the land, the Austrian Government persuaded the peasants to conclude the Ensisheim agreement early in June. But it broke the agreement very soon and hanged the preachers and leaders of the movement *en masse.* The peasants rebelled anew, and Sundgau was finally drawn into the Offenburg agreement (September 18).

Now it only remains to describe the Peasant War in the *Alpine regions of Austria.* These regions and the adjoining *Archbishopric of Salzburg* had been in continuous opposition to the government and the nobility since the *Stara Prawa.*[a] As a result, the Reformation doctrines found a fertile soil there. Religious persecution and arbitrary oppressive taxation precipitated a rebellion.

The city of *Salzburg,* supported by peasants and pitmen, had been in conflict with the Archbishop[b] since 1522 over its city privileges and religious practices. Late in 1524 the Archbishop attacked the city with recruited mercenaries, terrorised it with the cannon of the castle, and persecuted the heretical preachers. At the same time he imposed new crushing taxes and thereby irritated the population to the extreme. In the spring of 1525, simultaneously with the Swabian-Franconian and Thuringian uprisings, the peasants and pitmen of the whole country suddenly rose up in arms, organised under the commanders *Prassler* and *Weitmoser,* liberated the city and besieged the castle of Salzburg. Like the West-German peasants, they organised a Christian Alliance and formulated their demands in articles, of which they had fourteen.[341]

In *Styria, Upper Austria, Carinthia* and *Carniola,* where new extortionate taxes, duties and edicts had severely injured the basic interests of the people, the peasants rose up in the spring of 1525. They took a number of castles and at Goyss defeated Dietrichstein, the old field commander and conqueror of the *Stara Prawa.* Although the government succeeded in placating some of the insurgents with false promises, the bulk of them stayed together and united with the Salzburg peasants, so that the entire region of Salzburg and the bigger portion of Upper Austria, Styria, Carinthia and Carniola were in the hands of the peasants and pitmen.

In Tirol the Reformation doctrines had also found numerous adherents. Münzer's emissaries had been successfully active here, even more so than in the other Alpine regions of Austria. As elsewhere, Archduke Ferdinand persecuted the preachers of the

---

[a] See this volume, p. 4⁊0.— *Ed.*
[b] Matthäus Lang.— *Ed.*

new doctrine and impinged on the rights of the population by means of new arbitrary financial regulations. The result, as everywhere, was an uprising that broke out in the spring of 1525. The insurgents commanded by Geismaier, a Münzer man who was the only one of the peasant chiefs to possess any military talent, took a great number of castles, and carried on energetically against the priests, particularly in the South, in the Etsch^a region. The Vorarlberg peasants also rose up and joined the Allgäu peasants.

The Archduke, hard pressed from all sides, now began to make concession after concession to the rebels whom a short time before he had wished to annihilate by fire and destruction, plunder and carnage. He summoned the Diets of the hereditary lands and pending their opening concluded an armistice with the peasants. In the meantime he was arming for all he was worth, in order to be able to speak to the blasphemers in a different tongue in the nearest possible future.

Naturally, the armistice was not observed for long. Having run short of cash, Dietrichstein began to levy contributions in the duchies; besides, his Slavic and Magyar troops indulged in the most disgraceful brutalities against the population. This incited the Styrians to a new revolt. The peasants attacked Dietrichstein at Schladming in the night of July 3, and slaughtered everybody who did not speak German. Dietrichstein himself was captured. In the morning of July 3 the peasants called a jury and sentenced to death forty Czech and Croatian nobles among their prisoners. They were beheaded on the spot. That had its effect; the Archduke immediately consented to all the demands of the estates of the five duchies (Upper and Lower Austria, Styria, Carinthia and Carniola).

The demands of the Diet were also granted in Tirol, and thus the North was pacified. The South, however, stood firm on its original demands, scorning the much more moderate decisions of the Diet, and remained under arms. Only in December was the Archduke able to restore order by force. He did not fail to execute a great number of the instigators and leaders of the upheaval who fell into his hands.

Ten thousand Bavarians moved in August against Salzburg under Georg von Frundsberg. This impressive show of strength and the quarrels that broke out in their ranks persuaded the Salzburg peasants to conclude an agreement with the archbishop on September 1, which was also accepted by the Archduke. However, the two princes, who had meanwhile considerably strengthened their troops, soon violated the agreement and thereby compelled the

---

^a The Italian name is Adige.— *Ed.*

Salzburg peasants to start a new uprising. The insurgents held their own throughout the winter. In the spring Geismaier came to them and launched a splendid campaign against the forces approaching from every side. In a series of brilliant battles in May and June 1526, he successively defeated the Bavarian, Austrian and Swabian League troops and the mercenaries of the Archbishop of Salzburg, and for a long time prevented the various corps from uniting. He also found time to besiege Radstadt. Surrounded finally by superior forces, he was compelled to withdraw and fought his way out of the encirclement, leading the remnants of his troop across the Austrian Alps into Venetian territory. The Republic of Venice and Switzerland served the indefatigable peasant chief as starting points for new intrigues. For a whole year he endeavoured to involve them in a war with Austria, which would have given him an opportunity to begin a new peasant uprising. The hand of an assassin struck him down, however, in the course of these negotiations. Archduke Ferdinand and the Archbishop of Salzburg could not rest as long as Geismaier was alive. They hired an assassin who succeeded in ending the life of the dangerous rebel in 1527.[a]

---

[a] According to more precise data Geismaier was assassinated on April 15, 1532.—Ed.

The epilogue of the Peasant War closed with Geismaier's withdrawal into Venetian territory. The peasants were everywhere brought back under the sway of their ecclesiastical, noble or patrician overlords. The agreements concluded with them here and there were violated and the heavy services augmented by the enormous indemnities imposed by the victors on the vanquished. The most magnificent revolutionary effort of the German people ended in ignominious defeat and, for the time being, in redoubled oppression. In the long run, however, the situation of the peasants was not made any worse by the suppression of the uprising. Whatever the nobility, princes and priests could wring out of the peasants year after year, had been wrung out even before the war. The German peasant of that time has this in common with the present-day proletarian, that his share in the products of his labour was limited to a subsistence minimum necessary for his maintenance and the propagation of the peasant race. On the whole, nothing more could be wrung out of the peasants. True, some of the better-off middle peasants were ruined, hosts of bondsmen were forced into serfdom, whole stretches of community land were confiscated, and a great many peasants were forced into vagabondage or became city plebeians due to the destruction of their homes, the devastation of their fields and the general dislocation. But war and devastation were everyday phenomena at that time and, in general, the peasant class was at too low a level for increased taxation to cause any lasting deterioration of its condition. The subsequent religious wars and, finally, the Thirty Years' War [342] with its recurrent general devastation and depopulation affected the peasants much more painfully than the Peasant War. Notably, it was the Thirty Years' War which destroyed the most important part of the productive forces in agriculture, through which, as well as through the simultaneous destruction of many towns, the peasants, plebeians and ruined burghers were for a long time reduced to a state of Irish misery at its worst.

Those who suffered most from the Peasant War were the *clergy*. Their monasteries and endowments were burned, their treasures plundered, sold abroad or melted down, and their stores consumed. They were everywhere the least capable of resistance, and yet they were the main target of the people's wrath. The other estates— princes, nobles and burghers—even experienced a secret joy at the distress of the hated prelates. The Peasant War had made popular the idea of secularising the church estates in favour of the peasants. The lay princes, and partly the towns, determined to secularise the estates for their *own* benefit, and soon the possessions of the prelates in Protestant regions were in the hands of the princes or the honourables. But the power of the ecclesiastical princes, too, was impaired, and the lay princes knew how to exploit the people's hatred in this respect. We have seen, for instance, how the Abbot of Fulda[a] was relegated from feudal lord to vassal of Philip of Hesse. The town of Kempten forced its prince-abbot[b] to sell it a number of the precious privileges he had enjoyed in the town for a ridiculous trifle.

The *nobility* had also suffered considerably. Most of the noble-men's castles were destroyed and some of the most respected families were ruined and found a living only in the employ of the princes. Their weakness in face of the peasantry had been proved. They had been beaten everywhere and had been forced to surrender. Only the armies of the princes had saved them. The nobility was bound to lose more and more of its significance as an estate of the Empire, and to fall under the dominion of the princes.

The *towns*, too, generally gained nothing from the Peasant War. The rule of the honourables was almost everywhere re-established; the burgher opposition was broken for a long time. The old patrician routine dragged on in this way, tying up commerce and industry hand and foot up to the time of the French Revolution. Moreover, the towns were made responsible by the princes for the momentary successes the burgher or plebeian parties had gained within their borders during the struggle. The towns that had even previously belonged to princely estates had to pay heavy indemnities, to give up their privileges, and became defenceless prey to the avarice and

---

[a] Johann Henneberg.— *Ed.*
[b] Sebastian von Breitenstein.— *Ed.*

whims of the princes (Frankenhausen, Arnstadt, Schmalkalden, Würzburg, etc.). Towns of the Empire were incorporated into the territories of the princes (Mühlhausen, for example) or at least made morally dependent on the neighbouring princes, as was the case with many imperial towns in Franconia.

Under the circumstances, the *princes* alone had benefited from the Peasant War. We have seen at the very beginning of our account that the deficient development of industry, commerce and agriculture in Germany ruled out any centralisation of Germans into a *nation*, that it allowed only local and provincial centralisation, and that the princes, representatives of centralisation within disruption, were the only estate to profit from all the changes in the existing social and political conditions. The development of Germany in those days was at so low a level and at the same time so dissimilar in the various provinces that alongside the lay principalities there could still exist ecclesiastical sovereignties, city republics, and sovereign counts and barons. Simultaneously, however, this development was continually, though slowly and feebly, pressing for *provincial* centralisation, i.e. for the subordination of all the other imperial estates to the princes. That is why only the princes could have gained from the outcome of the Peasant War. And that is exactly what had happened. They gained not only relatively, from a weakening of their opponents—the clergy, nobility and the towns—but also absolutely, since they carried off the *spolia opima* (the main spoils) of all the other estates. The church estates were secularised in their favour; part of the nobility, fully or partly ruined, was obliged gradually to accept vassalage; the indemnities they received from the towns and peasant communities swelled their treasuries and, furthermore, the abolition of so many town privileges now afforded much greater scope to their favourite financial operations.

The chief result of the Peasant War, the deepening and consolidation of German disunity, was also the reason for its failure.

We have seen that Germany was split not only into countless independent, almost totally alien provinces, but that in every one of these provinces the nation was broken up into a multifold structure of estates and fractions of estates. Besides princes and priests we find nobles and peasants in the countryside, and in the towns we find patricians, burghers and plebeians, whose interests as estates differed radically even where they did not cross each other or come into conflict. Besides all these complicated interests there were still the interests of the Emperor and the Pope. We have seen how ponderously, imperfectly, and how differently in the various localities, all these interests finally gave shape to three major groups.

We have seen that in spite of this painful grouping each estate opposed the line indicated by circumstances for the national development, that each estate acted on its own, coming into conflict not only with all the conservative, but also with the other opposition estates, and that it was bound to fail in the end. That was the fate of the nobility in Sickingen's uprising, of the peasants in the Peasant War, and of the burghers in all of their insipid Reformation. Thus, even the peasants and plebeians in most parts of Germany failed to unite for joint action and stood in each other's way. We have also seen the causes of this fragmentation of the class struggle and the resulting total defeat of the revolutionary and partial defeat of the burgher movements.

How local and provincial disunity and the consequently inevitable local and provincial narrow-mindedness ruined the whole movement; how neither burghers, peasants nor plebeians could unite for concerted national action; how the peasants of every province acted only for themselves, as a rule refusing aid to the insurgent peasants of the neighbouring regions, and were consequently annihilated in separate battles one after another by armies which in most cases were hardly one-tenth the total number of the insurgent masses—all this should be sufficiently clear from this account. The various armistices and agreements concluded by individual troops with their adversaries represent just as many acts of betrayal of the common cause, and the fact that the only co-operation possible between the different troops was not according to the greater or lesser unity of their action, but to that of the particular enemy to whom they succumbed, is the most striking proof of the degree of the peasants' mutual alienation in the various provinces.

Here also the analogy with the movement of 1848-50 leaps to the eye. In 1848 as well, the interests of the opposition classes conflicted and each class acted on its own. The bourgeoisie, too developed to suffer any longer the feudal and bureaucratic absolutism, was, however, not as yet powerful enough at once to subordinate the claims of other classes to its own interests. The proletariat, much too weak to count on a rapid passage through the bourgeois period and on an early conquest of power, had already learned too well under absolutism the honeyed sweetness of the bourgeois regime and was generally much too developed to identify for even a moment its own emancipation with that of the bourgeoisie. The mass of the nation—petty burghers, their associates (artisans), and peasants—was left in the lurch by its as yet natural ally, the bourgeoisie, because it was too revolutionary, and partly by the proletariat, because it was not sufficiently advanced.

Divided against itself the mass achieved nothing and opposed fellow opponents on the Right and Left. As to provincial narrow-mindedness, it could hardly have been greater among the peasants in 1525 than it was among the classes participating in the movement of 1848. The hundred local revolutions as well as the consequent and unhindered hundred local reactions, survival of the separation of numerous small states, etc., etc.—all this is eloquent testimony indeed. *He who still dreams of a federated republic after the two German revolutions of 1525 and 1848 and their results, belongs nowhere else but in a lunatic asylum.*

Still the two revolutions, that of the sixteenth century and that of 1848-50, are, in spite of all analogies, essentially different. The Revolution of 1848 speaks for the progress of Europe, if not of Germany.

Who profited from the Revolution of 1525? The *princes.* Who profited from the Revolution of 1848? The *big* princes, Austria and Prussia. Behind the minor princes of 1525 stood the petty burghers, who chained the princes to themselves by taxes. Behind the big princes of 1850, behind Austria and Prussia, there stand the modern big bourgeois, rapidly getting them under their yoke by means of the national debt. And behind the big bourgeois stand the proletarians.

The Revolution of 1525 was a domestic German affair. The English, French, Bohemians and Hungarians had already had their peasant wars when the Germans began theirs. If Germany was disunited, Europe was much more so. The Revolution of 1848, on the other hand, was not a domestic German affair, and was an episode in a great European event. Its motive forces throughout its duration transcended the narrow limits of one country and even those of one part of the world. In fact, the countries which were the arena of revolution were the least active in producing it. They were more or less unconscious and hesitant raw material, moulded in the course of the movement in which the entire world participates today, a movement which under the existing social conditions may appear to us only as an alien power but which, in the end, is nothing but our own. This is why the Revolution of 1848-50 cannot end like the Revolution of 1525.

THE TWELVE ARTICLES OF THE PEASANTS

Handlung, Artickel, vnnd Instruction, so fürgenommen worden sein vonn allen Rottenn vnnd hauffen der Pauren, so sich besamen verpflicht haben: M: D: xxv:

TITLE PAGE OF THE
TWELVE ARTICLES

THE TWELVE ARTICLES OF THE PEASANTS*

THE fundamental and correct chief articles of all the peasants and of those subject to ecclesiastical lords, relating to these matters in which they feel themselves aggrieved.

M cccc, quadratum, lx et duplicatum
V cum transibit, christiana secta peribit.

Peace to the Christian Reader and the Grace of God through Christ.

There are many evil writings put forth of late which take occasion, on account of the assembling of the peasants, to cast scorn upon the gospel, saying: Is this the fruit of the new teaching, that no one should obey but all should everywhere rise in revolt and rush together to reform or perhaps destroy altogether the authorities, both ecclesiastic and lay? The articles below shall answer these godless and criminal fault-finders, and serve in the first place to remove the reproach from the word of God, and in the second place to give a Christian excuse for the disobedience or even the revolt of the entire Peasantry. In the first place the Gospel is not the cause of revolt and disorder, since it is the message of Christ, the promised Messiah, the Word of Life, teaching only love, peace, patience and concord. Thus, all who believe in Christ should learn to be loving, peaceful, long-suffering and harmonious. This is the foundation of all the articles of the peasants (as will be seen) who accept the Gospel and live according to it. How then can the evil reports declare the Gospel to be a cause of revolt and disobedience? That the authors of the evil reports and the enemies of the Gospel oppose themselves to these demands is due, not to the Gospel, but to the Devil, the worst enemy of the Gospel, who causes this opposition by raising doubts in the minds of his followers, and thus the word of God, which teaches love, peace and concord, is overcome. In the second place, it is clear that the peasants demand that this Gospel be taught them as a guide in life and they ought not to be called disobedient or disorderly. Whether God grant the peasants (earnestly wishing to live according to His word) their requests or no, who shall find fault with the will of the Most High? Who shall meddle in His judgments or oppose his majesty? Did he not hear the children of Israel when they called

* *Translations and Reprints from the Original Sources of European History*, Vol. II, published by the Department of History, University of Pennsylvania.

upon Him and saved them out of the hands of Pharaoh? Can He not save His own to-day? Yes, He will save them and that speedily. Therefore, Christian reader, read the following articles with care and then judge. Here follow the articles:

The First Article.—First, it is our humble petition and desire, as also our will and resolution, that in the future we should have power and authority so that each community should choose and appoint a pastor, and that we should have the right to depose him should he conduct himself improperly. The pastor thus chosen should teach us the Gospel pure and simple, without any addition, doctrine or ordinance of man. For to teach us continually the true faith will lead us to pray God that through His grace this faith may increase within us and become part of us. For if His grace work not within us we remain flesh and blood, which availeth nothing; since the Scripture clearly teaches that only through true faith can we come to God. Only through His mercy can we become holy. Hence such a guide and pastor is necessary and in this fashion grounded upon the Scriptures.

The Second Article.—According as the just tithe is established by the Old Testament and fulfilled in the New, we are ready and willing to pay the fair tithe of grain. The word of God plainly provided that in giving according to right to God and distributing to His people the services of a pastor are required. We will that, for the future, our church provost, whomsoever the community may appoint, shall gather and receive this tithe. From this he shall give to the pastor, elected by the whole community, a decent and sufficient maintenance for him and his, as shall seem right to the whole community (or, with the knowledge of the community). What remains over shall be given to the poor of the place, as the circumstances and the general opinion demand. Should anything farther remain, let it be kept, lest any one should have to leave the country from poverty. Provision should also be made from this surplus to avoid laying any land tax on the poor. In case one or more villages themselves have sold their tithes on account of want, and each village has taken action as a whole, the buyer should not suffer loss, but we will that some proper agreement be reached with him for the repayment of the sum by the village with due interest. But those who have tithes which they have not purchased from a village, but which were appropriated by their ancestors, should not, and ought not, to be paid anything farther by the village which shall apply its tithes to the support of the pastors elected as above indicated, or to solace the poor as is taught by the Scriptures. The small tithes, whether ecclesiastical or lay, we will not pay at all, for the Lord God created cattle for the free use of man. We will not, therefore, pay farther an unseemly tithe which is of man's invention.

The Third Article.—It has been the custom hitherto for men to hold us as their own property, which is pitiable enough, considering that Christ has delivered and redeemed us all, without exception, by the shedding of His precious blood, the lowly as well as the great. Accordingly, it is consistent with Scripture that we should be free and wish to be so. Not that we would wish to be absolutely free and under no authority. God does not teach us that we should lead a disorderly life in the lusts of the flesh, but that we should love the Lord our God and our neighbour. We would gladly observe all this as God has commanded us in the celebration of the communion. He has not commanded us not to obey the authorities, but rather that we should be humble, not only towards those in authority, but towards every one. We are thus ready to yield obedience according to God's law to our elected and regular authorities in all proper things becoming to a Christian. We, therefore, take it for granted that you will release us from serfdom as true Christians, unless it should be shown us from the Gospel that we are serfs.

The Fourth Article.—In the fourth place it has been the custom heretofore, that no poor man should be allowed to catch venison or wild fowl or fish in flowing water, which seems to us quite unseemly and unbrotherly as well as selfish and not agreeable to the word of God. In some places the authorities preserve the game to our great annoyance and loss, recklessly permitting the unreasoning animals to destroy to no purpose our crops which God suffers to grow for the use of man, and yet we must remain quiet. This is neither godly or neighbourly. For when God created man he gave him dominion over all the animals, over the birds of the air and over the fish in the water. Accordingly it is our desire if a man holds possession of waters that he should prove from satisfactory documents that his right has been unwittingly acquired by purchase. We do not wish to take it from him by force, but his rights should be exercised in a Christian and brotherly fashion. But whosoever cannot produce such evidence should surrender his claim with good grace.

The Fifth Article.—In the fifth place we are aggrieved in the matter of wood-cutting, for the noble folk have appropriated all the woods to themselves alone. If a poor man requires wood he must pay double for it (or, perhaps, two pieces of money). It is our opinion in regard to a wood which has fallen into the hands of a lord whether spiritual or temporal, that unless it was duly purchased it should revert again to the community. It should, moreover, be free to every member of the community to help himself to such fire-wood as he needs in his home. Also, if a man requires wood for carpenter's purposes he should have it free, but with the knowledge of a person appointed by the community for that purpose. Should, however, no such forest be at the disposal of the community let that which has been duly bought be administered in a brotherly and Christian manner. If the forest, although unfairly appropriated in the first instance, was later duly sold let the matter be adjusted in a friendly spirit and according to the Scriptures.

The Sixth Article.—Our sixth complaint is in regard to the excessive services demanded of us which are increased from day to day. We ask that this matter be properly looked into so that we shall not continue to be oppressed in this way, but that some gracious consideration be given us, since our fore-fathers were required only to serve according to the word of God.

The Seventh Article,—Seventh, we will not hereafter allow ourselves to be farther oppressed by our lords, but will let them demand only what is just and proper according to the word of the agreement between the lord and the peasant. The lord should no longer try to force more services or other dues from the peasant without payment, but permit the peasant to enjoy his hold-ing in peace and quiet. The peasant should, however, help the lord when it is necessary, and at proper times when it will not be disadvantageous to the peasant and for a suitable payment.

The Eighth Article.—In the eighth place, we are greatly burdened by holdings which cannot support the rent exacted from them. The peasants suf-fer loss in this way and are ruined, and we ask that the lords may appoint persons of honour to inspect these holdings, and fix a rent in accordance with justice, so that the peasants shall not work for nothing, since the labourer is worthy of his hire.

The Ninth Article.—In the ninth place, we are burdened with a great evil in the constant making of new laws. We are not judged according to the offense, but sometimes with great ill will, and sometimes much too lenient-ly. In our opinion we should be judged according to the old written law so that the case shall be decided according to its merits, and not with partiality.

The Tenth Article.—In the tenth place, we are aggrieved by the appropri-ation by individuals of meadows and fields which at one time belonged to a community. These we will take again into our own hands. It may, however, happen that the land was rightfully purchased. When, however, the land has unfortunately been purchased in this way, some brotherly arrangement should be made according to circumstances.

The Eleventh Article.—In the eleventh place we will entirely abolish the due called *Todfall* (that is, heriot) and will no longer endure it, nor allow widows and orphans to be thus shamefully robbed against God's will, and in violation of justice and right, as has been done in many places, and by those who should shield and protect them. These have disgraced and despoiled us, and although they had little authority they assumed it. God will suffer this no more, but it shall be wholly done away with, and for the future no man shall be bound to give little or much.

Conclusion.—In the twelfth place it is our conclusion and final resolu-tion, that if any one or more of the articles here set forth should not be in agreement with the word of God, as we think they are, such article we will willingly recede from when it is proved really to be against the word of God by a clear explanation of the Scripture. Or if articles should now be conced-ed to us that are hereafter discovered to be unjust, from that hour they shall be dead and null and without force. Likewise, if more complaints should be discovered which are based upon truth and the Scriptures and relate to offenses against God and our neighbour, we have determined to reserve the right to present these also, and to exercise ourselves in all Christian teaching. For this we shall pray God, since He can grant these, and He alone. The peace of Christ abide with us all.

REVENGE OF THE PRINCES
Trial, Sentence and Execution

NOTES
AND
INDEX

NOTES

Preface

[129] The *extreme Left* was one of the two factions of the Left wing of the Frankfurt National Assembly during the revolution of 1848-49 in Germany. The extreme Left, known as the radical-democratic party, mainly represented the petty bourgeoisie, but was nevertheless supported by a section of the German workers. The extreme Left vacillated and took a half-way position on the basic problems of the German revolution—abolition of the remnants of feudalism and unification of the country. Engels described the position of the petty bourgeoisie in the revolution of 1848-49 in his works, *The Campaign for the German Imperial Constitution* and *The Peasant War in Germany*

[130] This refers to Marx's works: *The Class Struggles in France, 1848 to 1850*, consisting of a series of articles written between January and October 1850 specially for the *Neue Rheinische Zeitung. Politisch-ökonomische Revue* and published in it under the general title "1848-1849" (see present edition, Vol. 10), and *The Eighteenth Brumaire of Louis Bonaparte*, written between December 1851 and March 1852

[131] On May 15, 1860, the Prussian Chamber of Deputies voted, at the Government's demand, for the allocation of 9,000,000 talers to the War Ministry till June 30, 1861 "for the temporary maintenance of the army in fighting trim and for the increase of its military might". The results of the voting (315 for, 2 against and 5 abstaining) showed that the Prussian bourgeoisie had in fact given in to the government over the reorganisation of the army.

[132] The *National-Liberals*—members of the party formed by the German, principally Prussian, bourgeoisie in the autumn of 1866 after a split in the Party of Progress. Their policy showed that a considerable part of the liberal bourgeoisie had abandoned its claims to extend its political prerogatives and had capitulated to Bismarck's Junker government as a result of Prussia's victory in the Austro-Prussian war and the establishment of her supremacy in Germany.

[133] Engels refers to the Austro-Prussian war of 1866 which wound up the long rivalry between Austria and Prussia and predetermined the unification of Germany under the supremacy of Prussia. Several German states—including Hanover, Saxony, Bavaria, Württemberg and Baden—fought on Austria's side. Prussia formed an alliance with Italy. After a serious defeat at Sadowa on July 3 Austria began peace negotiations and signed a treaty in Prague on August 23. Austria conceded Schleswig and Holstein to Prussia, paid small indemnities to her and gave the province of Venetia to Italy. The German Confederation, which was founded in 1815 by decision of the Vienna Congress and embraced over 30 German states, ceased to exist, and North German Confederation was founded in its place under Prussia's supremacy

Austria, Bavaria, Baden, Württemberg, Hesse-Darmstadt remained outside the Confederation. As a result of the war, Prussia annexed the Kingdom of Hanover, the Electorate of Hesse-Cassel, the Grand Duchy of Nassau and the free city of Frankfurt am Main. (On the events of the Austro-Prussian war see Engels' "Notes on the War in Germany", present edition, Vol. 20).

[134] In the German original the term *Haupt- und Staatsaktionen* (principal and spectacular actions) is used; this has several meanings. In the seventeenth and the first half of the eighteenth century, it denoted plays performed by German touring companies. The plays, which were rather formless, presented tragic historical events in a bombastic and at the same time coarse and farcical manner.

     Secondly, this term can denote major political events. It was used in this sense by a trend in German historical science known as "objective historiography". Leopold Ranke was one of its chief representatives. He regarded *Haupt- und Staatsaktionen* as the main subject-matter to be set forth. Objective historiography, which was primarily interested in the political and diplomatic history of nations, proclaimed the pre-eminence of foreign politics over domestic politics and disregarded the social relations of men and their active role in history.

135 Engels refers to the Kingdom of Hanover, the Electorate of Hesse-Cassel and the Grand Duchy of Nassau annexed by Prussia following the Austro-Prussian war of 1866.

136 Engels refers to what is known as Trans-Leithania

137 The *German People's Party* (Deutsche Volkspartei) was set up in 1865 and consisted of democratic elements of the petty bourgeoisie and partly of representatives of the bourgeoisie, chiefly from South-German states. As distinct from the National-Liberals (see Note 132), the People's Party was against Prussia's supremacy in Germany and advocated the plan of the so-called Great Germany uniting both Prussia and Austria. While pursuing an anti-Prussian policy and advancing general democratic slogans, the People's Party at the same time voiced the particularist aspirations of some German states. It was against Germany's unification as a single centralised democratic republic, advocating the idea of a federative German state.

     In 1866 the Saxon People's Party, whose nucleus consisted of workers, joined the German People's Party. This Left wing of the German People's Party had, in effect, nothing in common with it except anti-Prussian sentiments and the desire jointly to solve the problems of Germany's national unification in a democratic way; it subsequently developed along socialist lines. The main section of the Party split away from the petty-bourgeois democrats and took part in founding the Social-Democratic Workers' Party in August 1869.

138 In the 1860s a number of finance reforms in the interests of the bourgeoisie were carried out in the North German Confederation. In 1867 passports were abolished and freedom of movement and domicile established; in 1868 the system of uniform measures and weights was introduced and the trading code of the Customs Union extended to cover the entire territory of the Confederation. All these reforms undoubtedly facilitated the development of industry and the formation of the German nation.

     However, medieval guild regulations in Prussia during the mid-1860s was a great hindrance to the development of capitalism in Germany. In conformity with the bureaucratic system of regulating industry, there were branches in which no one could engage in business without a special license (concession). Only the Regulations of June 21, 1869 abolished the last remnants of guild privileges, and the law of June 11, 1870 provided for the establishment of joint-stock companies without preliminary permission.

139 The Basle Congress of the International adopted, on September 10, 1869, the following resolution on landed property proposed by Marx's followers:

     "1. That Society has the right to abolish private property in land, and convert it into common property.

     "2. That it is necessary to abolish private property in land, and convert it into common property."

Peasant War in Germany

²⁹⁴ Engels wrote *The Peasant War in Germany* in London in the summer and autumn of 1850. It was published in the double issue of the *Neue Rheinische Zeitung. Politisch-ökonomische Revue* (No. 5-6). In this momentous work the author generalises the experience of the 1848-49 revolution in Germany by comparing it with the revolutionary events of the period of the Reformation and the Great Peasant War of 1525. It is also one of the principal Marxist works on the liberation struggle led by the peasant and plebeian masses.

Engels' main source of facts was the book *Allgemeine Geschichte des grossen Bauernkrieges*, Th. 1-3, Stuttgart, 1841-43, by Wilhelm Zimmermann, a German democratic historian. In 1870 Engels wrote that for a long time this book had been "the best compilation of factual data". He found it an extremely useful large collection of documents, either quoted in full or in long excerpts. Engels thus quoted most original sources (Luther's writings, Münzer's pamphlets, leaflets listing the demands of the insurgent peasants) from Zimmermann's book. (In the footnotes and the Index of Quoted and Mentioned Literature, the editors of this volume supply bibliographical data on the first editions of the quoted material in the transcription of the time and indicate the pages of Zimmermann's book from which the quotations are taken.)

The Peasant War in Germany appeared repeatedly during Engels' lifetime. It was reprinted in the *Turn-Zeitung*, New York, Nos. 3-20 (January 1852-February 1853). In 1870, Engels and Wilhelm Liebknecht prepared the second edition of *The Peasant War*, originally as a reprint in the 29 numbers of *Der Volksstaat*, Leipzig (April 2-October 15, Nos. 27-83, at irregular intervals). Numbers 27 and 28 of the newspaper carried Engels' February 1870 Preface to this edition. Engels was not satisfied with the explanatory footnotes by Liebknecht (see Engels' letter to Marx of May 8, 1870).

In October 1870 this work was published in book form—*Der deutsche Bauernkrieg* von Friedrich Engels. Zweiter, mit einer Einleitung versehener Abdruck, Leipzig, Verlag der Expedition des *Volksstaat*, 1870.

A new, third, authorised edition came out in 1875: *Der deutsche Bauernkrieg* von Friedrich Engels. Dritter Abdruck, Leipzig, 1875. For this edition Engels wrote a special addendum to the 1870 Preface, dated July 1, 1874.

In the 1880s Engels intended to revise his *Peasant War in Germany* and incorporate extensive supplementary material on the history of Germany. In his letter to Sorge dated December 31, 1884, Engels wrote: "I am radically revising my *Peasant War*. The war of the peasants will be presented as the cornerstone of German history in its entirety." Work on the second and third volumes of *Capital* and other urgent matters prevented Engels from carrying out his intentions. In the 1890s he made another attempt at the supplement, but failed to complete it. Only an unfinished manuscript and several rough notes are extant. (The former was published under the editorial heading "Decay of Feudalism and Rise of National States".)

In this edition sources are quoted in the form given by Engels; whenever he introduces his own italics, this is mentioned in a footnote. Where the meaning differs significantly from that of the last authorised edition of 1875 and the previous author's publications of 1850 and 1870, this is also indicated in footnotes. Account is also taken in this edition of corrections made by Engels in his copy of the *Neue Rheinische Zeitung. Politisch-ökonomische Revue* .

[295] The *Hanseatic League*—a commercial and political alliance of medieval German towns along the southern coasts of the North and Baltic Seas, and their feed rivers; its aim was to establish a trade monopoly in Northern Europe. The Hanseatic League was in its prime in the latter half of the fourteenth century and the early half of the fifteenth century, and began to decay at the end of the fifteenth century.

[296] *Tributes*—one of the feudal obligations imposed on the holders of small plots of land.

Death taxes (*Sterbefall, Todfall*) were levied on the land and property inherited from the deceased peasant on the basis of the feudal lord's right (in France, "the right of the dead hand"). In Germany the feudal lords usually took the best cattle.

Protection moneys (*Schutzgelder*)—a tax levied by the feudal lord in payment for the "judicial protection" and "patronage" which he claimed to extend to his subjects.

[297] The "*general pfennig*" (*der gemeine Pfennig*)—a tax collected in German lands in the fifteenth and sixteenth centuries and appropriated by the Emperor; it was a combination of a poll-tax and a property tax, the main burden of which fell on the peasantry.

[298] *Annates* were lump sums paid to the Pope by persons appointed to church offices. In the fourteenth century they equalled half the first year's income or more. Holders of church benefices made up this loss by levying additional taxes and by extortions from the population.

[299] Engels is alluding to the German liberals who were in the majority in the Frankfurt National Assembly and in the assemblies of some German states during the revolution of 1848-49. In the first months of the revolution, liberals headed "constitutional governments" in a number of states (Prussia, for example), but were later replaced by members of the bureaucracy and nobility. The conciliatory tactics of the liberals were one of the chief reasons for the defeat of the German revolution.

[300] The reference is to Charles V's criminal statutes (*Constitutio criminalis carolina*), adopted by the Imperial Diet in Regensburg in 1532; the statutes prescribed extremely harsh punishments.

[301] The reference is to a religious philosophical doctrine opposed to the medieval Catholic Church and its orthodox teaching; mysticism was widespread in the twelfth and thirteenth centuries. Mystics, who believed it possible to know God through direct intercourse with the divine spirit, undermined the faith in the need for a church hierarchy. Particularly radical ideas were preached by the Italian twelfth-century monk Joachim of Calabria and other plebeian and peasant ideologists, with whom they assumed the form of a chiliastic dream of a millennium of equality (see Note 308).

[302] The *Waldenses*—a religious sect that originated among the urban lower classes of Southern France at the end of the twelfth century and later spread to Northern Italy, Germany, Bohemia, Spain and Switzerland. Its founder is said to have been Petrus Waldus (or Peter Waldo), a Lyons merchant who gave his wealth to the poor. The Waldenses repudiated property and advocated insubordination to the ecclesiastical and secular authorities; they condemned the accumulation of wealth by the Catholic Church and called for a return to the customs of early Christianity. Among the backward rural population of the mountainous regions of South-Western Switzerland and Savoy, the heresy of the Waldenses amounted to a defence of the survivals of the primitive communal system and patriarchal relations.

303 The *Albigenses*—a religious sect that existed in the twelfth and thirteenth centuries in the towns of Southern France (particularly in Provence and Toulouse) and in Northern Italy. This movement took the form of a "heresy", being directed against the power and doctrine of the Catholic Church, as well as against the secular power of the feudal state. Its adherents—the townspeople and the lesser nobility, supported by the peasants—were called Albigenses from the city of Albi, one of the sect's main centres. Between 1209 and 1229 the feudal magnates of Northern France, together with the Pope, waged wars against the Albigenses that wiped out the movement and resulted in a considerable part of Southern France being annexed to the lands of the French kings.

304 The *Hungarian teacher in Picardy*—a preacher by the name of Jakob said to be born in Hungary. He was one of the leaders of the anti-feudal peasant revolt in France in 1251, known as the shepherds' revolt, whose participants called themselves "God's shepherds".

305 The *Calixtines* (from *Calix*, the Latin for cup)—a moderate trend in the Hussite national liberation and reformation movement in Bohemia (first half of the fifteenth century) against the German nobility, the German Empire and the Catholic Church. The Calixtines (who maintained that the laity should receive the cup as well as the bread in the Eucharist, i.e. "*sub utraque specie*"—for which they were also known as Utraquists), supported by the burghers and part of the Czech nobility, sought no more than a national Czech church and the secularisation of church estates.

306 The *Taborites* (so called from their camp in the town of Tabor, in Bohemia)—a radical trend in the Hussite movement. In contrast to the Calixtines, they formed a revolutionary, democratic wing of the Hussites and their demands reflected the desire of the peasantry and the urban lower classes for an end to all feudal oppression, all manifestations of social and political arbitrariness. The Taborites were the core of the Hussite army. The betrayal of the Taborites by the Calixtines led to the suppression of the Hussite movement.

307 The *Flagellants* (from *flagellantis* in Latin, one who whips himself)—an ascetic religious sect widespread in Europe in the thirteenth to fifteenth centuries. They propounded self-castigation as a means of expiating sins.
     The *Lollards* (from the middle Dutch *lollaert*, literally, one who is murmuring prayers)—a religious sect (that originated in the fourteenth century) widespread in England and other European countries, which bitterly opposed the Catholic Church. The Lollards were followers of Wycliffe, the English reformer, but they drew more radical conclusions from his teaching and their opposition to feudal privileges took a religiously mystical form. Many Lollards, who came from the people and the lower clergy, were active participants in Wat Tyler's rebellion of 1381 and were cruelly persecuted in the late fourteenth century.

308 *Chiliasm* (from the Greek *chilias*, a thousand)—a mystical religious doctrine that Christ would come to earth a second time and usher in a millennium of justice, equality and well-being. Chiliastic dream-visions sprang up during the decay of slave-owning society; they were widespread among the oppressed during early Christianity and were continuously revived in the doctrines of the various medieval sects, which voiced the opinions of the peasants and plebeians.

309 The *Confession of Augsburg* (*Augsburgische Konfession, Confessio Augustana*)—a statement of the Lutheran doctrine read to Emperor Charles V at the Imperial Diet in Augsburg in 1530; it adapted the burgher ideas of a "cheap church" (abolition of lavish rites, modification of the clerical hierarchy, etc.) to the interests of the princes. A sovereign prince was to replace the Pope at the head of the

church. The Confession of Augsburg was rejected by the Emperor. The war waged against him by princes who adopted the Lutheran Reformation ended in 1555 in the religious peace of Augsburg, which empowered the princes to determine the faith of their subjects at their own discretion.

311 This date was cited by Zimmermann in the first edition of his book. According to later data Thomas Münzer was born about 1490 (the first date known from his biography, October 1506, is mentioned in his matriculation as a student of Leipzig University, when he was apparently sixteen years of age). In various sources, both, in his own works and in historical writings, his name is transcribed differently (Munczer, Muntzer, Müntzer). Engels writes Münzer, the way Zimmermann wrote it in Part Three of his book.

312 The *Anabaptists* (those who baptise over again) belonged to one of the most radical and democratic religious-philosophical trends spread in Switzerland, Germany and the Netherlands during the Reformation. Members of this sect were so called because they repudiated infant baptism and demanded a second, adult baptism.

313 Engels refers to the views of David Strauss and other Young Hegelians who treated questions of religion from a pantheist standpoint in their early writings.

314 According to later verified data Münzer went first to the imperial city of Mühlhausen, from where he was banished by municipal authorities in September 1524 for his part in disturbances among the city poor. From Mühlhausen Münzer came to Nuremberg.

315 The *Puritans* (from the Latin *puritas*—purity)—participants in a religious political movement in England and Scotland at the close of the sixteenth and in the early half of the seventeenth centuries. Their object was a Protestant Calvinist Reformation and purification of the Church of England of every trace of Catholicism (elimination of bishops, simpler church rites, etc.). They advocated modesty, abstinence, thrift, encouraged prudence and enterprise. The Puritans expressed the religious opposition of the bourgeoisie to absolutism and played an important part in the ideological preparations for the English bourgeois revolution.

The *Independents*—representatives of one of the Protestant trends in England. In the 1580s and 1590s they formed the Left wing of Puritanism and represented radical opposition to absolutism and the Church of England by the commercial and industrial bourgeoisie and the "new" bourgeois nobility. During the English revolution of the seventeenth century, the Independents formed a separate political party which came to power under Oliver Cromwell at the end of 1648.

316 The *Swabian League* of princes, noblemen and patricians of the imperial cities of South-Western Germany was founded in 1488. Its chief purpose was to combat the peasant and plebeian movement. The South- and West-German princes who headed this League also viewed it as a means to consolidate their oligarchic rule. The League had its own administrative and judicial bodies, and an army. It fell apart in 1534 due to internal squabbles.

317 This refers to the government of the viceregent of the Austrian Habsburgs in Ensisheim, the centre of the Austrian Forelands, the name used to denote the possessions of the Habsburgs and their immediate vassals in Upper Alsace, Upper Swabia and the Black Forest.

318 *Szeklers*—an ethnic group of Hungarians, mostly free peasants. In the thirteenth

century their forefathers were settled by Hungarian kings in the mountain regions of Transylvania to protect the frontiers. The region inhabited by them was usually called Szekler land.

319 The reference is to a popular rising in Sicily against the French Anjou dynasty, which conquered Southern Italy and Sicily in 1267. On the evening of March 31, 1282, the population of Palermo took the vespers bell-toll as a signal to massacre several thousand French knights and soldiers. As a result, the whole of Sicily was freed from French domination and came under the Aragon King.

320 Engels refers to the 95 theses that Luther (who began his clerical career as a simple monk in the Augustinian monastery in Thuringia) nailed to a church door in Wittenberg on October 31, 1517. The theses contained a vigorous protest against the sale of indulgences and the abuses by the Catholic clergy. They also presented the initial outline of Luther's religious teaching in the vein of burgher ideals.

321 *Burlesque*—satirical literature and parodies by writers of the Renaissance and humanitarian ideologists who ridiculed the high-flown style of court poetry and the strict behaviour of upper feudal society.

322 The *Wars of the Roses* (1455-85)—wars between the feudal Houses of York and Lancaster fighting for the throne, the white rose being the badge of the House of York, and the red rose of the House of Lancaster. The Yorkists were supported by some of the big feudal landowners from the south-eastern, more economically developed part of the country and also by the knights and the townspeople, while the Lancastrians were backed by the feudal aristocracy of the backward north and of Wales. The wars almost completely wiped out the ancient feudal nobility and brought Henry VII to power to form a new dynasty, that of the Tudors, who set up an absolute monarchy in England.

323 The reference is to the Polish national liberation uprising in November 1830-October 1831, and also to that in Cracow in 1846 (see Note 66).

324 See Note 317.

325 This refers to the black-red-and-gold banner symbolising German unity. The information on such a banner provided by Zimmermann is not, however, corroborated by contemporary sources, i.e. chronicles, etc. The usual peasant colours were red-white, red-black, etc.

326 Emperor Maximilian's edict ruled that only representatives of "noble" estates could be members of provincial courts.

327 Another big credit was advanced to Archduke Ferdinand by the Augsburg banking house of Fuggers, who owned vast tracts of land north of Lake Constance and had a vital interest in suppressing the peasant insurrection.

328 The reference is to the southern mountainous part of Baden adjacent to Switzerland. In the sixteenth century, part of this region was owned by the Margrave of Baden and the rest of it either belonged to the Austrian land of Breisgau or to petty ecclesiastical and secular feudal lords.

329 Engels refers to the anonymous pamphlet printed in Nuremberg in early 1525, entitled *An die Versammlung gemeiner Pawerschaft, so in Hochteutscher Nation und viel anderer Ort, mit empörung und uffruhr entstanden, ob ihr Empörung billicher oder unbillicher gestalt geschehn, und was sie der Oberkeit schuldig oder nicht schuldig seind, gegründet aus der heil. göttlichen Geschrift, von Oberlendischen Mitbrüdern guter*

maynung ausgangen und beschriben (To the Assembly of All the Indignant and Insurgent Peasantry of the Upper German Nation and Many Other Places on Whether or Not Its Indignation Is Just and What It Should or Should Not Do to the Authorities. Based on the Holy Scripture, Composed and Rendered with the Full Approval of the Highland Brotherhood). Wilhelm Zimmermann believed this pamphlet to have been written by Thomas Münzer (*Allgemeine Geschichte des grossen Bauernkrieges*, Th. 2, S. 113).

330 *Judica Sunday* (from *judex*—judge, literally "judgment Sunday")—the fifth Sunday in Lent.

331 The *small* and the *great tithe*—two varieties of tax paid to the Catholic Church. The size and nature of this tax varied in different parts of Germany, and in most cases greatly exceeded a tenth of the peasants' produce. As a rule the great tithe (*decima major*) was imposed on the corn and vine harvest whereas the small tithe (*decima minor*) was imposed on other crops.

332 The *Grand Chapter of Würzburg*—an ecclesiastical collegium governing the Würzburg bishopric, whose head, the Bishop of Würzburg, also had the title of Duke of Franconia.

333 The *Teutonic Order*—a German religious Order of knights founded in 1190 during the crusades. The Order seized vast possessions in Germany and other countries. These were administered by dignitaries known as commandores (or comthurs). In the thirteenth century, East Prussia fell under the rule of the Order after it was overrun and the local population exterminated. In 1237 the Order amalgamated with the Livonian Order, which also had its seat in the Baltic area. The Eastern possessions of the Order became a seat of aggression against Poland, Lithuania and the adjoining Russian principalities. After the defeat at Chudskoye Lake in 1242 and in the battle at Grunwald in 1410, the Order rapidly declined and was only able to maintain a small part of its former possessions.

334 Later research into the Peasant War in Germany proves that the Heilbronn Councillor Hans Berlin who, as Engels describes, became a traitor and negotiated with Truchsess, military chief of the Swabian League, on behalf of patricians and wealthy burghers (see p. 62 of this volume), and the author of the Declaration of the Twelve Articles who induced the peasant leaders to accept it, were two different people, the latter being the Heilbronn notary and procurator Hans (Johannes) Berlin.

335 The *agreement of Offenburg*, concluded by the Breisgau insurgents and the Austrian Government on September 18, 1525, stipulated the restoration of former peasant services and the institution of harsh measures against peasant societies and "heretics". For its part, the government undertook to pardon rank-and-file members of the movement and confine itself to relatively modest fines. The amnesty, however, did not extend to the leaders of the uprising. Even this agreement, unfavourable as it was to the peasants, was soon violated by the Austrian authorities and local feudal lords, who subjected the insurgents to bloody reprisals as soon as they had laid down their arms.

336 The agreement, concluded with the Austrian Government on November 13, 1525, forced the Black Forest peasants to repeat their oath of allegiance to the Habsburgs, to resume their former feudal services and not to interfere with the bloody reprisals of the victors against the town of Waldshut, headquarters of the movement. The defenders of Waldshut, however, stood their ground for several weeks, and the town fell only due to the treachery of the rich burghers.

337 Later research has proved that Münzer held no official post in the Mühlhausen "eternal council", but his presence at its sittings and his advice to the council made him the virtual head of the new revolutionary government.

338 Engels refers to Louis Blanc and Albert (Alexandre Martin), who represented the proletariat in the bourgeois Provisional Government of the French Republic instituted in February 1848.

339 See Note 11.

340 The Articles of the Alsàtian peasants not only defined more sharply the anti-feudal demands of the Twelve Articles (see this volume, p. 451) of the Swabian and Franconian peasantry (abolition of serfdom, return of common lands usurped by the nobility, etc.), but in many respects went even further. They were also directed against usurers (the clause on the abolition of usurers' interest, and others); they demanded the abolition not only of the small, but of the great tithe as well, and proclaimed the right of the local population to depose and replace officials with whom they were dissatisfied.

341 The Fourteen Articles of the insurgent peasants and pitmen of the Salzburg archbishopric in the main reproduced the demands of the Twelve Articles of the Swabian and Franconian peasants. In addition, they contained certain local demands. Among other things, the insurgents demanded that the independence of the courts from the influence of feudal lords and their puppets be secured, that the responsibility of the whole community for crimes committed on its territory be abolished and measures be taken to maintain roads in good repair and to protect trade.

342 The *Thirty Years' War* (1618-48)—a European war, in which the Pope, the Spanish and Austrian Habsburgs and the Catholic German princes rallied under the banner of Catholicism and fought the Protestant countries: Bohemia, Denmark, Sweden, the Republic of the Netherlands and a number of Protestant German states. The rulers of Catholic France—rivals of the Habsburgs— supported the Protestant camp. Germany was the main battle arena or the object of plunder and territorial claims. The Treaty of Westphalia (1648) sealed the political dismemberment of Germany.

INDEX

Albigenses, 14, 15
Albrecht, Duke of Saxony, 32
Alpine region, Austria, 76
Alsace region, 32, 74-5
Anabaptists, 21, 26, 27, 53
aristocracy, German nobility, and peasants, 44-6; and Reformation, 16-18, 32, 35, 38-9, 42-6, 48 ff., 55-6, 62-3, 79-82; Hungarian, 40- 44
Arnold of Brescia, 14
asceticism, 26, 29- 30
Augsburg, 2; Augsburg Confession, 18, 42
Aylva, Sjoerd, 32

Bach, Walter, 67; betrays peasants, 69
Ball, John, 14, 15
Baltringen Troop, 50, 52-3, 59, 60
Bantel, Hans, 37
Batory, Istvan, 40
Berlichingen, Gotz von, 54-6, 63; betrays peasants, 64
Berlin, Hans (Johannes), 56
Berlin, Hans, betrays peasants, 62
Bildhausen camp, 53, 74
Black Forest Troop, 50, 53, 60, 67
Black Troop (of Geyer), 54-5, 62, 64
Boheim, Hans, 29-33
bourgeoisie, viii, ix, xi
Bundschuh, 32-4; 14 articles of, 35; 39, 41, 42
burghers, 8, 28, 30, 82, 83; and clergy, 14; and heresy, 15
Burg-Bernheim, Gregor, 65

Calixtines, 14, 15
chiliasm, 16, 21
Christian Alliance, 52, 55, 56
Christianity, 13-19
class antagonism, 42-4, 71
class interests, 13, 69, 80
classes, in feudal society, 3-11, 13, 14, 16, 29-30, 33-4, 82
clergy, structure of, 5-6, 8, 80; and education, 13, and law, 14; and feudalism, 10, 52, 79,

81; attacked by nobility, 43; losses from peasant wars, 80
Common Gay Troop, see Gaildorf Troop
communism, utopian, of Munzer, 10, 12, 13, 16, 21, 23- 4, 33, 62
conservative Catholics, 16
courts, feudal, 5, 10, 13, 48, 49, 62

Diet, in Stuttgart, 37-8; again legalizes serfdom, 40; and Konrad 111, 56; in the Palatinate, 57
Dozsa, Georg, 38-9

Eitel, Hans, 50
Eisenhut, Anton, 61
Elector Palatine, Ludvig V., 38, 45, 63, 65

farm labourers, xiii, xiv feudalism, church and, 4-7, 13, 14; division of labor in, 1-6, 9, 30, 66; hierarchy of, 3-4, 8, 20, 44
Ferdinand I, Archduke, 49, 57, 68, 76
Feuerbacher, Matern, 57, 60, 61
Flagellants, 15
Forner, Anton, 53
Franconia, 27, 53, 69, 72-76
Franconian Tauber Troop, 56, 63, 64
Frisian revolt, 32
Fritz, Joss, 34, 35, 36, 41
Frundsberg, Georg von, 69, 77
Fulda Troop, 73; Abbot of, 73, 80

Gaildorf Troop, 56, 57, 63, 66
Gau peasants, 61
Gay Bright Troop, 54, 56, 57, 63, 64
Gay Christian Troop, 58, 60, 61
Gay Troop, 54, 64
Geismaier, Michael, 77-79
Gerber, Erasmus, 75
Gerber, Theus, 58, 61
Germany, fragmentation of, 2-3, 12, 33, 43-4, 46, 62, 81-83; taxayion in, 3-7, 10, 15;
Geyer, Florian, 54, 56, 59, 63, 65-6
Grebel, Konrad, 27
Gugel-Bastian, 39

Habern, Wilhelm von (Marshal), 57, 67
Hanseatic League, 1
Hegau troops, 60, 67, 68
Heilbronn program, 61, 62
Helfenstein, Ludwig von, 45-5, 63
heresy, heretics, 14-17; 19-21; 24-5
Hesse, 70-71, 73-4
Hipler, Wendel, 53-5; 62, 64
Hosszu, Anton, 40
Hubmaier, Balthasar, 27, 47
Hus, Jan, 14
Hussite movement, 14-16, 21, 29
Hutten, Ulrich von, 18, 43-46, 67

Joachim of Floris, 21
Judica Sunday, 52-3

Kleeburg troop, 75
Kolben troop, 75
knights, 3-5, 39, 43-46, 82; join with towns, 15
Knopf von Leubus, 69

Lake Troop, 50-51, 52, 53, 59-60, 64
Leipheim Troop, 50, 54, 57F 59, 61
Letter of Articles, 52, 57
Lollards, 15
Lower Allgau Troop, 50, 50
lumpenproletariat, xii, 8-9, 51
Luther, Martin, opposes Catholic Church, 17; sides with burghers & princes, 18; stoned by peasants, 19; denounces peasant revolt, 20; denounces Munzer, 26, 27; Theses of, 42
Lutheran reform, 16
Lutheranism, 24-8, 42-3, 47

Mantel, Dr. (Johann), 27
Maximilian 1, 34, 38, 40, 49
Menzingen, Stephan von, 53, 66
Metzler, Georg, 53-55, 62, 64
Muller, Hans, 47, 48, 50, 67; betrays peasants, 68
Munzer, Thomas, and plebians, 9-10; and mysticism, 14-16, 21; and utopian communism, 16; and revolutionary party, 17, 27, 28, 51; theology becomes more political, 22, 23; and Union of the people, 24, 47-8; publishes ideas, 24, 25, 26; denounces Luther, 24; and Twelve Articles, 49; and "eternal council," 70-71; as prophet, 72; executed, 74

mysticism, 14-16, 21, 42

Niklashausen, 29, 30
nobility, 5, 6, 10, 11, 34; demands of, 43; income, 44; and Reformation, 16-18, 32, 35, 38-9, 62-3, 79-82

patricians, 7; see also nobility
peasant war, causes of, 3-7, 10-11, 29, 69, 76; demands, Twelve Articles, 47-8, 51, 52, 62, 76; Heilbronne program, and burghers, 7-9, 12, 14-22, 25-28, 42, 61, 62, 66, 72, 80; peasant-plebian radical wing, 6-12, 14-23, 26, 28, 33, 42, 52, 62, 66-7, 69; repressive terror, 20, 26, 49, 54, 61, 63-66, 70, 72, 75, 77; in Alpine Austria, 76-78; in Hungary (Dozsa), 34, 38-41, 83; in Swabia and Franconia, 27, 33, 41, 47-69, 70, 71, 72, 74, 76; in Thuringia, 9, 19, 22, 24-27, 53, 70, 72, 74, 76; causes of failure, xvi, 2, 11, 14, 28, 36, 48, 51, 55-6, 59-61, 66, 67, 77, 79-83.
peasants, xiii; burdens on, 4, 10, 11; need for allies, 11; and nobility, 45; union of, 47; waverings, 60-61, 79-81; movements of, 11, 16, 29-30, 32-39, 40, 41
Pfeifer, Heinrich, 70, 74
Philip I, Landgrave of Hesse, 45, 72-3, 74
plebians, 8-9, 10, 15-19, 27-8, 33-6, 42, 58, 79, 81
political party, 9, 28, 42-3, 70-71
Poor Konrad, 34, 37, 39, 40
Pope, the, 6, 20, 35 81
Pregizer, Kasper, 37
princes, viii, 3-4, 19, 43, 45; benefits from peasant war, 81, 82

Rabman, Franz, 27
Reformation, class interests in, 16; of propertied class, 50; rapid growth of, 42; seeds of discord, 42-3. see also Luther
religion, 13-15, 22-3
Revolution of 1848-49, viii, 7, 8, 16-20; results of, 12, 18, 56, 71, 82-4
Rohrbach, Jacklein, 54, 55, 57, 58, 61
Rothenburg camp, 53

Salzburg, 143-45
Saxony, 24, 25, 27
Schappeler, of Memmingen, 27, 68
Schmid, Ulrich, 50
Schneider, Georg, 35

Schon, Ulrich, 59
serfdom, 20, 40, 44, 52; and peasants, 3, 4, 6-8, 10, 16, 79
Sickingen, Franz von, 18, 43, 45-6, 82
Singerhans of Wurtinger, 37
Slovenia peasant uprising, 40 Ff.
Stara Prawa, 40, 76
Stockach provincial court, 49; and 16 articles, 48
Storch, Niklas, 21
Swabian League, 47-8, 51
Szaleresi, Ambros, 39; betrays peasants, 40

Taborites, 15, 16
Teutonic Order, 55
Thirty Years' War, 79
Thunfield, Kunz von, 22, 28
Thuringia, 9, 70, 72-5
Truchsess, Georg, 48, 49; and Swabian League, 51, 59; vs. Ulrich, 51; defeats peasants 58-69; avoids defeat, 60
Tubingen agreement, 38

Twelve Articles, 47, 48, 49, 50, 52, 58, 62, 76; of Alsace troops, 74; Declaration of, rejected by peasants, 56

Ulrich, Duke of Wurttemberg, 37-8; 49, 51
Union Shoe, 50-52; Upper Rhine, 54, 56-59
Upper Allgau Troop, 50, 53, 60, 78
Upper Swabia, 47, 57
usury, 7, 32

vagrancy, 8, 9, 34-5, 79

Waldenses, 14
Wars of the Roses, 44
Wat Tyler's rebellion, 15
Wehe, Jakob, 27, 51, 59; executed, 54
Weingarten agreement, 60, 68
working class, ix, x, xi, xii, xiii
Wurttemberg Troop, 63
Wurzburg, 29, 56, 65-67, 81

Zapolya, Johann, 40